SAVING ALEXANDER

Susan Mac Nicol

SAVING ALEXANDER

Famous author though he may be, Alexander Montgomery is not someone you take home to meet your mother. Seriously flawed, damaged by a horrific past, he's trying hard to claw his way back to normality. But how can anyone respect what he truly is? His therapy involves regular sessions at Study in Scarlet, an exclusive S&M club.

Then comes Sage. Tall, with black hair and blue eyes, an up-and-coming actor with impossible charm and boy-next-door good looks, he's the perfect choice to play the leading man in a TV adaptation of Alex's latest best-seller. Even more, he *is* a man you introduce to your family. Which Alex would do—if he weren't taken by another man who offers the punishments Alex prays will wipe away the past and make him the person he wants to be. Yet, perhaps there is another path to redemption. If only the solution would reach out and touch him.

SAVING ALEXANDER

Susan Mac Nicol

www.BOROUGHSPUBLISHINGGROUP.com

SAVING ALEXANDER
Copyright © 2013 Susan Elaine Mac Nicol

Digital edition created by Maureen Cutajar
www.gopublished.com

ISBN 978-1941260128

In 2007, I lost someone very close to me. My younger sister, Carol, was a romance buff, a woman who always wanted people to have a happy-ever-after. She would be terribly amused to see that her big sister—the one who always pooh-poohed romance stories and told her she was a softy—is now writing them for a living. Alex's birthday is the same as hers, the 27th September. He's a Libra, too, a peace-lover. In this way I hope she lives on in other memories like she does with our family.

Miss you, sweetheart. Always.

ACKNOWLEDGMENTS

I'd like to thank the wonderful Elizabeth Cummings from Dallas, Texas, for being my partner in the sense of checking psychological aspects and character motivations in this book.

And, as always, a shout-out to my wonderful family for putting up with me while I ponder out loud the use of whips, floggers and sex in Alex's life....

CONTENTS

Chapter 1

Alexander Montgomery was in a lot of pain. Pain of his own choosing but pain nonetheless.

He watched as Eric Rossi, hair as darkly red as his name suggested, tightened the bindings around his wrists, slowly trailing the custom-made leather whip down his naked body. Alex's torso was already marked with the various slashes Eric had made on his stomach, buttocks and hips, and Eric's willing prisoner held his breath as he waited to see what came next.

Eric walked around to stand before him as Alex hung by his wrists on the smooth gunmetal St. Andrews standing cross embedded in floor of the luxurious basement, this place Alex came when he needed solace. Eric grinned widely, showing off perfect white teeth. His tongue crept out of the corner of his mouth as he teased Alex, deciding where and how he should strike next.

Eric's lean, well-defined body was sweaty and shiny, clad in only a pair of unzipped white denim jeans, the colour stark against his dark tan, the skin tone he'd inherited from his Argentinean father. As was his usual fashion, he wore no underwear and Alex saw his impressive cock, deeply purple and swollen, jutting out from the opening. Alex's own cock stood up like a rocket and he winced at the dull, aching sensation in his groin.

"Alex, are you all right?" Eric said solicitously, even though Alex knew Eric didn't really care. "You're looking a little pale."

Eric reached out a hand, tweaking Alex's nipple then leaning down to claim it with his mouth. Alex closed his eyes at the feel of his wet mouth and ravenous tongue.

His Principal's mouth travelled across his chest and up his throat, coming to rest beside his ear. Eric bit the lobe viciously. Alex winced. *That* would go with the bite marks on other parts of his body that Eric had made tonight.

He knew if he cried out Eric would simply hurt him again, worse than before. And he knew he still had a fair amount more of this oh-so carefully orchestrated brutality to endure. He'd rather not add to it. Even he had his limit. Eric took deep breaths as he moved around behind Alex, running his hand over his naked back down to his clenched buttocks. He slapped him hard-on his backside. He did it again and again, each time harder than the last.

Alex bit his lip to keep from crying out. Eric finally stopped and Alex heard the whip flick. It smacked him hard, once, then again on his lower back. He gritted his teeth, but when Eric struck him across his shoulders he cried out at the shock of stinging pain, unable to maintain the silence required to make his tormentor gentler.

He sensed rather than saw Eric shaking his head. "Alex. What have I told you? Your rules, remember? No crying out, no whimpers, no groans. Or it just gets worse. Now I have to punish you. Are you ready?" He reached around, stroking Alex's cock, his fingers lightly touching the tip.

Alex gasped with the feeling as the pressure built and his hips pushed out uncontrollably toward Eric's hand.

Eric chuckled. "You know better than to come unless I tell you that you can. So restrain yourself." His voice was harsh.

Alex made an effort to suppress the overwhelming need to orgasm, bracing himself for a slash of Eric's whip, clenching his teeth together. The crack never came.

Eric chuckled quietly. "Sometimes I like to exercise my prerogative and change my mind. You've been through enough tonight. Time to end it, don't you think?"

The distinct desire in his voice was evident and Alex thought Eric had chosen to end it for his own pleasure, to finish off the evening for him in the way Eric liked most. Inside Alex.

Flickering lights highlighted the sweat on Eric's face as he circled Alex like a hungry tiger. Alex stood on a small square of dark wooden floor in the centre of an ornate Rococo room. Glittering chandeliers lit the room dimly, casting shadows around the richly decorated walls. The roof was sculptured with decadent images that in normal circumstances would catch the eyes and made one breathe a sigh of wonder.

Baroque figures scattered about the room watched Alex and Eric with dead eyes, their faces pastel white and non-judgmental. The sheer opulence of the room was overwhelming.

But for Alex, this place was not about the décor or the ambience. His world revolved around the four square feet he stood on and the man standing in front of him. Eric wore a look of sheer avarice. *This* constituted Alex's solace and universe when he was here. Alex's body was bound right in the centre of this sacred space, his arms outstretched and secured to the cross. The green silk ropes binding his wrists were tight, the long, loose ends trailing down his arm, brushing his body as he moved. It tickled, the sensation sometimes driving him crazy. His legs were spread apart, ankles secured to large, golden hoops on the floor, the same type of silk ties binding them fast. He was almost on tiptoes and the muscles in his long, strong legs threatened to cramp and seize up with the effort.

Eric lifted Alex's chin with one hand. "Look at me!" he commanded, brushing his fingertips against Alex's two-day-old stubble.

Alex levelled his eyes to Eric's, and he lost his breath at the greedy look in them. Not for the first time Alex wondered whether these sessions were for him or for Eric. The lines between customer and seller seemed to blur. The other man seemed to take such special pleasure in Alex.

Eric spoke huskily. "I'm going to let you go now. You know what to do." He reached up, untying Alex's arms and dropping the ties onto the floor. Alex stood unsteadily before him. Eric motioned imperiously with his hand. Alex walked over to the large four-poster bed in the corner of the room, lying down on his stomach and turning his head away from Eric, his arms above his head. The silk sheets felt cool and slippery against his skin, soothing the welts and injuries on the front of his body. His cock was hard, needy and he desperately wanted release. He pressed himself harder into the bed, trying to ease the ache and throbbing in his groin.

The bed was used only after the flogging was over, when Eric granted them both the release they needed. Sometimes Alex was simply handcuffed to one of the posts of the bed, standing upright while Eric had his way. Other times he was spread-eagled out flat with Eric pounding away behind him. Alex was never quite sure which scenario was going to play out. Alex didn't want the emotion and discipline that went with a typical Dom/sub relationship. He was simply a paying customer with a set of rules that his "Principal," Eric, would enforce. Alex, Eric's "Charge," refused to call Eric Master or Sir.

Behind him, he heard Eric's jeans drop to the floor, then felt the bed move as Eric lay down next to him. He heard the snap of a bottle opening and imagined Eric coating his fingers with lubricant.

It was obviously going to be lying down tonight.

Eric's slippery hands slowly trailed their way from the back of Alex's neck down his spine and into the crease of his buttocks. Alex hissed in satisfaction as Eric slid a finger slowly into his hole, which immediately clenched around the man's fingers.

Eric's breaths were deep gasps of air, indicating his arousal as he pushed a second finger inside Alex. Alex moaned silently at the feeling those scissoring fingers invoked, craving the sensation as Eric got him ready for his cock. He pressed his face into the pillow lest he cry out.

If he made any noise, Eric may not finish it.

He'd been known to leave Alex dangling at the precipice of satisfaction and go off and indulge himself with someone else as a punishment. Not often, but it had happened.

"You feel so good, Alexander. I did well." His voice was deep and husky with desire. Alex's buttocks rose in rhythm with Eric's fingers toward the man who controlled him with every stroke.

Eric moved over him, covering his body. Alex winced at the pain of the lacerations and welts on his back and buttocks as he felt Eric's hardness, slick and velvety smooth, pressing into his buttocks, teasing, not quite willing to give Alex relief.

He licked Alex's ear, removing his fingers from Alex's anus as his mouth sucked at the skin on the back of Alex's neck.

Alex knew from experience he'd have bruises on his fair skin.

Alex's cock felt ready to explode and he gritted his teeth, trying to hold it back until he was commanded to come. Eric's fingers slid inside him again, thrusting deep. Alex bit his lip as he pressed his face even harder into the pillow.

Eric growled. "Raise yourself," he commanded. Alex obeyed, lifting to his knees and presenting himself. His own cock stood hard and rampant against his stomach, and he wanted nothing more than to feel Eric's hands on it, stroking it to release.

That would only come later.

Eric reached over his body to the table, taking the condom and ripping the packet. He sighed deeply.

Sheathing his cock was something Alex insisted on, despite Eric's sulky entreaty that he was clean and had no need of condoms. Alex point blank refused to go bareback.

Finally ready, he grasped Alex's hips, his hardness ramming into Alex's entrance deeply from behind, filling him so completely Alex thought there was no room for any more of him. The sound of skin slapping skin as he drove into Alex echoed in the room. Alex pressed back against him, wanting more, wanting to drive him deeper and harder.

Eric grunted in satisfaction, finally taking hold of Alex's cock with one hand as he started to work it, deep, hard strokes that Alex knew wouldn't take long to bring to him to orgasm.

"Come, Alexander," Eric commanded as he drove his cock into Alex. Alex's heart beat faster, the warmth of his climax already spreading through his loins, flooding him with sheer erotic heat.

He groaned loudly into the pillow as hot spurts of his semen covered Eric's hands, his wrists, Alex's stomach and the sheets below. His body shuddered as Eric let go of his cock and gripped his hips tighter, going deeper, until finally he called out loudly, using Spanish words when he climaxed.

Alex felt the throbbing inside his passage as Eric collapsed, groaning, on top of him. Alex's eyes filled with tears as he lay there under the other man's body. Fiercely he blinked them away.

It always happened after one of his sessions with Eric. The release of his orgasm at the end of the night's activities never completely assuaged the emptiness inside him.

Their breathing slowed and finally Eric rolled off Alex's back, allowing him to turn over. Eric removed the semen-filled condom, tied it and placed it on the bedside table.

Alex ran his hands through the other man's thick, short, deep-red hair, loving the crisp feel of it and marvelling once again how a man of Latin descent could have hair this colour. Eric had told

Alex laughingly in one of their more playful moments that his mother had been a wild redhead from Scotland and he seemed to be a throwback to her Gaelic ancestors. It made for a very unusual and striking combination.

Eric leaned over, moving a strand of hair from Alex's forehead. "Do you feel any better after that?" His hands caressed Alex's chest as he slid his fingers gently across his flat stomach.

Alex sighed. "I always feel better after that. You are definitely one of the best at what you do. Perhaps I need to make it more than once a week, but I'm not sure I could afford any more."

Eric sat up, regarding him thoughtfully. "I've told you before. We can take this outside our current relationship. I'm happy to see you outside of Study in Scarlet where I can give you some more personal attention." He leered at him.

Alex shook his head. "You know my answer to that. I'm not interested in a relationship outside of Scarlet. That would be far too complicated. And I don't like complicated." He ignored Eric's frown, swinging around to get off the bed to stand up. "There's a reason I come here. It's to keep my two lives apart—the one I choose to show to everyone and the other one that I hide inside me."

The one he hid concealed a need he didn't want anyone to know about.

Alex walked over to the corner of the room where his clothes lay in a heap on the floor after Eric had undressed him, or rather, ripped off his clothes. He'd lost count of how many times he'd had to replace his shirts at the buttons because of Eric's passion but he was relieved to see this time his clothing was intact.

Alex was conscious of Eric's eyes following his every move as he dressed. He spoke gently. "You're very good for me. You give me what I need and take the urge away for a little while. But I need to keep it separate or God knows what'll happen."

He finished dressing and turned to see the mutinous look on his Eric's face. Alex smiled. "Eric, go out and find some gorgeous bloke who's not as fucked up as I am. He can make you happy. I can't."

The words rang with finality as Alex opened the door and stepped out into the dimly lit corridor of the basement of Study in Scarlet.

Chapter 2

Christopher Sage breathed in the welcome scent of warm horse, sawdust and straw as he stroked the nose of his grey mare, Tallulah Briar.

She's bloody skittish. I need to keep her calm.

That was no surprise considering the wound on the horse's side.

Better known to friends and family as Sage, the young man leaned forward as the mare snickered, moving around the stable nervously on the cool April afternoon. Sun streamed in through the thin cracks in the wood slats that made up the stable, slivers of pure light criss-crossing the ground like a tic-tac-toe template.

"Relax, Lulah, easy now." Sage murmured to his horse, his soft, slightly lilting Irish tone soothing the anxious beast.

Miles Conway, the vet, examined a nasty gash on the horse's left haunch. He scowled, his grizzled face close as he peered at the wound. "Keep her still, Sage," he said quietly. "I'm nearly done."

Sage nodded, rubbing her flanks and stroking her sides as Miles finished his inspection. The vet sighed and stood up, his hands rubbing his back as he winced. "Jesus, my boy, I'm getting too bloody old to be doing this still. I'm supposed to be retired."

Sage chuckled. "Come on, old-timer. You live for this stuff. What's the prognosis?"

"She'll be fine. I'll patch her up, give her a shot and she'll be as good as new until the next time she runs into a bloody broken tree branch."

Sage heaved a sigh of relief. Tallulah was his favourite. "Good. Shall I grab your bag and you can get started?"

He didn't wait for a reply, leaving the stable with long strides across the yard, returning in a few moments with Miles' black medical bag. Sage watched as the vet prepared the dressings. He crooned to his horse and held her halter as Miles administered an antibiotic shot deftly to her rear.

Tallulah reared slightly and Sage once more coaxed her into submission.

"You have a way with animals," Miles said quietly. "Pity you can't do the same tricks with your men."

Sage scowled at his godfather, knowing the barbed comment referred to his latest breakup with a long-standing boyfriend. "Horses are easier to understand than people. They don't need as much attention. They also don't lie to you."

Miles laughed. "I don't know what I'm going to do with you. Thirty-four years old, men throwing themselves at you and you still end up going to bed alone most nights." He smiled slyly. "Apart from the occasional itch-scratching I'd guess. But I'm too old to remember those times. Now I'm lucky if I get to see a woman naked, let alone get into bed with her, and God forbid I actually get to do something with her."

He shut his bag, looking at Sage, who was smiling widely.

"You're only sixty-four, old man." Sage loved teasing Miles. "There's hope for you yet."

He frowned as his mobile rang, drawing it out of his jeans pocket and answering. "Chris Sage."

"Sage, it's Jenny. I have great news for you, hon. That part you auditioned for in that new Moorcroft Film production? It's yours if you want it."

His agent's voice was teasing. Jenny was well aware he coveted the part of the feisty and independent photographer, Carter

West, who travelled the world, managing to cause havoc wherever he went. It was a part Sage knew he could really do justice to.

At her words a surge of sheer happiness flooded his body. "That's great news, Jenny. The best I've had all day. Tell them of course I'll do it. It's a great script and the storyline is really appealing."

Jenny chuckled. "I'm glad you're happy. Can you come in tomorrow around ten A.M. and I'll give you the packet and we'll get everything formalised? I also want you to meet the writer of the series, Alexander Montgomery. He's really keen to see you again."

Sage remembered the man from his audition a few days ago, a rather stunning dark-haired fellow who'd stood quietly on the periphery of the set watching the performances. He hadn't been sure what his role was in the proceedings until someone had pointed him out as the creator, the author of the books.

"Of course I will. I'll see you at your office tomorrow morning then. Ten A.M. Cheers, Jen. You just made my bloody day."

He finished his call, beaming from ear to ear. "I just got offered the lead part in that TV series I told you about, *Double Exposure*. We start filming in a month's time from what I remember of the schedule."

Miles hugged his godson with pride. "I told you they'd give it to you. They'd be fools not to. That part sounds like it was made for you."

Sage frowned. "Strange you should say that. Apparently the writer insisted I audition. The film company already had me in mind and it was apparently written into the contract that the author have a say on the main character casting. It's unusual but I'm not complaining."

"Who is the author?" asked Miles.

Sage shrugged. "I don't know much about him. His name's Alexander Montgomery. He's written these books and they've become an instant hit, so the producers sniffed around, sensing a buck or two. Now that I remember, I've seen some pictures of him in the entertainment magazines. He's quite a looker with black hair and really odd eyes."

Miles leered at him. "There you go, then. You can get stuck into that one."

Sage grimaced. "Jesus, give it a rest, will you? After Mason I'm quite happy to vow off men for the short term. I'll concentrate on the career and get my nooky where I can when I need it. No ties, no responsibilities."

Closing the stall door, he gave Tallulah one final stroke on the nose before turning to Miles as he made his way to the front door of his thatched cottage.

"I suppose I need to make you tea and feed you Hobnobs before you go?" he said to Miles in resignation.

Miles nodded, rubbing his hands together in satisfaction. "That you do, lad. It's a tradition isn't it? You can't break with tradition."

Sage's cottage was set in Finchingfield in the northwest of the county of Essex. It was a small, picturesque village and Sage owned the cottage and two acres of land. His mother and father had been killed in a plane crash when Sage had been nineteen. Luckily the life insurance payout had been generous, allowing him to keep the house and still fund his drama studies at the University of Essex.

He'd lived in this cottage all his life, with horses and various farm animals that his mother had kept. The farm animals had gone but two horses remained, Tallulah and a stallion called Mixed Jack, a huge black beast that was probably more trouble than he was worth but as he was family, Sage kept him on.

Miles had always been there for him, a surrogate father. As Sage's career had taken off and he'd landed various roles in both London theatre productions and various mainstream TV series,

Miles kept the home fires burning and looked after the two horses when Sage wasn't around. His godfather lived only a mile down the road, in an old barn that had been converted to something fairly comfortable and modern.

Sage bent his six-foot-plus frame just to make it under the oak beams to get into the kitchen. Miles, being fairly short, had no such problem. They sat down to tea and biscuits at the old wooden table in the kitchen.

"So then, I suppose this means you'll be in London at the film studio more often than not?" Miles looked at the younger man with raised eyebrows.

Sage looked guilty. "I suppose so. I guess I'll stay with Dan whilst I'm there and that'll save the commute. I'll find out more about it when I see Jenny tomorrow morning. Apparently the writer will also be there."

Dan Costyn was an old friend of Sage's who lived in a fancy apartment in Chelsea and was always amenable to having Sage lodge with him.

Sage hoped fervently that Dan hadn't shacked up with some woman since he last talked to him. He'd best call tomorrow, perhaps pop round and see him.

"So that means I'll be taking care of the animals and the house while you're gone." Miles sighed in mock exasperation. "You really take the mick out of your godfather, don't you? You think that Irish charm will get you in my good books, son?"

Sage grinned. "It's worked for most people so far, hopefully it'll still work on you." His look turned serious. "I do appreciate you. I don't know what I'd do without you being around."

Miles shook his head. "I promised your folks I'd always take care of you. It's no hardship, I promise." He regarded Sage fondly. "You just get up to that studio and blow them away. You're a fine young actor and this part could be just what you need to launch you firmly into the big time."

He narrowed his eyes. "Didn't you tell me this series was about some photographer chap who meets a woman through some quite dangerous circumstances and they start a relationship?"

Sage nodded. "Yes, that's the gist of it. They meet in the hospital after being involved in a bombing, and the series is really all about all the things they have to overcome. It's quite violent actually, with lots of action and some unexpected turns of events. I really enjoyed the books, strangely enough for what's billed as a romantic suspense novel. The main protagonist, Carter West, the part I'll be playing, is really quite a character. I can do a lot with him."

"Hmm, sounds titillating. Is it sexy?" Miles looked at Sage slyly.

Sage flushed, something that had been the bane of his life since he was a boy. He'd been called "Rosy Sage" when he was younger, a name he hated with a passion. "It is a bit. I've never really done many sex scenes on camera before, so it'll be a real eye opener." He shrugged. "But it's all experience. I'll be fine."

"I suppose it depends on the woman you're having pretend sex with," Miles commented drily. "Do you know who'll you be having it off with yet, then?"

Sage laughed at his godfather's choice of words. "The female lead is Dianne Cunningham."

"Wow!" Miles whistled, impressed. "She's a beauty. Even though you don't bat for that team, my boy, you're a lucky man to get close to that one."

Sage grinned. "I can kiss a woman as well as a man when it comes to acting. Of course it would be much nicer if it was someone who was my gender and looked like Tyler Hoechlin, but I can't be fussy." He leered mockingly at Miles.

Miles shook his head. "There's no hope for you, young Sage."

He finished his tea and stood up, stretching as he did so. "Right. I'd better get off, let you get yourself sorted before tomorrow. I'll come by and sort the horses out at some stage, don't you worry. I'll get young Annie down the road to help me. You know she loves them and she'll take them for a bit of exercise."

He hugged his godson, picked up his tweed hat and disappeared out the front door. Sage heard him whistling as he walked toward home.

Sage smiled. He was really very lucky to have Miles. Closing the cottage door, he went back into his small lounge to sit down and finish the rest of his tea and biscuits, his mind in a whirl. He had a good deal of arrangements to make before tomorrow.

Chapter 3

At nine forty-five, Alexander sat in the office of the TV casting agent, Jennifer Miles, waiting for Christopher Sage to arrive for their ten o'clock meeting. He smiled at Jenny as she bustled into the office bearing a tray with two cups of coffee and a small plate of biscuits.

"Here we go, Alex. An early pick-me-upper, my very own brand of Columbian and a Jammie Dodger. You can't get any better than that."

Alex chuckled as he took a biscuit and a cup of coffee. "Thanks, Jen. We live for the little pleasures in life, don't we?" He dipped his biscuit in his coffee and nibbled it.

Jenny sat down behind her desk and looked at Alex curiously. "So tell me, put me out of my misery. I know the film team had already considered Sage for this part but I heard it was your conviction he was so right for it that sealed the deal. Why did you fancy Christopher Sage for the part? I know he'll do it justice, but I'm curious."

Alex shifted on his seat. "He's incredibly talented and very versatile," he said. He grinned inwardly at "versatile," wondering if it was true. "I've had a bit of a crush on him since he was in that first series where he played a doctor's son. I started writing *Double Exposure* and he just evolved into the character. I thought that perhaps if I wrote the part with him in mind, one day I'd get to meet him. I know it sounds stupid, but—" he shrugged. "He's really sexy and his looks certainly help. That Irish look, the black hair and blue eyes."

Jenny smiled and he flushed slightly. "You think I'm some sort of fan groupie now, don't you?"

She laughed loudly. "Sweetheart, I'm fifty-five and I'd like to do him if he was into ladies. He's scrumptious and a really nice person as well. And you're right that he's one of the most talented actors I have on my books and he deserves every break he can get. I'm glad you went all gooey-eyed. He is so right for this part. I can feel it in my bones—this series is going to be good for all of us."

Alex shrugged. "If it takes off like the books, I couldn't ask for anything more." He smiled wryly. "Becoming a New York Times best-selling writer went beyond my wildest dreams. I'm still not sure how it all happened."

Jenny chuckled. "The readers saw something they liked, your publisher did an amazing job in promoting you and, most of all, it was a great series of books, well-written and appealing. And I'm sure there's a little luck and good timing somewhere in there."

Alex shook his head. "Whatever it was, I'm damn grateful."

Jenny cocked her head as they heard her secretary greeting someone. She stood up, patting Alex on the shoulder.

"I think that might be young Sage arriving."

Alex winced at the woman's touch. His shoulders were still sore from the previous night's session with Eric, the weals still bruised and painful.

Jenny bustled over to the door as someone appeared. "And here he is, my star of the moment. Sage, darling, come on in. Let me introduce you to Alexander Montgomery."

Alex stood as Christopher Sage entered the room and kissed Jenny in greeting. The older woman smiled delightedly, giving him a warm hug.

Alex studied the man who had invaded his dreams more than once and been instrumental in bringing his sexual fantasies to a literal climax.

He was even more delicious in person. And the man was gay. That was a real bonus.

Six-foot-and-some tall, longish curly black hair, deep blue eyes that crinkled when he smiled and a rangy body that looked as if it were made to wear fine suits or nothing at all. In tight blue jeans and a checked long sleeve shirt with a white tee shirt underneath, Sage looked very relaxed.

Alex had a sudden image of peeling off the shirt to find a nice set of pectoral muscles beneath, then running his hands over them. The other man's mouth was extremely kissable, with generous lips that Alex wanted to nibble. His cock shifted in his chinos at the images his mind was conjuring up and he cursed the sudden rush of heat to his groin.

Jesus, where was his professionalism now? He needed to get a bloody grip before anyone noticed his raging hard-on.

He reached out his hand to Sage, who was returning the scrutiny. Sage's hand was warm and firm with long fingers and clean, shaped nails. Alex's breath deepened at his touch. He hoped Sage hadn't noticed.

The reality of feeling his warm skin in his own hands was infinitely better than the dream.

Sage met his gaze and narrowed his eyes. "Heterochromia iridis. I've never seen it in a human being before. Very striking."

Alex stared at him. Most people simply squinted and looked at him strangely before they asked him how his eyes came to be two different colours—one green, one blue. Actually hearing someone who *knew* what the condition was called was slightly disconcerting. Especially when rendered in that very charming slight Irish accent.

"I was born like this." He shook Sage's hand firmly. "Not many people seem to know what it's called though."

Sage smiled. "I had a horse once with the same condition. He was a Pinto. It's quite common in that breed."

Alex raised a dark eyebrow. "Comparing me to a horse? Well, that's one way to start a relationship."

Sage raised one eyebrow back. "Is that what we're doing? Starting a relationship? I thought we were here to discuss business."

He grinned as Alex felt himself flush, then turned to face Jenny, who'd been watching the interchange with amusement.

Sage gestured towards the biscuit plate. "You don't mind, do you? I'm bloody starving."

He helped himself to one of the biscuits and munched with satisfaction. Alex felt slightly out of his depth with this man and needed to bring the conversation back to what he knew best: business.

"May I call you Sage?" he enquired.

Sage waved the biscuit at him and nodded, his mouth full.

"I'd like to welcome you on board. The part of Gillian was offered to Dianne Cunningham and she's agreed to do it." Alex stopped to take a breath.

Sage regarded him curiously. "Why me?"

"I beg your pardon?"

"I know the production company wanted me to audition in the first place. But what made *you* recommend me so highly over everyone else? Not that I'm complaining, of course."

Alex certainly wasn't going to tell him about his crush. He shrugged. "To me, you were simply the best fit for the part based on your past performances. And your audition was incredible." He saw Jenny grinning at his evasiveness.

Sage nodded. "Thanks. I'm very pleased of course. I really enjoyed the books. I'm not one for romance novels but these were rather different. Perhaps because they were written by a man? I'm not sure, but they were a lot grittier and down to earth. I thought the characters were very well developed. I'll enjoy playing the part of Carter."

Alex was surprised. "You read all three books then?"

Sage nodded in amusement. "Yes, I actually can read and I have. I thought if I was auditioning I needed to. It wouldn't have been fair to you otherwise." He reached over and took the last biscuit from the plate as Jenny shook her head. "Sage, would you like coffee to go with that?"

He grinned. "I thought you'd never ask. Yes, please. Just black."

Jenny disappeared to go brew him a cup of her Columbian.

Sage regarded Alex curiously. "Jenny says she's got the full draft script already for the first three episodes. I read just a few pages for the audition." He sat down in Jenny's chair, his blue jeans-clad legs up on the table, his worn brown boots showing traces of straw and mud.

Alex wondered where he'd been to get his boots in that condition. He noticed they were at least a size eleven and he had a sudden thought in his head about men and big feet.

Sage saw him looking at them and coloured slightly, removing his feet from the desk. "Sorry. Bad habit. I shouldn't really be doing that here. I've been mucking out stalls."

"You have horses?" Alex didn't know anyone else who actually had any, let alone mucked them out.

Sage nodded. "I have two back home. They keep me grounded when I need the distraction from show business."

"Where's home, then?"

"I have a cottage with a fair bit of land in Finchingfield, a small village in North Essex. But London will become my home whilst we're filming the TV series. I'll be at your beck and call." He smiled slightly. "I understand you intend being on-site as we do the day-to-day filming?"

Alex heard the amusement in his voice and bristled. "I'm not one of those controlling author freaks who want to vet everything that gets done or tell everyone what to do," he said sharply. "I was offered a collaborative role with the film company and I thought I could learn something about the business while I worked, something I've always wanted to do. It made sense to be there to help out where I can."

And I have nowhere else useful to be. I may as well get the next book written in my spare time.

Sage nodded, obviously not believing him from the look on his face. "Of course. I understand."

Alex scowled at him as Jenny walked in with the coffee. "Sorry it took so long. I took a couple of calls in between. I hope it's still hot."

She placed Sage's coffee on the table, looking at them both. "So have you two been getting to know each other? What do you think, Sage? Do you think the two of you will work nice together?" She frowned. "Is that mud on my blotter? Have you had your feet on my desk again?"

Sage grimaced and stood up, brushing the dried mud off onto the floor with his hands. "Sorry. There, all clean now. I was telling Alex I intend on staying in London whilst we film so I'll be around twenty-four seven."

Alex grinned at the exchange. "Janine Fortress is the scriptwriter and Luke Belmont is directing. I believe you've worked with him before?"

Sage nodded, looking pleased. "Luke directed the last TV series I was in. He's incredibly talented and focused. It'll be good to work with him again. He's slightly crazy and unorthodox but pretty much a genius."

Alex laughed softly. "He's one helluva live wire and his reputation for being a little eccentric certainly precedes him. I thought he was a real character." Alex looked at Jenny. "I imagine you'll be giving Sage the full script to read and he can start thinking about his character? We start filming in four weeks' time."

Jenny tapped a finger on the manila envelope on her desk.

Alex looked over at Sage. "Where are you going to be staying then if you're not on your farm in Finchingfield?" Moorcroft Studios in London wasn't far from where Alex lived so the commute would be convenient for him.

Sage smiled, a little edgily, he thought. "It's not a farm; it's a cottage with horses. And I intend staying with a friend in Chelsea so the film studio is just a tube hop away."

Alex wondered with a slight pang what kind of a "friend" it was, surprised at himself for even having such a thought. With his background, he knew he'd never have a normal relationship with any man.

Jenny snorted. "Good God, Sage, don't tell me you're staying with Dan? The two of you together is a recipe for disaster. I remember the last episode the two of you got involved in."

Sage's face went deeply pink and Alex gazed at him in amazement. He'd never seen a man blush like that before. It was adorable.

"That was a one-off," Sage muttered. "It won't happen again, I promise you. "

He looked at Alex uneasily and Alex made a mental note to interrogate Jenny later and find out what had happened. This story sounded very interesting.

Jenny snorted. "This is Dan we're talking about. I'd be careful if I were you."

Sage changed the subject. "I googled you, Alex." He sounded more than a little curious.

Jenny sighed. "You are such a nosey parker, Sage. You just can't bear going in blind, can you?"

The man grinned in agreement but all Alex felt was a sense of dread.

"There's not a lot on the web about you, other than when you started writing and became this best-selling novelist. Are you a man of mystery then?"

Alex knew Sage was probably just teasing, but his words struck a chord of fear that he hadn't felt in a while. "I'm a very private person," he said curtly, probably too curtly from the expression on both Sage and Jenny's face. "I don't like talking about my private life. The only detail anyone needs is on my website." The only personal thing he'd made no secret of was the fact he was gay. That was all the information he was prepared to release.

There was an awkward bit of silence broken by Sage, who regarded him thoughtfully. "I'm sorry," he said quietly, inclining his head. "I wasn't trying to probe. I can see I hit a nerve there. I won't do it again."

Jenny watched Alex curiously and his heart sank. He'd stupidly overplayed that out of fear. The last thing he wanted to have was anyone wonder about him and try to investigate his past.

"I suppose that's it for today then?" Sage picked up his envelope, waving it with a flourish. "I have my usual *Mission Impossible* self-destruct manila envelope with all the script and the paperwork."

Jenny nodded. "That's it, I think. We'll start the publicity as soon as the contracts are signed. I hope you're ready for this, both of you. It's going to mean a lot of appearances and talk shows. Sage, my darling, I need you to be your charming Irish self and get everyone interested in Carter West, photographer extraordinaire. This role will put you a lot more in the public eye so you'll need to manage the paparazzi when they start hounding you."

Sage chuckled, kissing her cheek. "I'll try my best to live up to your expectations. As for the reporters, I'll sort them out, have no fear." His tone was slightly threatening.

Jenny sighed. "You do realise you need them, Sage? Please be on your best behaviour. I know you're not fond of having everything splashed out there after the last time but you need this exposure."

Sage nodded, his eyes flinty. "I'll be a good boy, Jen. Just as long as they know their boundaries."

Alex knew Sage had taken a lot of flak some years ago. He'd thrown his then-fiancé out of their shared flat after finding him in bed with another friend. Unfortunately, a reporter had been nearby. The incident had made most of the newspapers.

Alex stood watching them both as Sage turned to him and extended his hand politely. He noticed with a pang he seemed a lot cooler that he had been.

"Alexander. It's been a pleasure meeting you. I imagine I'll be seeing you on set in a few weeks' time."

Alex shook Sage's hand, watching as he left the office. He turned to Jenny with a smile. "I suppose I'd better get off too. Thanks for the coffee and biscuits."

Jenny grasped his arm softly. Alex stifled a moan of pain. She hit one of the spots Eric had bitten last night.

Thank God he could wear long sleeves and shirt collars to hide the bite marks and bruises. He tried to move his arm away without seeming rude.

The agent smiled at him. "We're probably going to be seeing a fair bit of each other. I want you to know that I'm a good listener in case you ever want to talk. I understand your views on being in the public eye. I'll try not to make you uncomfortable."

Alex smiled. "Thanks. I appreciate the offer." He knew he'd never take Jenny up on it but there was no point in being churlish. Alex left the office conscious of Jenny's eyes boring into his back.

Chapter 4

Sage boarded the tube on the way to Chelsea to meet Dan for a drink at lunchtime and plan Sage's move to London. He held onto the rail, thinking about Alexander Montgomery as the tube hurtled toward Sloane Square. The novelist was certainly a very attractive man and had the bonus of batting for his side to boot. Sage had watched the re-run of the man's last interview on the television last night in an effort to see whom he was getting involved with. Montgomery was about thirty, he guessed, with short, brush-cut black hair, pale skin and those incredible eyes in an extremely sexy package. Tall and lithe, his shoulders broad and taut from what Sage had managed to see despite the closely buttoned up shirt. He'd been very aloof and contained. Sage's comment about googling him had certainly made the man uncomfortable. Sage wondered what he was trying to hide.

He'd been very attracted to the other man, the spicy smell of his aftershave alluring, the intense and brooding expression on his face one that Sage would love to replicate in a film scene.

Well, he wasn't going to lose sleep over it.

He'd sworn off relationships for the short term. The only men he was interested in were the ones who serviced his needs and went home in the morning.

Dan Costyn was waiting for him at the Chelsea Brasserie in Sloan Square. From the looks of him, he'd already had one too many. Sage sighed. Dan could be a lot of work when he was this way. He walked over to his friend, who was currently chatting up the blonde waitresses giving him what was obviously at least his third drink.

At the sight of Sage, Dan stood up, waving his drink around in abandon, narrowly missing sloshing it all over the man seated next to him on the barstool.

"Sage, buddy. Come and have a drink." He turned to the bartender. "Whisky for my friend, please, and make sure it's Irish."

Sage sat down on the barstool on Dan's other side and set the manila envelope on the bar. "You look as if you've had enough for both of us," he remarked drily as Dan struggled to stay balanced on his stool. "Please tell me you won't do anything yet that'll get us kicked out of here."

Dan chuckled, punching Sage on the arm. "You worry too much, old son. I was just asking this lovely lady over there—" he waved vaguely in the general direction of the waitress, "if she wanted to come back to our place for a bit of you-know-what." He leered. "She even has a friend for you. Caitlin says he's blond, hung like a gorilla and she can *so* see the two of you together."

"Jesus, Dan, don't start that malarkey. That's the kind of thing that got us into trouble last time." Sage shook his head in irritation. "Can we not just sit and have a drink without you wanting to fix me up with every guy you hear about?"

Dan was very adventuresome in his sexploits and always wanted to include Sage in them. His friend chortled and took another gulp of his drunk.

Sage sipped his whisky, regarding his friend thoughtfully. "I take it you're still happy for me to stay with you whilst I'm filming?"

At the word "filming" Sage noticed the waitress turn and smile at him. Sage knew he was fairly well known but not yet a mainstream presence. It was amazing though how even a minor celebrity seemed to attract people.

"Are you a film star then?" She batted her eyelashes at him. "My friend loves film stars."

Sage was about to answer her when Dan threw his arms around his shoulders and gestured expansively. "This man is about to become an even bigger force to be reckoned with. He's just landed himself the leading role in the new *Double Exposure* TV series." He smiled proudly at his friend.

The waitress's eyes went even bigger. "Oh my God. I've just read two of those books. They're amazing." She looked at Sage. "You're going to play Carter West?"

Sage nodded, feeling a little uncomfortable as he wasn't quite sure when it was to be announced. He'd been so distracted by the sexy author he'd forgotten to ask. Jenny would kill him if she found out he'd leaked something he shouldn't.

Dan and his bloody big mouth!

The waitress leaned forward, muttering in Dan's ear before walking away saucily. He grinned widely.

Sage looked at him suspiciously. "What did she say?"

Dan hooted. "She really wants to come home with me now so she can say she's been in the flat with somebody famous. She's gone to tell her friend. I think we both just got really lucky." He raised his palm in a high five.

Sage slapped it. "Sorry to disappoint you but I'm not participating in any bloody foursome tonight. You can have them both."

Dan looked crestfallen. "But I'm not gay, Sage. I just want her. I think they're a package deal though."

"I'm going back home tonight, alone," Sage said firmly. "I have a ton of stuff to sort out and a script to start reading. I can't do that when I'm playing top to someone's bottom." He chuckled at his friend's disappointed expression. "Sorry, old lad. It's just not going to happen."

Dan scowled. "I hope you're going to be more bloody fun when you're staying with me or you're no use to man or beast."

Sage laughed as he ordered himself another whisky. He'd have one more then get on his way. An hour later, all good intentions of script-reading forgotten, he was still sitting bleary eyed at the same bar stool, with his fourth empty whisky in front of him, telling Dan all about Alexander Montgomery.

"I mean, the man is absolutely gorgeous, Dan, especially with those odd eyes. But he's a real cold fish. He got all uppity when I told him I'd googled him. You'd have thought I'd told him I was a stalker or something, the way he looked at me."

Dan held up a finger, wagging it in Sage's face. It made him feel ill and he reached up and grabbed it.

Dan giggled. "Sage, you're my best friend, you know that. But you worry too much about what goes on in men's heads and less about what goes on down there. I mean their 'down there,' not yours, although that counts as well."

Sage found this rambling discourse from his very drunk friend highly amusing and snorted with laughter.

The two men giggled drunkenly as they balanced unsteadily on the barstools. Sage had already seen their prospective dates leave earlier with a dirty look at them both as if they'd been cheated out of their night's entertainment. He hadn't quite fancied the look of the man anyway. Much too butch for his tastes.

The barman, busy polishing a glass, approached them with a resolute look on his face. "Lads, as much as I always love your combined company, I think you two have had enough. Can I call you a taxi to get you somewhere?"

Sage looked at him, trying to be as serious as possible. "Dan has a flat not far from here. I think we can walk."

The bartender didn't look convinced but shrugged his shoulders. "Well, I suggest you both have a quick cup of coffee, on the house, seeing as how you're both regulars. Then you'd better get home. If you can find home the state you two are in."

He grinned and walked off, still polishing his glass.

Sage looked at Dan. "He's always pretty nice to us. Shall we take him home for me?"

Dan howled at this and they rolled around on the stools, tears streaming down their faces until the bartender put two cups of black coffee in front of them.

"Drink," he said and it wasn't a request. The two picked up their cups, still trying to stifle the giggles that threatened to choke them.

Five minutes later they found themselves staggering down the road in the late-afternoon sunshine toward where they thought Dan's flat was. What should have been a brisk ten-minute walk took them nearly half an hour and they finally found themselves at the entrance to Dan's apartment building. On the fourth floor, after fumbling about for about five minutes, Dan managed to get his flat door open and the two men stumbled inside.

"You have the spare room," muttered Dan. His face looked a little green. "Feel free to make it yours. I really need the bathroom."

Sage nodded then wished he hadn't. The room spun and the contents of his stomach threatened. Other than the biscuits he'd had at Jenny's office that morning, he'd eaten nothing and he was certainly feeling the effects of four double whiskies. Dan was in the bathroom and Sage heard him retching. He swiftly made his way to the kitchen sink where he too promptly vomited. He could have kicked himself for getting into this state. He'd feel like crap in the morning. Sage groaned loudly as he was sick again. Finally, his heaving finished, he rinsed the kitchen sink, making his way over to the spare room. He didn't bother getting undressed, just flopped down on the bed, closing his eyes.

* * *

Alex awoke in a cold sweat, painfully aroused, sitting bolt upright in his bed. He couldn't remember what had woken him up, just that it had been something he needed to leave behind. His heart raced and he swallowed, feeling the dryness in his throat as if he'd been talking or snoring in his sleep. His bedroom was quiet with just the ticking sound of the Arti and Mestieri clock on the bedroom wall cutting into the silence.

He leaned back against the wall, passing a trembling hand across his eyes. God, he needed a drink. He looked at the bedside clock. Two A.M. Late and early enough to have one, he thought as he got out of bed, looking around for his robe. He slept naked, not liking the touch of clothing whilst he slept. He found it and slipped it on, enjoying the feel of the silk against his skin as he moved over to the minibar he kept in his room, opening the fridge, taking out a bottle of ice-cold peach schnapps. Alex poured a tumbler full and drank it in one swallow. He poured another one, walking to the window as he sipped. He stared out into the darkness beyond.

His groin ached, his erection swollen and throbbing. He felt a sense of unease and need in his mind and chest like an oil slick that slowly threatened to suffocate him. His hands trembled as he held the glass, the clear liquid shuddering gently. He watched the movement for a minute, then in a fit of violence threw the glass at the wall, smashing and splintering it into pieces. He choked back a sob, his eyes filling with tears as he slid down against the cool wall. Sitting on the floor, tears trickled down his cheeks and he tasted their saltiness. An essence of spilt peach permeated the room.

His hand slipped beneath his robe and he grasped his cock, moving in slow strokes as he pleasured himself, thinking of the man he'd met that day, the broad shoulders, the smiling eyes and the lips that just begged to be kissed.

He kept up his frantic movements, then his legs tensed against the cold floor, thighs like steel cables as he came with no sound, biting his lips to keep the sound inside. His ejaculate coated his hand and robe, slippery and warm, the room scented with its familiar smell.

Alex closed his eyes, hitting the back of his head, once, twice against the wall, then continued, the action growing in intensity and violence until finally he could no longer bear the painful throbbing in his head. He curled into a foetal ball on the hard stone floor, wrapping his thin robe tightly around his shivering body, closing his eyes, willing the night to be over.

Chapter 5

Seated at the kitchen breakfast table, Christopher Sage's head was splitting and his stomach queasy while the dryness in his mouth rivalled the Sahara. He groaned, wishing he was dead as he looked at the equally stricken Dan Costyn seated across from him.

The only saving grace was the script had made it to Dan's home with him.

The two men regarded each blearily. They'd slept all evening and night and had finally woken up around eight A.M.

"I wish I'd never bloody met you yesterday." Sage glared at his friend. "The only time I ever seem to feel this way is when I've been with you."

Dan squinted at him from bloodshot eyes. "That's a bit harsh, Sage. It also sounds a little bit wrong, you know? I'm not sure I would have phrased it that way myself."

He took a gulp of the piping hot black coffee in front of him. The friends were silent as they watched the news on the TV, the sound turned down because of their headaches.

"And we didn't even get to go home with the waitress and her friend." Dan's face was comical. "At least if we had, this might have been all worthwhile."

Sage looked at him in amazement. "Dan, if we'd gone home with them yesterday the only thing either of them would have seen would have been us puking our guts out, then falling comatose on the bed. I doubt either of us would even have been able to find it, let alone get it up."

Dan looked at him. "Speak for yourself. I know where mine bloody well is." He chuckled.

Sage grinned weakly. "I have to set some ground rules, Dan, if I move in here. I won't be able to do this. I need to be sure I can get up in the morning or no one's going to take me seriously. I really want this TV series to be a success. Do you promise me that when I say no I mean it?"

Dan laughed. "No means no. I'll try not to corrupt you too much whilst you're here. Scout's Honour."

"I don't bloody well believe you, but it'll do for a start." Sage stood up slowly, lest he lose his balance, still feeling fairly drunk despite the long sleep and vowing to turn over a new leaf. "I need to get off home and get cleaned up. I feel bloody awful and I smell it too." His nose wrinkled in distaste.

Dan nodded. "Fine, buddy. I promise to behave, honestly. I know how important this job is to you." He narrowed his eyes. "Just as long as you promise to keep those Irish moods at bay. Sage in a strop is one of the most bloody annoying creatures I've ever seen."

Sage grimaced. He didn't do it often but he'd inherited his father's predilection for what he'd affectionately called "The Black Irish," and what his mother had tautly called a "sulk and a fucking menace."

When Sage's mood crept up he knew he became sullen, moody and impossible to talk to. While it lasted, he was a definite downer on anyone around him. His mother had to put up with the two men in her life being awkward sods, and how she'd done it without taking a knife to their throats whilst they slept had always confounded both Sage and his father.

Sage reached over, gripping his friend tightly on the shoulder. "Thanks. I appreciate that. I promise I'll try and keep the moods to a minimum. I'll probably get here a few days before we start filming, just to settle in. I'll give you a call. I've got the spare key anyway, so I can let myself in if you're at work."

Dan worked as an investment advisor at one of the major London banks. He kept long hours and made an obscene amount of money, hence the three-bedroom luxury apartment in King's Road and the natty suits he wore.

The two friends could not have been more different. But they'd known each other since they were twelve years old and at school together. Dan had helped Sage through many a crisis in the course of his burgeoning understanding of his homosexuality. There wasn't a man Sage trusted more, other than his godfather.

Sage finally made it home to his cottage just after lunchtime. He was glad to see the familiar sight of his front door as he let himself in, making his way straight to the bathroom. Shedding his clothes in an untidy mess as he crossed the floor, he stepped into the shower and turned on the taps. Jets of steaming water cascaded over his body, washing away the sweat and stale smell of vomit that clung to his body. The taxi driver had sniffed in ire more than once. When Sage finally wrapped the towel around his waist and brushed his teeth, he felt more human.

He made himself a quick plate of scrambled eggs on toast, eating it whilst he read through the script. He had to admit he was impressed. The script was punchy, witty and well written. He could see the definite influence of Alexander Montgomery's writing. The writer had a unique style, one that was entertaining, dry and in places downright sarcastic. He could see why his books had such an impact.

The basic premise of the series revolved around Carter West, a world-renowned photographer, used to taking pictures in war zones, jungles and other far-flung places, and a fashion model called Gillian Banks.

The two of them meet in Egypt after a bomb explodes at the Cairo restaurant where they were both dining. Carter's best friend is killed in the explosion. Gillian is injured and Carter ends up at the hospital with her.

Sage chuckled when he read the fairly misogynistic viewpoint of the lead character, a fiery exchange in which Carter gave a no-holds-barred discourse of his view of fashion models.

Needless to say, tempers flared. From that point on, it became a case of bumping into each other all over the city. Finally they admit their attraction to each other and take the relationship to the next level.

Sage really liked the drama within the drama. Things always seemed to go wrong or one of them was in the wrong place at the time. The dialogue was quirky, tender and at times bitingly funny.

His mobile rang just as he was getting to the part where both characters were due to attend some photography awards ceremony and she couldn't keep her hands off him. It was all fairly erotic and he had to say he looked forward to testing his acting skills in this bit. He answered his phone feeling fairly put out at the interruption.

"Chris Sage."

"Christopher? It's Alexander Montgomery."

He was fairly surprised when he heard who it was. "Alexander. Hi. How are you? And please call me Sage. Christopher is normally only used when someone is really mad with me. What can I do for you?"

"Call me Alex, please. I just wanted to call and say I'm sorry for being a bit short yesterday. I tend to value my privacy and I get a little antsy when people talk about me. But it's not your fault, really."

Sage frowned slightly. "It's fine, don't worry about it. Everyone deserves privacy. Believe me, I know better than most."

"How are you finding the script?" Alex sounded a little wary.

"I'm busy with it now. It's really good. I'm very impressed and looking forward to getting started. What about you? Are you ready to have your words made into film? It must be quite an honour to have that sort of attention."

"It's all a bit overwhelming. But Luke and Janine are really professional and they're good teachers."

Sage chuckled. "They are that, quite the characters, the pair of them. I look forward to working with you. I'm sure we'll get to do a lot of really good stuff together as a couple."

He flushed as he realised what he'd said. "I mean, what with the publicity and the interviews of course, we'll probably be together a lot…" His voice tailed off and he shook his head in despair.

How did this man manage to make him say the wrong thing all the time?

"I'll be moving across to London a few days before we start filming. I've had a quiet word with the friend and asked him to help me keep on the straight and narrow so I don't get into any more trouble."

Alex chuckled softly and Sage's heart beat faster at the sound. It was extremely sexy, like the man himself. "I can only imagine what the two of you got up to, so one day you'll have to tell me the whole story. I've got to go now but I look forward to seeing you on set."

"Good. I'll see you soon then. Thanks for the call, Alex."

He disconnected the phone and whistled softly.

Well, he seemed to have come around.

It might be more fun working with him than he'd realised.

* * *

Alex put the phone down with a smile. Sage was absolutely charming with that sexy Irish voice of his. That bit about being a couple had made him want to laugh. He *had* felt bad about snapping at the actor. After all, Alex had created this character especially for Sage because he had such a thing for him.

He couldn't afford to alienate him.

Alex had a feeling in his gut this charming man was going to be trouble for him. He'd need to be very careful that he didn't get too close. Sage could never understand this side of him or be able to meet his special requirements. It was why Alex paid Eric, who he was going to see in just over an hour. He'd bought an extra session this week. Madame Duchaine had been most accommodating in freeing Eric up from his other clients. He looked at himself in the mirror. Tonight he was feeling especially needy; the dream of the previous night still preyed on his mind, even though he couldn't remember it clearly. At least that what's he told himself.

If he let the memories in he'd go crazy.

Chapter 6

Eric Rossi watched in satisfaction as Alex tried to suppress his cries. The man's stomach was a mass of short, narrow weals. Blood dribbled down his hardened stomach toward his shaved groin. Eric loved looking at Alex marked this way. He loved his job, loved inflicting pain and getting paid a lot of money to do it. He was *very* good at it.

Eric moved forward, his breathing laboured as Alex looked at him out of those strange eyes, eyes Eric thought made him look like some sort of devil. He ran his fingers down Alex's stomach, through the blood and the sweat, then lifted his fingers to his mouth to suck.

"You taste good, Alex," he whispered as he leaned in, his tongue darting in and out of Alex's ear, his hands slowly caressing the weals on his stomach.

"Here, try some." He thrust his bloody fingers into Alex's mouth and Alex sucked them greedily, his breathing deep, his eyes closed in supplication. He was in his usual position, Eric's favourite, bound to the posts, his body naked with the marks of the last session's ministrations still visible.

He'd been surprised when Madame had told him he had another session with Alex. Normally once a week was enough for his client, though he'd like to have him more.

He really must be going through some serious stress to come back so soon.

Eric had been harsher with his guest this evening, at his request. Alex was obviously punishing himself for something; they all were in some way. Eric didn't know why and he never asked. Alex never volunteered the information.

He leaned in toward Alex's face, his mouth just short of brushing his lips. One of Alex's cardinal rules was no kissing. Eric wasn't allowed to take Alex's mouth with his and it frustrated him. Sometimes he really wanted to kiss him, taste him, feel Alex's tongue in his mouth, but he knew Alex would choose someone else if he disobeyed. It was probably why he treated him harsher than his other clients. He didn't like being denied something he badly wanted.

He was naked, his white jeans in a pile by the door. Tonight he'd wanted Alex to see all of him as he tamed his client. As he walked around Alex, his hand stroked his cock, revelling in the feel of his own fingers against his swollen and upright member.

"Do you see what you do to me, Alex?" he murmured, caressing himself, his breath getting deeper and deeper with each touch. "You make me extremely horny and I expect you to satisfy me later."

He raised the whip again, seeing his prisoner tense, expecting the crack. Eric smiled, thinking there was no point in disappointing him. The whip struck Alex's buttocks hard, and he jerked in pain. Tears welled in Alex's eyes, trickling down his cheeks. Eric moved around and licked them as he stroked Alex's smooth groin gently with his hand and then without warning, slapped it hard, causing a hiss to escape from Alex's mouth as he raised his whip again.

"Chrysippus," Alex whispered softly.

Eric stopped in disbelief. Alex had spoken his safe word. He had never heard him say it in the two years he'd been coming here. He laid down his whip, undid the silk ties, then watched Alex walk unsteadily to the bed and lower himself down with his head turned to the side. He must have been in pain from the lashes on his stomach but he said nothing.

Eric walked over to the bed, lying down beside Alex.

This ritual never changed. There would be no talking. It was always the same position, the same way of entering him, never from the front when he could see Alex's face. This was something else Alex demanded that frustrated him.

It was one of the things Alex had stipulated when he'd joined, as well as not being able to go down on him, something else he really wanted to do. He wanted to taste the other man's musky scent on his lips, feel his tongue slip around his lovely cock, feel him throbbing beneath his lips as Alex came in his mouth.

But even that was denied him, as was Alex giving *him* a blowjob. It wasn't on the list of "permitted activities." He would have liked nothing more than to have Alex's beautiful, sensual lips wrapped around his cock, tonguing him with deep abandon, taking his balls in mouth and sucking him until he came.

He ran his fingers down Alex's back, touching the weals on his buttocks then kissing them. He reached for the lube and coated his fingers, sliding his fingers inside Alex, feeling him arch back against him as he pushed into Alex's wetness and heat. When he'd finished his teasing and finally was ready to enter Alex, his cock sheathed once again in the condom that he hated using, it was with all the frustrated force he could muster and Alex's body responded to his violence in kind as he pushed back, wanting him deeper inside him.

The noise of skin on skin, sweat on sweat and the smell of blood was intoxicating. As he rammed himself into the needy man panting beneath him, Eric wondered not for the first time what this man thought he had done to deserve such treatment. Alex was his most extreme client. The man took more punishment that anyone he'd ever seen and still came back for more.

As Eric climaxed, his body spasming in his need of Alex, he broke the rules and cried out his name.

Chapter 7

Melanie van Pelt regarded the man sitting opposite her with thoughtful eyes. In her three years as Alexander Montgomery's therapist she'd never quite seen him as fidgety or anxious as he was now. She wondered what had changed in his life to orchestrate such a change.

Melanie leaned forward, toying with the pen she held. "So, Alex. It's been a little longer than usual since I saw you. What's been happening in your life since we last spoke?"

Alex didn't look at her directly as he usually would but instead sat back on the soft leather couch, looking at her hands rather than her face, his long legs crossed at the ankles and his arms folded across his chest in a classic defensive pose.

"Well, I'm still seeing Eric." He hesitated before going on. "I needed to see him more than usual this week."

"More than once? That's not a step forward. What's going on?"

Alex sighed, finally looking up at Melanie, his eyes shadowed. "I had the dream again. And the whole TV series thing has got me a bit spooked. It's one thing writing novels in the solitude of my apartment but now I have to interact with people every day. It's a little overwhelming."

Melanie shook her head. "We talked about this. You felt you'd be all right with the whole public thing. Something else has driven you to this, not just your sudden visibility." She leaned back in her chair. "Have you met someone? That's normally a trigger of your need to self-punish more."

Alex shook his head vehemently. "No, I'm not involved with anyone."

Melanie could tell Alex was not being particularly truthful. She'd known him too long, too intimately. She sighed. "Something or someone *has* triggered this. You may not realise it yet but I can see it from the outside. Who have you met recently that's making you feel this way?"

Alex clamped his lips together mutinously, saying nothing.

Melanie knew better than to push him. "Tell me about the dream," she asked quietly. "Were you back at Bohemia with Rudy?"

Alex flinched, his eyes closing momentarily. "Yes," came back the whispered reply. "I was in the dungeon again. Rudy was there with me." He swallowed, his voice breaking. "I woke up and couldn't remember my dream but the memories it brought back were so vivid I couldn't sleep. I wanted Eric there with his whip. What kind of monster does that make me?" His voice was harsh.

Melanie sighed. "Alex, you aren't the monster. Rudy was the monster. You were a seventeen-year-old boy. He broke you down until there was nothing left but what he wanted. You're stronger than that now. You know you are. It takes time to break down eight solid months of abuse."

Despite her professionalism, Melanie's heart broke as she saw the desperation in Alex's eyes. She was glad that cult-leader bastard was dead. What he had done to this young man was beyond despicable.

"I just want to be normal." Alex's words were flat and dead. "I want to be able to have a normal relationship with a man that doesn't involve the things Eric does to me. But I can't. I'm not capable of it."

Melanie felt a stirring of unease. Alex had been doing so well but all of a sudden he seemed to have regressed. She had to find out what lay beneath it.

"Alex. Tell me about the last couple of weeks. I remember you telling me at our last session you were planning some auditions for your TV series. How did that turn out?"

She didn't miss the flicker of animation that appeared in Alex's eyes at her words. This was something she definitely needed to pursue.

Alex swallowed. "It went very well. We held the auditions and chose the leads. We start filming in two weeks' time."

"Who are the leads? Anyone I'd know?" Melanie acted nonchalant but she knew in her bones this was the key to Alex's current predicament.

Alex was quiet for a while, twisting his hands and watching the play of knuckles as he flexed his hands. "The female lead is Dianne Cunningham. I'm sure you know who she is. She's been in quite a few films. The lead man's name is Christopher Sage. You've probably seen him in the TV series *Dalton Hospital* and the remake of *King Solomon's Mines* that aired recently."

Melanie did indeed know the young actor. He'd been making quite a splash in the newspapers and gossip magazines now that he was single and eligible again. He was also gay. She chuckled, trying to ease the tension in the room. "He's very personable, I must say. Very good-looking and a great actor to boot. You must be pleased he's playing one of your characters."

Alex nodded and looked up at Melanie, a slight smile on his face. "I am. He's perfect for the part and I think he'll bring my work to life. He's very professional and he seems to really like my books. He said he'd read all three."

Melanie felt they were finally getting to the heart of the matter. Alex felt something more for this man than he was ready to reveal.

In the past, when Alex became interested in someone, the spiral downward began.

Melanie had always had the feeling Alex held something back from her. It frustrated her that she'd never managed to get to the bottom of it. "I suppose you've spent some time with him. What's he like?"

Alex shrugged. "He seems very down to earth, very charming. He keeps horses."

Melanie nodded. "I see, an animal lover. Well, that makes him all right in my book. Animals always know a cad when they see one." She grinned at Alex, who relaxed slightly and smiled back for the first time since the session began.

"You'll be working quite closely together then, I imagine. How do you feel about that?" Melanie watched Alex's face closely. She didn't miss the faint softening of his face as Alex thought about her question.

"I think it'll be okay. We've already had our first little spat when he told me he was googling me and couldn't find anything. I might have overreacted but I called him to apologise." Alex smiled

Melanie nodded. "You know they shouldn't be able to find anything under your current name as it was all kept so quiet, but I know you had worries before you started writing the books."

"You know me, Mel. I can deflect with the best of them." Alex's voice was hard and steely. "The need I have for Eric is my own. No one deserves to know about that. It's what keeps me going in the normal world."

"You are capable of a fulfilling sexual relationship with a lover, Alex. You've done it before even if it didn't quite work out." Melanie said gently.

"Yes, I know. But no man is going to take me on full time when he finds out I visit an S-and-M club that specialises in bondage and whipping." He laughed bitterly. "'Babe, I'm home.

Just don't mind the whip marks and the bite marks on my behind or my stomach or the stench of another man inside me.' What man could share that with me?" He was quiet then spoke again, more resigned. "Until I can get the need to be punished out of me, there's no point in starting any type of relationship. It's just not fair on the other man." Alex looked at his silver Armani watch. "I'm five minutes over, shame on you. You might have someone out there chewing off their fingers because they feel unloved."

His tone was wry but Melanie sensed the slight edge to it. He stood up, stretching his arms. "I'll see you next week, same time, same place then. Thanks, Melanie."

Melanie nodded as Alex disappeared out the back door, then sighed. She felt a little worried about Alex's regression. She'd write up her notes later. She had the video of the session. Perhaps she'd watch it later and try to come up with a strategy Alex might use to deal with his current change of situation, she thought as she went out to the front office to welcome her next patient.

"Mr. Smith? Won't you come in? I'm terribly sorry I'm late."

Chapter 8

Christopher Sage sat in the Moorcroft Films studio office, his long legs propped up on the desk as he read the week's filming schedule. He had to admit so far it all seemed to be going like clockwork. He'd been here two weeks now and was really getting into the part. He looked up as his co-star, Dianne Cunningham, came in.

She grinned when she saw him. "Sage, those feet of yours are going to get you into a ton of trouble. You know how possessive Luke is about that antique desk. And here you are with your great big clodhoppers all over it. "

He smiled. "These boots are clean. Stop worrying."

She smiled slyly as she studied his boots. "Tell me. Is it true what they say about men with big feet? Do they really have big dicks?"

She chuckled as he went pink. "God, you are the only man I've ever met who blushes. What the hell are you going to do when we hit the sex scenes? Are you going to self-combust and take me with you?"

He scowled at her. "Thanks for that. I'll be fine. I'm a professional too, remember? I'll manage to keep it on track." He waggled his eyebrows at her comically.

She spluttered with laughter. "God, please don't do that to me on set, I'll die laughing."

Sage chuckled. The actress leaned toward him, kissing his cheek briefly.

"You are such a darling. I love working with you. You're incredible."

Sage watched her affectionately as she darted around the office like a hummingbird. She was a real character. Lithe, attractive, blonde and a consummate professional. It was easy to be good in a part when you had a co-star like Dianne.

Dianne flitted over to him, her eyes mischievous as she perched on the desk. He could see her rather striking cleavage and the freckles on her throat and he averted his eyes.

Dianne looked at him in amusement. "So tell me. What do you think of Alexander?"

Sage was a little discomfited by the question. During the past two weeks, he'd seen Alex, but the writer had been aloof. Civil enough, but Sage couldn't seem to get to know him better, despite all his very considerable efforts.

He didn't think anyone on set had made any inroads in getting to know him. "He's very professional and seems to be fairly well liked by everyone."

He trailed off as Dianne shook her head. "No. I mean what do you think of him as a man? Do you find him attractive? None of the other gay guys on set have managed to get more than a little smile out of him despite their best efforts. They even doubt that he's gay at all."

Sage frowned. "Christ, Dianne, I'm not going to talk about someone I hardly know like that. It's a little unfair, don't you think? Besides, given the state of that lot out there," he gestured with his hand, "I'd say not being able to get him in their sights is no reflection on Alex, more on them. They can be a bunch of randy pillocks." He scowled fiercely.

Dianne batted him playfully on his arm. "Come on. Surely you've thought about it, getting him into the sack?"

He shook his head, not wanting to admit he had indeed had those thoughts about Alex. They generally involved him moving up and down Alex's body slowly, tasting every inch of him, sucking whatever he had beneath the chinos Alex favoured and then finally plunging himself inside the man as he cried out Sage's name in sheer ecstasy.

"Well, I'm not one of the other guys," he lied. "He seems to want his privacy, and to be honest, I can see why if you're all talking about him behind his back." He stood up and heard a noise at the door. He turned to see Alex standing there, a strange expression on his face.

"Thank you, Sage," Alex said quietly. "I appreciate you fighting in my corner for me."

Dianne laughed softly. "Honey, it's just office gossip, nothing more. This is show business. You get used to people talking about you. Even Sage knows that's true. You've been talked about in the past, haven't you?" She raised her eyebrows suggestively. "But it's all in good fun, I promise."

She stood up and walked past him out of the office.

Sage looked at Alex, whose face was paler than normal. "You need to ignore their gossip. They're bloody vicarious. Don't let it worry you."

Sage's heart ached at the lost look on Alex's face. He'd never seen anyone look so—abandoned. He moved over him instinctively, placing a comforting hand on his shoulder. Alex hissed in pain, jerking away. "Please don't touch me." His voice was low.

Sage stepped back in confusion. He'd only just touched Alex lightly, nothing to warrant such a reaction. "I'm sorry. I didn't mean to hurt you."

Alex turned away to stare out of the window. "I have a slight injury to my shoulder. It wasn't your fault. I just don't like being touched."

Sage sighed. "I seem to have a habit of upsetting you. I promise you it's not intentional."

Alex turned back, looking at him with those incredible eyes. Sage's chest tightened. Where he'd thought he might see disdain he saw something else entirely. Affection.

Alex shook his head. "Sage, you're great. It's me that's the problem. I'm a little complicated, I'm afraid. Some would say peculiar." He smiled.

Sage grinned back. "You look fine to me," he murmured. "You look even better when you smile. You should do it more often."

"I'm trying, I'm really trying." Alex's voice sounded tired suddenly and the camaraderie that Sage had seen just a few moments ago dissipated. But a slight grin remained on Alex's face. "I promise you I'm not into women though. *That's* not one of my vices."

Sage thought Alex's voice sounded rather droll, as if there was a hidden message in there.

"Glad to hear it," Sage murmured. "That'd be a real waste for men like me everywhere."

Even as he said it, he marvelled at the fact that he was actually managing to flirt with this very unusual man. Alex's quiet chuckle at his words made the hairs on Sage's arms stand up and his erection grow.

Christ, what this man did to him. He hadn't had a boner like this in a while.

Sage tried to ease the growing turmoil in his groin by walking over to the window and gazing down into the street. Alex moved up behind him, touching his arm gently. A charge like a slow flick of fire licked against the skin under Sage's shirt.

Alex spoke softly. "The reason I came in here was to tell you Luke was looking for you. He and Janine had a script change they wanted to run by you. They're in the staff room."

Sage nodded, moving over to the door, brushing past Alex as he did so. He was sensually aware of the stubble on Alex's chin and the scent of his aftershave, something spicy, a smell that teased Sage's nostrils and made him extremely horny. Not for the first time he cursed the fact that a man's primal reaction to someone he found attractive could happen at the most inopportune of places and times. Sage found Luke and Janine sitting poring over a wad of documents in the studio staff room.

Luke waved him over. "Sage, there you are. Christ, I was about to send out a search party. Did you get my message?"

"Loud and clear," Sage affirmed. "Sorry, I got a little sidetracked. What's up?"

The rest of his afternoon was spent with Janine and Luke discussing alterations to some of the scenes to be filmed the next day. It was almost nine p.m. when Sage finally went to fetch his denim jacket from his locker. He saw Alex still sitting in his office staring at his computer screen.

He popped his head in. "Alex? Isn't this a bit late for you to be here?"

Alex looked up at him. "I was catching up on some business stuff. My publisher insists I keep a blog so I was updating it." He sighed wryly. "It's been a bitch of a day today, so I haven't had time to do all the social networking stuff I'm expected to do."

"How are you getting home? Do you live far?"

The other man shook his head. "I have an apartment in Brook Green about a five-minute walk from here. It's pretty convenient actually."

"My tube stop is that way. Maybe we could walk together?" Alex looked at Sage and Sage thought he was going to refuse his offer.

Alex's face changed to an expression that was resolute; then he smiled. "It would be nice to have company, thanks. Let me just pack up my stuff and I'll be with you."

Sage nodded and went to wait in the foyer for him. Alex joined him a few minutes later.

"Have you had the apartment long then?" Sage watched his face as they walked.

Alex nodded. "About eighteen months. I bought it with some money I inherited. It's pretty nice, two bedrooms and a small walled garden. A ground-floor flat. I love it. It's very private."

He looked at Sage mischievously. "How are you doing with your friend Dan? I'm very intrigued to hear more about that episode Jenny referred to when we first met."

Sage groaned. "Don't remind me. I'm still trying to forget the whole blasted thing."

Alex looked at him enquiringly. "Are you going to tell me about it then?"

Sage smiled. "Suffice it to say we'd both had a bit too much to drink and ended up in our underwear chained to some old railings outside the Royal Hospital in Chelsea. It wasn't one of my finer moments and it was a long time ago, when luckily I wasn't really known. I'm sure the footage will be somewhere on YouTube, though."

He heard Alex's snort of laughter and was pleased he'd made him laugh.

"Why would you do that?" Alex finally managed to ask.

Sage pretended to reflect seriously. "Some young lady Dan was interested in dared us to do it and we both felt honour bound to fulfil the dare. My date scarpered the minute he saw what was happening. What can I say? We were both bloody stupid. Dan tends to bring out my bad side. He's a bit of an animal."

Alex chuckled. "I'd like to meet him one day. He sounds — interesting."

Sage looked at him. "Perhaps one day you will. We can always invite you round for takeout at our place. I'm afraid neither of us cooks particularly well."

"Maybe one day I'll take you up on the offer." Alex sounded wistful but Sage didn't want to push.

Alex motioned toward a fairly imposing red brick building ahead with railings surrounding it. "That's my building there." He glanced at Sage slyly. "Perhaps you'd like to chain yourself to those railings in your underwear? I won't mind, I promise."

Sage laughed loudly, glad to see Alex flirting back with him. "I think once in a lifetime is enough for that. Although if you dare me when I've had one too many, I might oblige. I don't like turning down a dare or a bet. It's a family trait. My dad was a bit of a gambler and he'd take a bet on anything."

Alex stopped at the entrance to his building and hesitated. Finally he spoke quietly. "Would you like to come in for coffee? I'm sure I can scrounge up a Jammie Dodger or something for you. I know how partial you are to biscuits."

Sage smiled. "I'd like that, thanks." He'd appreciate any opportunity to get to know this man better. He followed Alex into the grounds, down a small flight of stairs to a large basement apartment with a wrought-iron gate. Alex opened the gate and they walked up to the very secluded front door.

"It's like having your own secret entrance," Sage said admiringly. "Not like my place where anyone can pop in anytime. I hardly ever lock the door. I think perhaps I should start," he said gloomily. "The other day I was in the kitchen in the altogether and the gardener came in to ask me about lawn cuttings. I don't know who was more shocked."

Alex laughed loudly as he unlocked the front door. "What the hell were you doing naked in the kitchen anyway?"

Sage looked at him in indignation. "It's my bloody house! I can walk around naked if I want to. I'd just got out the shower and was making a quick cup of coffee."

Alex shook his head in amusement. Sage whistled as he walked into the front room. "Wow. This is incredible. It looks like something out of an interior design magazine."

Alex's lounge was decorated in shades of grey and purple, with artwork adorning the walls and many sculptures and glass bowls scattered around in various cubist pieces of furniture. The lighting was dim and subdued and there was a faint odour of sandalwood in the air. Sage stood and admired it. "It's lovely. It looks like somewhere you can retreat and just lose yourself. Not like my place, which is a constant hive of activity."

Alex looked pleased at his comments. "I'm glad you like it. Make yourself comfortable and I'll make you that coffee I promised."

He disappeared into a large, airy kitchen to the left of the lounge. Sage wandered around the room, inspecting the artworks and various knickknacks. There were no photographs scattered around and nothing personal on show. "Do you take sugar or milk?" Alex called out.

"Just black please. No sugar." Sage called back. He sat down in an easy chair. Alex soon appeared with his coffee and a plate filled with various biscuits. "Sorry, no Jammie Dodgers. Just chocolate digestives and the ginger nuts."

Sage took his coffee and smiled. "I'm not fussy when it comes to biscuits." He took a chocolate one, dipping it into his coffee.

Drops of liquid dribbled down his chin and he wiped them absently with his sleeve.

Alex shook his head in amusement. "You're very unusual, Sage. Very down to earth, not at all like I'd imagine an actor to be."

Sage peered at over the rim of his coffee cup as he sipped it. "Do you think we're all living the high life, in suits and classy outfits, always at shows and with a different person on our arm each time?" He raised an eyebrow in query.

Alex mused for a moment before replying. "I suppose I'd say yes. It seems to be what it's all about. But you're different. You stay away from the limelight. Shun it, almost."

Sage looked down at his coffee cup. "I'll do whatever's needed to promote myself and the film or TV series that I'm in. Jenny makes sure of that; it's her job and mine. I have a responsibility toward the producers, the film's shareholders and the rest of the cast. But that doesn't mean *I'm* always available to be on show. I value my private life. I've had it invaded once before and that didn't turn out so well. So now I play it by my rules, where I can at least." He smiled wryly. "Sometimes it isn't possible."

Alex nodded. "I understand that philosophy. I like to do the same as you've noticed." Sage noted Alex didn't ask him about his cryptic comment about his life being invaded.

I suppose he feels he doesn't share his past, so why would I return the favour? I admire him for that.

"I like your Banksy piece." Sage waved toward a large print on the wall depicting a street artist. "I've always liked his sense of irreverence when it comes to what he paints."

Alex nodded. "Me too. It's a little unorthodox." He yawned, covering his mouth with his hand. "Sorry. It's not your company. It's just been a long day." Alex looked at Sage curiously. "Tell me about your dad. You said he was a bit of a gambler. What did he gamble on?"

Sage smiled. "Horses of course. We've a bit of a family tradition when it comes to the ponies. In fact I have two of them at home. My dad was a trainer for some horse owners in Southern Ireland where I lived after I was born, in a town called Shannon, in County Clare.

"We moved to England when I was twelve. Of course Dad always had to put a bet on the horses." He grinned. "My mum was always very tolerant of his gambling but when he pinched her housekeeping money one day to place a bet, she laid down the law. He had to tone it down a bit after that. Mum was fairly fiery. You wouldn't have wanted to get on the wrong side of her." He smiled at the fond memory.

"Do they live close by then or are they in Ireland?" Alex asked curiously.

Sage's face shadowed. "My folks were killed in a plane crash when I was nineteen."

"God, Sage. I'm sorry. That must have been very difficult." Alex laid a hand on Sage's and Sage clasped it, enjoying the feel of another man's warm skin beneath his. His groin still tingled with the Alex's nearness.

Sage nodded, his eyes distant. "Dad had got his pilot's licence and he bought himself a small plane, a little Cessna 152. He and Mum used to go back to Shannon to see my aunt and uncle. They'd only been flying about half an hour and a flock of birds flew straight into the propeller. We're not hundred percent sure, but the crash investigators said it looked like Dad was forced to pull back fairly sharply on the control wheel and the engine stalled. There were no survivors." He shrugged his shoulders. "It was just one of those things, no one's fault." He sat silently, remembering the tragedy and the pain he'd felt when Miles had come to break the news.

Alex squeezed his hand. "I am so sorry. You sound as if you were close to your parents."

"I was and I was very fortunate to have them for those nineteen years," Sage said quietly. "Some people aren't so lucky, I guess." He looked at Alex. "How about you? Do you still have family around?"

Alex took his hands away from his as he smiled tightly. "No, no family. There's just me." Alex offered nothing more. Again Sage wondered at this man's need to keep secrets about his personal life.

Sage finished his coffee, putting the cup down on the coaster on the table. "I should be getting off." He stood up and stretched. "Thanks for the chat and the coffee. I suppose I'll see you in the morning?"

Alex nodded. "I'll be there. Where else would I be?"

Sage picked up his jacket and slung it over his shoulder. He made his way to the door and opened it, stepping into the warm June night air. "Goodnight, Alex. Sweet dreams." Sage turned and walked up the steps to the pavement, feeling Alex's eyes on him as he headed toward the tube station.

He'd enjoyed that little glimpse into the elusive Mr. Montgomery's private world and thought he might have been fairly privileged to see the inside of his home. He imagined Alex didn't share it with many. That alone made him feel special.

Alex was certainly growing on him even though his caginess about the other areas of his life continued to intrigue him. Sage wondered exactly what secrets he held in that head of his. He wasn't sure whether he had the patience to find out, as much as he wanted to. He sighed as the train rumbled into the station and he jumped onto the tube that would take him toward Chelsea. But he certainly might give it a try if the right opportunity presented itself and he could break through that wall the man had put around himself.

* * *

Alex closed the door to his apartment, leaning against it with both a sigh of relief and regret. Relief that Sage had finally gone and he could relax and stop wondering what the actor looked like with his shirt off, wanting to run his hands through his curly black hair, place his mouth against his and taste him and feel him inside him.

Regret saddened him. All he had was the fantasy because he didn't have the courage to do any of those things. His groin ached with his need for Sage and he felt bereft now that he'd gone.

What the hell is going on with me? I hardly know the man except through work yet it feels like I've known him longer. He has this effect on me. It must be because he's been in my head so intimately as Carter West that I almost feel I know him. It's as if part of him belongs to me because I created him.

Since leaving the studio, he hadn't even thought of Study in Scarlet or his next session. Why was it when he was with Sage he could forget his seedier side? Alex took the coffee cups to the kitchen and actually drank the dregs of coffee in Sage's cup from the side where he had sipped it.

He was mortified at himself.

Christ, Alex, you're like a mooning hormonal teenager. Get a grip on yourself.

That night when he finally went to bed around eleven, he made sure Sage starred in his fantasies. When he finally climaxed, murmuring Sage's name, he imagined Sage's hands on his body, Sage's warm mouth on his, and for the moment he was content.

Chapter 9

The following morning Alex was sitting at his desk in his office at the film studio when he heard a soft knock on his door. His face brightened when he saw Sage standing there, dressed in tight blue jeans and a well-worn green checked shirt. Alex thought he looked as sexy as hell.

"Morning." Sage grinned. "Did you sleep well last night?"

Alex flushed, remembering what he'd done last night with this man in his mind. He nodded. "I did. It must have been the biscuits and the conversation."

Just then, Sarah Brose, a member of the canteen and cooking staff, walked in. Alex saw her look at Sage and her nostrils flared slightly as if she didn't like something. He wondered what that was all about.

Sarah brushed past Sage, ignoring him, and walked over to Alex with a bright smile.

"Your coffee, just the way you like it. I asked the kitchen staff to make you one of those chicken sandwiches you like for lunch so it'll be ready when you go down to the staff room."

Alex was touched. For some reason Sarah had taken quite a shine to him, making sure Alex didn't want for anything. In fact, it was getting a bit stifling but he didn't want to offend the woman. Sarah was a stereotypical spinster of indeterminate age, but Alex guessed about sixty, with greying hair, granny glasses and a matronly figure, quite a large and powerfully built woman. The cast and crew seemed fairly scared of her.

Alex also had the strangest feeling that he had seen the woman before but he couldn't think where that might have been. "Thanks, Sarah. That's very sweet of you. You really don't have to do this for me, you know."

Sarah shook her head emphatically. "It's the least I can do for you. Your books are a wonderful inspiration to me and you're such a talented writer. You also need to keep your strength up to write that next novel you're busy with."

Sage so far had kept quiet. Alex presumed he was as much in awe of Sarah as the next man.

At the implication Alex was writing another book his ears pricked up. "You're writing another book? I didn't know that. What's this one about then? Or is it a secret?"

Sarah scowled at him. "If he wanted anyone to know he'd tell them. Don't be so bloody nosy. Alex, don't forget your sandwich." She turned and left.

Sage watched her go with an open mouth. "Jesus. Is it just me she doesn't like or is she that way with everyone?"

Alex was nonplussed at her rude behaviour. "She's a little bit overpowering, I confess. But her heart seems to be in the right place."

"I'd say. I think it's in bloody Hades with Satan." Sage frowned, his eyes flashing dangerously.

Alex had just taken a sip of coffee and at Sage's words he laughed and spluttered his coffee all over his chin and the keyboard in front of him.

Sage came over to him, chuckling at his predicament, taking his shirt out of his jeans and offering it to Alex as a cloth. "Sorry about that."

Alex accepted the oddly intimate gesture and dabbed his mouth with Sage's shirttail, glimpsing Sage's naked torso as he wiped his mouth.

Alex definitely liked what he saw.

Taut stomach muscles and the indentation of Sage's hip bones in their V shape as they disappeared into the waistband of his jeans, a line of hair down to his groin that looked very inviting for either his hand or mouth to trail down. The man had an amazingly sexy torso. Alex's cock moved in his pants like a small animal trying to get out. He was glad he was sitting down, hidden from view.

Sage said teasingly, "I can take the shirt off if you like and you can wipe down the computer?"

God, had he seen him looking?

Alex found his voice. "Sage, I think that might be taking it too far, as much as I'd like that. I've got tissues somewhere in the drawer; I'll use those."

He scrabbled around in the desk drawer, becoming aware Sage had gone quiet. Alex looked at him and saw Sage regarding him with eyes that suddenly looked quite sultry.

"Really?" Sage's voice was now an even more pronounced soft Irish lilt that turned Alex's bones to jelly. "You'd like to see me with my shirt off? Is that an invitation?"

Alex swallowed, not sure what to say. This sudden openly uber-sexy and flirtatious Sage was someone he wasn't sure about, although he was causing havoc with his nether regions.

Sage moved around to Alex's side, taking the tissues from his clenched hand and slowly wiping the keyboard free of coffee. Alex leaned back in his chair, breathless. The pressure between his legs grew in intensity. Sage was so close to Alex he could smell his aftershave and see the dark hairs on his arms at his wrists. Alex could also see the hardened ridge of Sage's own erection lying against his leg in his tight jeans.

God, he must be able to smell how bloody aroused I am. And he feels the same about me, obviously, if that monster in his pants is anything to go by.

They were both aware of the effect they was having on the other. Alex saw it in the slight smile on Sage's face and the way he deliberately moved closer to him as he used the last of the tissues.

Sage threw the sodden lump accurately into the wastepaper bin on the other side of the desk. "There. All cleaned up. Now where were we before you so rudely expelled everything in your mouth over the desk? Oh yes, you were going to tell me about this book you're writing."

Sage still stood close, not moving, watching Alex's face with intense eyes that made Alex's insides churn and his mouth dry.

"I've only just started it," Alex said huskily, looking up at Sage's unwavering stare. "It's another romance trilogy but it's quite different than the last one. This one's a little darker and much sexier."

"I like the sound of that. Is there a part for me in it again in case they make another TV series?" Sage said teasingly.

Alex was a little unnerved at both Sage's statement as well as the mischievous expression on his face. "I haven't thought that far ahead yet. Like I said, it's in the early stages."

Sage nodded. "Have you got a name for it yet?"

"Only a working title. I'll probably change it later as the story develops."

"What's it about?" Sage asked curiously.

Alex shook his head firmly, trying to get back on safer ground. His insides churned at Sage's nearness. "You are so quizzy, aren't you? You'll find out when you read it one day. Do you ask an artist to tell you all about the painting he's doing whilst he's busy? No, you wait for it to be finished. Well, you'll have to do the same with this one."

Sage stepped away from him and Alex could breathe again.

"Well, that's telling me," Sage murmured with a smile on his face. "I suppose I'll have to wait then, won't I?" To Alex's relief, Sage tucked his damp shirt back into his jeans.

Luke Belmont appeared in the entrance to the office. "Sage. We're all ready to rock and roll, old son. Get yourself geared up. We'll start in about an hour." He grinned. "Give you plenty of time to get that ugly mug all made up and pretty for the cameras."

Sage grinned back. "I'll be there." He took one last lingering look at Alex and disappeared behind Luke. Alex sat there, feeling slightly shell-shocked.

What the hell had just happened? To put it mildly, Sage's sex appeal had just flared like a flame turned up on a Bunsen burner. Alex had simply folded like a newly laundered sheet.

He turned to his computer, hitting the *esc* button to awaken the system. The cursor on page eighty of the new story winked at him, inviting him to write more words. He swallowed, shifting uncomfortably in his chair to relieve the tension in his groin.

Perhaps he'd jump straight into the sex scenes. They'd be as hot as hell the way he felt right now.

* * *

Sage had a distinctly uncomfortable feeling down below as he made his way to the studio makeup room. He hoped like hell no one else noticed the bulge in his crotch. He knew Alex had. The man's eyes had widened and he'd licked his lip, almost causing Sage to come in his jeans. He'd have to try and conceal his arousal somehow until it subsided.

What the hell had possessed him to approach Alex all "come hither" like that? Jesus, he'd been like some sort of male escort tempting a customer. What was it about this man that bought out the man-slut in him?

He'd got the distinct impression Alex had felt the same way from the way his nostrils flared when Sage was near, and the needy expression in his eyes took his breath away. He'd quite enjoyed testing Alex's reaction to his nearness.

I could have swept everything off the desk, ripped his trousers right off that sexy tight arse of his and taken him right there. God, that would have felt so good.

He sat in the chair with a towel in his lap whilst Amy did his film makeup. She chatted, keeping him distracted whilst he went over his lines in his head, trying to get back into character. By the time the hour had passed he was feeling more comfortable, the steady mantra of lines he repeated in his head keeping him focused. He was ready to start filming. He sighed. It would be a long day but he was ready for it. There was time enough to think about Alexander Montgomery later tonight when he was alone in his room.

Chapter 10

Three weeks later, Alex sat in Melanie's room, his hands gesturing animatedly as he talked to his therapist.

"He's driving me crazy, Melanie. He's funny, he's pretty cute and he's sexy as hell. I hardly ever think about anything bad when I'm with him. He makes me laugh. And we haven't even slept together. But we have been spending quite a lot of time together on set and having the occasional evening drink."

He wasn't going to tell his therapist about the fantasies he'd been having or the fact the man made him want to rut like an animal. The last drink he and Sage had shared together, he'd been sure Sage had been about to kiss him. Instead Alex had gone to bed so sexually frustrated he'd jacked off twice to get his satisfaction, all the time imagining Sage's naked body and his hot, greedy mouth.

All Alex could think about was the feel of Sage inside him, filling him and the taste of the man on his lips.

Melanie smiled in pleasure. "I've never seen you this animated about someone before. I like the fact you're not obsessing about Eric or your needs. Every little moment you aren't thinking about that is a step forward. It just goes to show that perhaps you're ready to have a relationship with a man other than Eric."

Alex's face shadowed. "I wouldn't go that far." Then his expression changed. "I can tell he definitely likes me. He can be quite a flirt, which seems to surprise him." He grinned. "He's been a complete gentleman so far, unfortunately." He smiled ruefully.

"You need to trust your instincts. From what you tell me, he's not really the wham-bam-thank-you-ma'am type. His last relationships were long term and committed. I don't know why they broke down but I'd imagine there was a good reason."

Alex shook his head stubbornly. "I shouldn't get emotionally involved. You know I can switch off. It just needs the right trigger and I'll bury the emotions."

Melanie sighed wryly. "By trigger, I assume you mean when you find a man you could care about you find an excuse to sabotage the relationship."

She smiled as Alex scowled at her words. "I think you might be misleading yourself on this one. I don't think you'll find it as easy with Sage to push him away."

She took a sip from her water glass. "When was the last time you saw Eric?"

"Three days ago," Alex said without meeting her eye. "I tried so hard not to. I'm trying to reduce them. Eventually it got too much and I needed a session." He frowned. "But something was different. I didn't feel as committed as I normally do. Even Eric asked me what was wrong. He said I seemed to be more distant, less participating. He actually sounded worried about me."

"Alex, I think you actually need this less than you think you do. You're punishing yourself for something you haven't shared with me yet."

Alex felt his face flush.

"I think Eric is less worried about *you* than the fact that he's had you to himself for two years now and he sees you almost as a relationship in itself. He's a purist when it comes to what he does for a living. He needs to be totally in control. He won't like the fact you might be seeing another man, if it eventually happens." Melanie spoke softly, her concern for Alex evident in her voice.

Alex waved a hand. "Nonsense. I'm just a paying client, nothing else. He does what the customer wants and he's got no emotional investment. What I do outside of Scarlet is of no concern to him."

Melanie was quiet for a while. Finally she spoke. "I disagree. But we'll leave it there for now."

"I googled Sage." Alex picked at a piece of imaginary fluff on the couch arm. "I remembered he said there was some invasion of privacy in his past life and I wanted to find out about it."

"And what did you find out?" Melanie made a notation in her pad.

Alex looked down at his trendy designer loafers. "It was all over the news at the time. He found his fiancé in bed with one of his friends. He kicked them both out. A journalist who had followed him home caught it all on camera, him shoving the guy out of the apartment with his then-fiancé, both of them half-naked. The papers made quite a big thing about it. Apparently they were due to have their civil partnership in a month's time."

He shook his head in sheer disbelief and continued. "Why would you want anyone else if you could have that man all to yourself? He split up with his current lover about eight months ago. He seems to have a run of back luck. I hope he's not some sort of freak." Alex smiled slightly.

Melanie nodded her head. "Poor man. Maybe he just chooses the wrong partners."

Alex looked at her carefully. "He's had some bad times too. When he was nineteen, both his parents were killed in a plane crash. His father was an amateur pilot and the plane they were flying in had an engine failure when they flew into a flock of birds."

Melanie pursed her lips as she looked at Alex. "So he's had his fair share of drama then as well. Perhaps not as horrific as yours, but he knows tragedy and heartbreak. Perhaps that's formed some sort of kinship between you."

She looked at Alex in compassion. "Have you thought about what you'll do if this relationship goes to the next level and you decide to act on the attraction you both seem to have? What will you tell him about the scars you have? And if you've been to see Eric recently, how will you explain the marks away?"

Alex looked down at his feet again. When he spoke his voice was sombre. "I have rules to help me with that, Melanie. No lights on, always in the dark. I try keep to my place where I can control the lighting. I insist on keeping my shirt on so no one sees the scar tissue. As for Eric—I'll make sure I start to heal up. Eric can switch to the chamois flogger. I'll limit where he hits me. It's not ideal but"—he shrugged—"it sort of gets the job done. I'm thinking of jumping Sage's bones soon, which, God help me, I really want to do. I'm not sure how much longer I can hold out. The man's a bloody sex bomb." His smile was twisted.

Melanie was out of her depth. She had no idea that there were different types of floggers. But in some bizarre way, she knew Alex was actually moving forward. He'd actually accepted that he might start a normal relationship and was willing to take steps to reduce both the number of visits and his level of discomfort at the sessions with Eric in order to do so. That was definitely a step in the right direction. It still remained to be seen how Eric would feel about that. Melanie still had a feeling of unease, despite Alex's assurances, that Eric might just be the thorn on the rose that ended up drawing blood.

* * *

Eric Rossi scowled fiercely as he readied himself for his session with Alex. He'd been given his new instructions by Madame and he wasn't pleased with them at all.

The chamois flogger, for God's sake? You might as well whip the man with a damp dishcloth. He'd also been requested to limit himself to Alex's back and buttocks, nothing in the front.

It had been nine days since he'd last seen Alex, longer than normal. He wasn't sure what the reason was but tonight he was damn well going to find out.

Eric entered the basement room where his client normally waited for him. Alex knelt on the sumptuous floor cushion in his usual spot. He wore his chinos, no shirt, and his arms rested loosely at his sides. He looked up as Eric entered but kept silent.

He looked delectable, Eric thought, his groin stirring. "Alex, I missed you. But I'm glad you're here now."

He moved over to Alex and pulled him to his feet. He stood quietly, head slightly bowed as Eric caressed his cheek.

"I understand you've requested a change to the programme. You'll have to tell me all about that later. I'm interested to see what's changed in your life."

It could only be a man, he thought savagely as jealousy surged through him. His imagination had been running riot that morning as he'd pondered the possible reasons for Alex's change of heart.

He's found himself some nice vanilla that probably fucked him from the front and was actually able to kiss him and see his face when he came.

That's why he didn't want any marks on his stomach. Marks on the back could always be hidden if you were doing it missionary or cowboy style.

Eric's resentment built in his chest and he reached out, roughly unzipping Alex's pants and thrusting them down his legs.

Alex flinched but continued to keep his head bowed.

Eric motioned to Alex to step out of the trousers puddled at his ankles.

Alex did as he was instructed and Eric kicked the trousers across the floor. Alex stood naked in front of Eric, his cock hard and already leaking. Eric ran his hands over the healing welts from the last session.

The bruises had faded and Eric felt a sense of loss.

Alex's breathing deepened as Eric touched him and satisfaction flooded Eric's body. At least he hadn't lost the ability to turn Alex on. Eric licked Alex's left nipple, then bit, hard. Alex hissed and Eric smiled, then his mouth travelled upward to Alex's neck. He sucked the skin, intent on leaving a bruise. Alex pulled away and Eric heard his next words in amazement.

"No biting, Eric. I thought Madame would have told you. I asked her to."

Not only had Alex spoken, which was one of the cardinal sins of the game, but he'd done so with such determination that Eric was very taken aback.

"Have the game rules changed so much then?" Madame *had* told him about the new no-biting rule but Eric had chosen to ignore it. Alex nodded. Eric stood back, looking at his charge in displeasure.

"This whole thing doesn't leave room for me to do much, does it? You're becoming soft." Eric walked around Alex, inspecting a body he already knew so well.

Alex was lean and muscled, with strong, slim legs covered in fine, dark hair. His stomach wasn't a defined six-pack but rather tight and smooth. His backside was a pleasure, with taut cheeks and a swell that Eric loved to slap. He had broad shoulders and a narrow waist and his shaven groin was always a turn-on.

Eric insisted Alex shave it because it made the slapping and whipping so much more effective. He could see the welts and scars left from the whippings so much more clearly. Alex's cock was a thing of beauty too. It wasn't the biggest Eric had seen but it beautifully formed, wide and strong with a slight curve toward his stomach. It stood out now, rampant against his lightly tanned skin, proud and twitching with each touch of Eric's hand on Alex's body.

Alex's body was a canvas of past abuse. Alex wouldn't talk about the marks and scars no matter how hard Eric tried.

Small scars dotted his lower stomach from what looked like cigarette burns and when Eric stepped around to Alex's back, there were more scars. Cigarette burns as well as four deep parallel scars ran from his left shoulder blade to just under his right arm, long, deep indentations that could only have been done by a knife.

He'd been curious about the origin of those violent marks. Alex's hip also had a four-inch-long jagged puckered scar on it. It looked like it hadn't healed properly.

Finished with his inspection, Eric pulled Alex over to the posts and Alex stood meekly whilst Eric tied his wrists to them. He bound his ankles with the silk, caressing the inside of his thigh as he straightened up. Alex shivered.

Eric unzipped his own trousers, freeing himself, as he reached out his hand, taking Alex's chin, pulling it up. Alex's eyes looked at his unwaveringly.

Eric picked up the flogger that was not his favourite toy of choice. A short-handled crop with seven-foot strands of soft chamois leather. It was almost a party toy compared with what he was used to. A tool a bored housewife might give the pool man to use when she was in the mood. It did sting but left much less of a mark on the body than his custom-made rawhide crop.

He'd have to make up for the lack of whip strength in the number of strokes he inflicted. There'd been no talk about restricting that. Alex still had his "Get out of jail free" card, the safe word.

Eric leaned forward, trailing his tongue over Alex's nipples and sucking them deeply, hearing him sigh. He stood back, sliding the fronds of his flogger through his fingers, then used light strokes at his back and backside, as instructed. Alex's sudden intake of breath invigorated Eric and his strokes grew harder.

The chamois left thin strips of colour across Alex's body, but there would be no weals that would be felt when a man ran his hands across Alex's skin. The thought incensed Eric and he continued his mission, and he watched as Alex crumpled in pain.

At one point Eric thought Alex would use his safe word.

He whispered in Alex's ear. "If you suck me off, Alex, or allow me to go down on you, I'll stop the flogging,"

Alex tensed at his invitation.

"It'll be a small price to pay and save you from anymore pain. Perhaps we can change the rules a little just this once? I'd love us to taste each other."

Alex shook his head vehemently and Eric felt an irrational burst of anger. "Fine, if that's how you want to play it, so be it."

He increased his flogging efforts. Alex took his punishment quietly until finally Eric stopped, his chest heaving from his exertion. He reached up to undo the bonds and Alex fell into his arms as he released him. Eric roughly supported him as Alex righted himself and walked over to the bed, once again lying face down.

Alex's back showed a mass of pale pink streaks, the earlier ones already beginning to fade.

Eric's frustration at being held back from his full service intensified and he dropped his trousers, quickly sheathing himself. He lowered himself on top of Alex, reaching down between his legs to grip his cock roughly as he forced himself inside the man beneath him with no lubrication. Alex arched and tossed beneath him but Eric wasn't sure if it was to escape the rough assault of his arse or if passion caused the movements.

Eric thrust in and out as his hand continued working Alex's cock. Finally Alex shuddered and Eric recognised the tremors oscillating through his body as he climaxed. Eric's anger and irritation was evidenced in every violent thrust of his body into Alex, whose face remained buried in the bed.

Eric heard his gasps as he fucked him deep and hard. Eric cried out loudly as he came, his semen filling the condom, his hips still plunging into the man beneath him.

Finally Eric's orgasm abated and he slumped on top of Alex. When he lifted his head, he felt a sense of satisfaction at the bruises forming on Alex's hips where he'd gripped him so tightly. The deep crescent marks of his fingernails on Alex's tanned skin thrilled him. At least he'd left his own marks on him, Eric thought savagely. Let the other man see those and know that he'd been there first.

Finally, his lust and anger spent, he rolled off his charge, his eyes gazing at the ceiling above.

Alex turned to face Eric, his face white, his eyes glittering, before climbing off the bed in obvious pain. "That was too personal, Eric. I told you what I wanted and you disobeyed the instructions."

Eric shrugged. "Alex, you got what you paid for. I didn't do anything against your wishes; it was just a little rougher than normal. I thought you liked that."

Alex's lips pressed together as he ignored Eric. He moved to the corner of the room to pick up his clothes and dressed swiftly, leaving the room without looking back. Eric watched in satisfaction. He'd re-established some control. The fact that Alex seemed to be slipping away from him had infuriated him.

In his world, when Eric was wielding the whip and the flogger, he was king.

Chapter 11

Sage glanced up from the sitting area outside Alex's office at the man seated inside. The past few days Alex had been very quiet, keeping to himself, and no amount of conversation seemed to draw him out. He was a different person to the one Sage had flirted and laughed with over the past few weeks.

Their evening drinking sessions had come to an abrupt end and Sage had no idea why. He'd honestly thought he'd been gaining some ground with Alex. He wondered what had happened in the days between that flirty Alex and the one he saw now.

These weeks passed, Sage had to control himself like hell to not gather Alex's body to his and take his mouth in a kiss that he just knew would be absolutely mind blowing. Instead he'd given Alex the space he so obviously needed and hadn't acted like a caveman.

Sage was in between filming scenes and he decided he'd try once again to talk to Alex.

Alex looked up as Sage came in. He seemed very tense.

"Alex, is everything okay?" Sage perched his backside down on the desk beside him.

Alex moved back slightly. "I'm fine. I've just not been sleeping well and I'm tired."

"I'm worried about you; we all are. You haven't been eating and you look very pale." Sage smiled as he said the words but the other man's expression stayed stoic with no flicker of real life in his eyes.

"Everyone needs to stop worrying about me. I'm a big boy. I can look after myself. I wish everyone would bloody leave me alone." He leaned forward, looking at his computer screen intently.

Sage stood up, conscious that he'd been dismissed. "Well, if you need to talk, you know where I am."

Alex nodded but he didn't seem particularly concerned in Sage's whereabouts. A prickle of temper began in Sage's chest at Alex's disregard of his concern. He felt the Black Irish creeping up on him.

He was only trying to help for fuck's sake!

He'd thought they'd started making a breakthrough but this man was just unreal.

He really should give it up and find someone who isn't so bloody temperamental and secretive, just like he promised himself he would.

Sage shrugged. "Suit yourself. It seems like you think you can do everything on your own. We'll all leave you to it then, shall we?"

He hadn't meant to sound bitchy but this man bought out the worst in him. He scowled then turned as someone came in behind him. It was Janine Fortress, looking fairly harassed.

"Sage, have you seen Dianne anywhere? We're due to start filming in twenty minutes and nobody's heard from her. Luke is getting a little pissed off with the delay. Her phone is off and no one can get hold of her. Has she called you?"

Sage frowned, pulling his mobile out of his pocket. He shook his head. "No. No call, no text. That's very unlike Dianne. She's normally very punctual."

Janine looked fed up. "Thomas last saw her this morning. She was only scheduled to be here at two p.m. She had some beauty treatment this morning and she was coming in from there. Thomas called them but they said she left a long time ago."

Alex looked up with a frown on his face. "That isn't like Dianne at all."

Sage was perversely glad to see something shocked the man's current air of disinterest in everything around him. "I imagine she's just lost track of time, Janine. I'm sure she'll be here soon."

He moved out of the office onto the main studio floor, Janine following him like an anxious puppy. Diane's husband, Thomas Cunningham, was on his mobile on the other side of the floor and Sage walked up to him, placing a hand on the man's arm.

"She'll pitch up, Thomas. Stop fussing."

Thomas scowled, looking harassed. He finished talking to whoever was on the phone then put it back in his shirt pocket with a vexed sigh. "Absolutely no one has seen her since this morning. I don't know where the hell she can be. I've even called her friends and they haven't spoken to her today either. She was supposed to give her sister Jem a call too to find out how Natalie was and even she hasn't heard from her."

Sage frowned. "Natalie is your niece, if I remember?"

Thomas nodded. "Yes. She's been ill lately and Dianne calls Jem in the US every day to check how she is." He checked his phone screen again.

Out of the corner of Sage's eye he saw Alex talking to Luke. He wandered over. "Luke, I suppose we'd better put the next scene on hold and do something else until Diane turns up. Any suggestions on which one you want to do and I'll get it sorted?"

Luke looked grateful. "Perhaps we can shoot that one scene in the casino that didn't need Dianne. That was all set up to go next anyway. We'll just bring it forward if you're okay with that."

Sage nodded. "No problem, I'll get kitted up in my James Bond suit."

Luke chuckled. "That'll make the ladies and gents squeal in delight. Did you see that last magazine article from when you attended that summer fashion event a couple of weeks ago? Maggie said your bloody fan mail went ballistic after that photo was published with you in your tux with that gorgeous model Maddox on your arm. They had to hire extra help just to get through it all." He laughed softly. "You're becoming a fashion plate, a real-live sex symbol. I believe you've even got a modelling job on the catwalk next week, right? That should be something to watch."

Sage flushed, wishing this propensity for blushing would disappear. *It's a real bloody nuisance*, he thought, conscious of Alex's eyes on him.

"You say the nicest things, Luke. Yes, I'm doing a charity function next week, wearing some designer's new suits or something. As for Maddox, I'd have thought she would have been the one most people were focusing on. She has the longest legs I've ever seen on a woman. She's a stunner."

Luke chuckled. "As the saying goes, a man would like those legs wrapped right around him. She's bloody gorgeous. Pity I'm already in a relationship."

Sage grinned. "Lizzy would have your balls if you even so much as mentioned that, Luke. Your wife is one woman I wouldn't want to mess with." He walked over to the dressing room. The tuxedo for the casino shoot was already hung up, ready to wear. He dressed quickly, trying to get the bow tie on, swearing softly to himself with his lack of success. Something made him look up to the mirror and he started, seeing Alex standing behind him. Sage ignored him and continued trying to get the dickey bow straight.

Alex chuckled softly as he moved in front of him. "Here. Let me help you with that. You're all thumbs, it seems."

Sage watched as Alex reached up, taking the bow tie in his fingers. He had long, shapely fingers with square nails. Sage's imagination worked overtime imagining where else those hands might be right now. He was very conscious of Alex's scent and the nearness of Alex's forehead to his chin. He was confused. One minute Alex didn't want to know him, the next he was so close Sage could have kissed him. His groin tingled and he muffled a groan.

Simmer down, Sage. You're filming in a few minutes. You don't need another bloody hard-on now.

Alex finished with the bow tie and stepped back to see the effect. "You look very dashing in a tux. I can see why the ladies like it." He flashed a smile. "I daresay all the men too."

Sage stood back. "Thanks. And thanks for fixing the bow tie. I've never been able to get them right." He was determined to keep this professional and not revert into man-slut mode even though he felt the character coming on. He turned to walk out of the room.

"Sage?" He turned back at Alex's quiet voice. Alex was looking at him with an expression on his face he couldn't quite fathom. Sage raised his eyebrows.

"I'm sorry about earlier." Alex said softly. "I shouldn't have been so rude. You were just—caring. I'm not used to anyone doing that. It's been a bit of a difficult week."

Sage regarded the other man. "Perhaps you need to start getting used to it. A film set is like a family. We all look out for each other. It's best to fit in or you get left out."

He turned, walking out of the office. Sage needed to focus now, not have some emotional conversation with a man who was like Jekyll and Hyde. The next scene would be fun to shoot but it was intensive and Sage needed all his wits about him.

* * *

It was close to six p.m. when Alex saw one of the receptionists call Thomas over to answer a call on the studio phone. He then saw Thomas almost fall down as he nearly dropped the phone and grabbed the nearest table for support. His face was dazed and uncomprehending.

Alex gasped, hurrying over to him. Thomas' face was grey as he listened to the news on the other end of the phone. Finally he ended the call.

"That was the police. Dianne is in the hospital. She was injured earlier in an explosion, apparently after she left the beauty salon. They've only just been able to track me down. She's at North Middlesex Hospital. I have to get there."

Alex took him by the arm. "Thomas, you're in no shape to drive. Let me find someone to take you. If someone has a car, I'll drive you there." He caught Janine's eye and waved her over.

Janine bustled over, her round face full of concern. "Alex? What's up?"

Alex explained the situation and Janine's face paled.

"Jesus. Come on, Thomas, I've got my car here, I'll take you to the hospital. Alex, tell Luke and Sage what's happening when they finish this scene. I'll call from the hospital and let you all know what's going on." Janine took Thomas by the arm and the two of them left. Alex made his way over to the film set, standing on the perimeter whilst he watched them wrap up the last few minutes. The casino scene had been a favourite of his when he'd written it. It involved Carter West charming a bevy of lovely ladies and insulting a rather large man playing a bodyguard to a very rich and powerful gambler with whom Carter had a past.

Alex watched Sage with a smile as he played his part, his portrayal of sardonic Carter West in this scene particularly powerful. Alex felt guilty about being a bastard to him earlier. He knew Sage had only been trying to help. But the rough time with Eric recently was unsettling him and Alex was starting to doubt that any expectations he'd had about healing his tortured psyche with Sage were just pipe dreams.

Could Sage really expect anyone to understand what Alex did and why? Wasn't that being selfish, to expect that kind of commitment?

Finally the scene was complete and Sage conversed animatedly with Luke before walking off into the dressing room. Alex hurried over to Luke, who smiled at him.

"Alex. What did you think of that take? Sage was pretty incredible in this scene I can tell you."

"He's always incredible. Listen, I have some bad news." Alex succinctly explained the situation.

Luke gasped in horror. "Did they say how she was? Is she all right? How badly was she hurt?" He pulled out his phone and tried to call Thomas with no success and then got the number for the hospital. On calling them, the hospital refused to give out any information.

Sage came in at the last leg of the conversation, towel drying his shower-wet hair, more casually dressed in his usual jeans and tee shirt. He frowned when he saw them together. "What's going on?"

Once again Alex explained.

Sage looked at him in disbelief. "Dianne was injured in an explosion? How's that bloody possible?" He paced around frantically, his hands waving animatedly. "Why did it take them so long to get hold of Thomas?"

Alex shook his head. "We don't know. I imagine we'll find out when we get to North Middlesex."

Sage ran a hand through his hair. "I need to get down to the hospital. I can't sit here. I need to see how she is." He pulled out his mobile, making a quick call to order a taxi. He finished the call and looked at Alex and Luke. "We can leave Aaron here to lock up and all go down to the hospital. The taxi will be here in five."

He darted off in the direction of the studio entrance, Alex and Luke following him. Forty-five minutes later they'd arrived in the hospital and waited for someone to tell them where to find Thomas and Dianne. Sage paced impatiently.

Alex sighed, laying a hand on his arm. "For God's sake, Sage. You're wearing out the pattern on the floor. Calm down. I'm sure someone will be here soon to take us there."

"All I want to know is where to find them in this bloody place." Sage continued walking back and forth impatiently. "How long does that bloody take?"

Five minutes later a nurse appeared with a smile. "Mr. Sage? Your friend is on the second floor, Room 203. You can take the stairs or the lift over there." She pointed toward the far corner.

"Thanks." Sage hot-footed it up the stairs, Luke and Alex behind him. A few minutes later they were in the corridor outside Room 203, which was crawling with police and hospital staff.

Sage looked at the mass of people outside the room. "This is a helluva lot of attention. It must have been a really serious incident." His face was perplexed. "What the hell is going on?"

Alex frowned as he moved forward to the entrance of the hospital room, spotting Thomas inside sitting on a chair by the bed. He caught his eyes and Thomas waved him in but not before a rather large and burly policeman held out a hand to stop Alex.

"I'm sorry, sir. You can't go in there."

"I'm a friend," Alex said quietly. "We work together." He saw Thomas stand up as Sage and Luke joined him either side.

"It's all right, officer," Thomas said tiredly. "They're friends. You can let them in."

The policeman nodded, moving his bulk to admit them entrance. Sage barrelled past Alex to hug Thomas.

"Jesus. How's Dianne doing?" His voice was soft as he gazed over at the supine form of Dianne Cunningham in the hospital bed. Her face was pale and marked with blemishes and cuts.

Thomas sighed tiredly. "Dianne will be fine. She's got grazes and cuts to her face and body but the doctor says she'll be fine once she wakes up. They've given her something to make her sleep. She was a bit hysterical earlier."

"What happened?" Sage moved over to the bed, his face grim, taking Dianne's hand in his. Alex stood beside him as they all gazed down at the unconscious woman.

"They don't really know. They found Dianne slumped in the entrance to some old derelict restaurant, with a blanket over her. There were shreds of an envelope next to her. The police think it was a letter bomb."

Thomas's voice was sombre. There was silence as everyone digested this information.

"Who in hell's name would send Dianne a letter bomb and then wrap her in a blanket in front of an old building?" exclaimed Sage. "Why would she even be opening a letter there in the first place?"

Thomas nodded wearily. "I have no idea. It's why the police are here. Something funny's going on and they want to get to the bottom of it. They said it looked staged." He looked bewildered. "Staged? Who the hell would stage something like this? Why? I don't understand. Who'd want to harm Dianne?"

A trickle of fear caressed Alex's spine at Thomas's narrative and he swallowed. "It sounds a bit like the start to my book. First the bomb in the restaurant and then Gillian being injured and being given a blanket when she went into shock," he said.

Sage looked at him with narrowed eyes. "Why would anyone do that?" he muttered. "It sounds like a horrible publicity stunt." His voice trailed off and he looked horrified. "Hell, that's what everyone's going to think."

Alex stared at him. "They couldn't possibly think that, surely."

Sage laughed cynically. "Of course that's what everyone will think. The press have never been particularly good at playing these sorts of things down. They're going to milk this for everything they can and we'll come off worse. Trust me." He looked at Luke, his face hard. "Luke, you need to call Jennifer. She needs to manage this situation or it's going to turn into a bloody circus." He looked over at Dianne, his face softening as he reached out, brushing a strand of hair from her face. "Thomas, she's going to need protection. I assume you've asked the police to keep an eye on her?"

Thomas nodded. "I've organised my own bodyguards for her. They should be arriving soon. A couple of mates of mine I can trust."

A policeman walked in, looking at Thomas enquiringly. "Could I have a word with you outside, please, sir?" Thomas nodded, following the man into the hospital corridor.

Luke sighed. "Well, if Dianne's all right and surrounded at the moment by the men in blue, then I guess I'd better call Jenny and see if we can contain this situation." He too went into the corridor to find somewhere to use his mobile.

Sage and Alex stood together, looking down at Dianne. "Who the fuck would do something like this?" Sage muttered.

Sage's words startled Alex. He'd never heard him really swear before.

Alex shook his head. "I really don't know. The mind boggles. I just hope the police get to the bottom of it."

"Someone's playing games and I'd like to get my hands on them. I'll bloody throttle them." Sage's anger was plain to see and Alex thought he was seeing a side to him that probably didn't go on show often.

Alex reached out, rubbing his arm gently. "Dianne will be fine. Thomas will make sure of that."

Janine appeared with a large cup of tea. "I heard Thomas talking to the doctor outside earlier. He says she was very lucky that the cuts were mostly superficial and the letter bomb was fairly mild, designed to scare more than maim."

Alex nodded, pleased at that news. "Are you going back now?"

She shook her head. "I'll stay and give Thomas a lift home later."

Sage nodded curtly, passing a hand over his eyes in exhaustion. "That's a saving grace, then. Fuck me, what a bloody mess. I suppose I should be getting home. Dan will be wondering where I've got to." He looked at Alex. "Do you want to share a taxi? It's a bit too far for either of us to walk home." His face darkened, his tone growing harsher. "Unless you want to be by yourself? I know you have a need to be on your own and I wouldn't want to intrude." His tone was sarcastic.

Alex nodded. "No, we can share a ride home, that's fine."

Sage nodded curtly. "Fine, I'll call a taxi."

He disappeared into the corridor. Alex said goodbye to Janine and stepped out of Dianne's room to follow him, staring bemusedly at his retreating back. The man was more than a little prickly all of a sudden. Alex knew he deserved it and he supposed miserably that Sage was getting tired of trying to make the effort with him, something he certainly couldn't blame him for.

The journey home in the taxi was quiet. Sage gazed out of the window into the darkness beyond, hardly speaking a word, answering Alex's attempted efforts at conversation with staccato sentences and an air of complete disinterest.

It was most unnerving given this man was usually one of the most gregarious people he knew. This dark mood of his was unfamiliar to Alex.

They were stopped in front of the door to Alex's apartment building. It was dark, quiet and the street was deserted. "Do you want to come in for coffee?" he asked quietly.

Sage shook his head. "No thanks. I'm knackered and need to jump into bed. The taxi will drop me home."

Alex nodded, feeling a little awkward. "Well, thanks for the company."

Sage nodded, turning away. Alex hesitated, reaching out to touch his arm. Sage turned back and Alex reached over, kissing his cheek softly, hearing Sage's slight hiss of breath at the unexpected gesture.

"Please don't give up on me," Alex murmured, then left the cab and walked to his apartment as he heard the cab pull away.

Chapter 12

Sage finally got back to his and Dan's apartment feeling tired, fractious, horny and terribly confused. His black mood had risen, determined to take him over. It was like a fire blanket and he embraced its cold caress.

The mixed signals he kept getting from Alex were hard to figure out. When Alex had been saying goodbye in the cab Sage had wanted nothing more than to pull him close and kiss him.

He let himself into Dan's apartment and came face to face with a woman, barely twenty-five years old he guessed, clad in nothing but a blue bra and a thong. She was extremely pretty, very curvy with long blonde hair, a pert nose and even perkier breasts.

He stared at her, a little nonplussed. "Hi." He watched her warily. "I'm Sage. I live here with Dan."

Her face cleared. "Oh. You're his gay roommate. I'm Cherry." She smiled. "My God, what a waste. But Bri is just going to love you." Her eyes looked at him hungrily. Sage gazed at her in confusion.

Who the hell was Bri?

Sage simply nodded, skirting her carefully, moving over to his room. As he was about to go in, Dan came out of his own bedroom wearing just his boxers, with yet another woman on his arm. This one was totally naked, with dark, lustrous skin, long black hair and an oriental slant to her eyes. Dan saw Sage and waved an introduction.

"Sage! Meet Akira and Cherry. They're from the hotel down the road. They're receptionists." He drawled the word out languorously. "I'm glad you're home. You're later than I expected and your present is waiting in the lounge." He chuckled, pulling Cherry closer to him.

Sage shook his head, even more perplexed. "Dan, I'm very appreciative of the offer but I've had a crap evening. I've been at the hospital all night and I just want to get into bed. I'm not in the best of tempers I'm afraid, so I'd really be no fun." He wondered with trepidation what the hell the present was in the lounge.

Dan moved over to his friend. "God, I'm sorry. What happened?"

Sage shook his head tiredly. "One of the cast—Dianne Cunningham—had an accident. She's fine but it's been a little stressful. I'll tell you all about it tomorrow. I don't want to put a downer on whatever you had planned."

He turned, forcing a smile at the two women. "Ladies, it's been lovely meeting you both. Look after him and make sure he doesn't eat after midnight. It drives him crazy."

He went into his bedroom. He undressed, dropping his clothes by the bed, going into his en-suite bathroom to shower. When he came out, he was once again on the back foot. Naked in his own room, Sage found himself with a long-limbed, highly aroused and very naked man curled up on his bed, eyes watching him. From the grin on his face, he was liking what he saw. The man—who was probably in his early thirties himself—smiled, stretching like a cat, his cock bobbing as he did so, looking very inviting.

Sage was drawn to it and the lean lines of the other man's body, the hair on his sculptured chest and the sexy come-hither look in the brown eyes. A strand of long, dark hair fell across his forehead.

Sage's feeling of extreme exposure lingered as his cock hardened and came to life but he was damned if he was going to go all girly and cover his naughty bits with his hands. Instead he stood there, getting slowly bigger and harder with every lick the other man made of his rather luscious lips. Sage looked back at him, feeling his heart beat a little faster with his sudden desire to get physical despite his bad mood.

"My name's Brian. I've been waiting for you for ages." The man pouted. "Dan thought you might be a bit tense and he asked me to take a look and see if I could relax you." He chuckled softly, moving off the bed and over to Sage. "I told him that I liked my men tense, at least in certain places, but I'd certainly see what I can do for the rest."

Brian reached out, teasingly drawing his fingers down Sage's chest toward his groin. He leaned in, kissing Sage, his mouth warm and hungry, his tongue darting into Sage's mouth as his warm, firm hand gripped Sage's very needy member, sliding down the length of him, causing Sage to gasp with the sensation.

"Wow. You're a really big boy, aren't you?" *Bri* murmured huskily. "I like it when a man fills me up."

Sage felt a perverse need to show both himself and Alex he wasn't above getting his own action and using the tools he had at his disposal. He was at full attention now as Brian's mouth moved lower toward his belly and his accomplished hands continued their artful stroking. As Brian took him into his hungry mouth, Sage thought that perhaps the evening might not be such a loss. After all, it was rude to refuse a present and it had been a while. And it may just be the very thing he needed to lift his spirits.

* * *

The following morning Sage woke up in a far better mood that the one he'd been in the night before. He showered again and changed, getting into the studio around ten o'clock. He'd even spoken to the paparazzi camping outside the studio and managed to be courteous, which he thought was quite a coup for him.

His evening had certainly been memorable as Brian had proven himself to be a very talented and extremely lusty young man. Sage had finally got to sleep around two A.M. but he'd been woken up around seven by Brian for a quick morning shag and a fairly mind-blowing blow job. He'd left Brain curled up languidly in his bed like a cat. On his way in, Sage realised he'd left his annotated script at home. He'd called Dan, who'd promised to bring it in on his way into work. Sage saw Luke and Janine sitting at the studio table and he sauntered over, whistling.

Janine peered at him from over his bifocals. "Good morning, Sage. You look fairly pleased with yourself today. Anything we should know about?"

Sage grinned. "Nothing that a gentleman would talk about. Have you heard from Thomas this morning? How's Dianne?"

Luke smiled. "She's doing well. She'll be coming home later today and Thomas is going to take a couple of days off with her until Monday. We'll reschedule Dianne's scenes for then. So I'm afraid the pressure is going to be all yours for the next few days." He smiled slyly. "From the glow you have I have to ask—did someone get lucky last night?"

Sage chuckled. "Stop fishing. I have nothing to tell either of you." He turned as a voice echoed across the studio floor. Dan stood there, waving a sheaf of papers.

"Got to go, Dan's brought my notes in." He turned and sauntered over to where his friend stood. Dan had a wide grin on his face and Sage laughed at the knowing glint in his eyes. He held up his hands in supplication. "I agree I was uptight and I needed to release some pressure. Thanks for looking out for me. It was definitely fun."

Dan chuckled. "They're all friends and came as a package deal and I couldn't refuse. Brian really liked you. He said, and I quote, 'He was so hot and needy.' Unquote. Suffice it to say he was impressed with your large manhood and your sucking skills. That's as much as I'm telling you or else you'll go all red and 'Aw, shucks' and I can't stand that at this time of the morning. I'm telling you, Sage, you should see him again. He's very into you. You need to fuck him again."

Sage chuckled. "Jesus, Dan, he told what we did? Hell, we're not eighteen any more. Have *some* decorum and stop broadcasting my bloody sexploits all over the studio."

Dan's eyes widened at something behind him. Sage glanced back, seeing Alex standing there. His face was pale and he looked ill. Sage groaned silently, wondering if he'd heard any of their conversation. He fervently hoped not. Despite his irrational need to get back at him last night, in the cold light of morning it was something he'd rather have him not know about.

"Alex, hi. Let me introduce you to Dan. You remember I told you about him."

Alex nodded, holding out his hand to Dan who shook it. Dan smiled at him. "So you're the mysterious Alex this bugger keeps talking about. Glad to meet you at last. Sage tells me you're a very gifted writer and that you're busy with another book? I haven't read them yet myself but Sage here is very taken with them."

"I'm glad he enjoys them." Alex turned and looked at Sage. "Luke asked if you could see him when you have a moment. Apparently there's been a bit of a mix-up with some of the scene sequences and he needed to run something by you."

Alex turned to Dan. "Lovely to meet you, Dan." He walked away.

Dan whistled. "Jesus, Sage, if I wasn't straight, I'd fancy him. Those eyes are just something else."

Sage watched after Alex with a sick feeling in his stomach. He knew he had nothing to feel ashamed about. He and Alex weren't an item, even though in his wild fantasies he'd thought they could be if he tried hard enough.

But the man was such bloody hard work! So why did he feel like such a heel?

He said a distracted goodbye to Dan, citing the fact he needed to get to work. He went in search of Alex, finding him in the office in front of his PC. Alex glanced up at him as he came in.

"Alex, can I have a word?" Sage didn't quite know what he was going to say.

Alex shrugged, looking relaxed. "I have time. What's up?"

Sage cleared his throat. "I wasn't sure how much you'd heard about what Dan said. I didn't want you to get the wrong impression. Dan has a certain way of saying things which can be— misconstrued if you don't know him."

Alex cocked his head in amusement. "Oh, I don't know about that. He was very clear from what I heard. You banged someone called Brian last night who thought you were hot and apparently your oral skills are really good. What's to misconstrue?"

Sage's face flooded with heat. If the room had been any darker he'd have been a beacon lighting the way home.

Alex carried on. "You're a grown man, Sage. You can do what you like. I'm glad you pulled. That at least makes one of us." He looked at Sage. "Is that all you wanted to say? Not that I'm rushing you or anything, but I have some feedback to give for a proposed scene change and Janine will kick my arse if I don't get it to her soon."

"That's all," Sage said quietly. "Sorry to disturb you." He turned, leaving the room, hearing the click of the keyboard as he did. He didn't know what he'd expected. In hindsight it had probably been a stupid thing to try and explain. Alex obviously didn't really care one way or another, so that should actually make him feel better.

So, why didn't he?

"Bloody man," he muttered fiercely. "He's got under your skin, Sage, and you need to dig him out."

Sage scowled fiercely, muttering to himself as he made his way to the dressing room to change. "You promised yourself you weren't going to get involved with someone for a while. Best keep that bloody promise."

* * *

Back in the office, Alex stopped typing, heaving a shuddering sigh. His hands were cold and wouldn't stop trembling. He'd had to use every acting skill he'd got to pretend he didn't care about Sage's little fuck session last night.

It had driven a nail through his chest hearing Dan's casual words and knowing Sage had been intimate with another man— *very* intimate based on what he'd heard. Some other man had gotten the chance to do what so far Alex had only fantasised about doing. Alex knew he'd no right to judge because he'd done nothing to make Sage feel he had a real chance with him; in fact, he'd done everything he could to do the opposite and he couldn't expect the man to wait forever.

Alex reached inside his jacket pocket and pulled out his mobile, scrolling down the favourites contact list until he hit the familiar number.

Time to stop kidding himself that he could have a normal life and go back to what he was used to, what he deserved. No holds barred this time—he'd tell Madame Duchaine it was business as usual.

Chapter 13

Dianne Cunningham came back to work two weeks after the incident. Sage sat talking to her after filming late one evening. They'd had a lot of catching up to do and Dianne had insisted they work extra hours to make up the lost time. Her facial cuts were healing and with makeup and the right camera angles, one could hardly notice the faint scars.

"I was petrified, Sage," she said softly as they sat on the sofa in the staff room. "I was walking away from the beauty salon to get to my car. Some young man came up and handed me an envelope. He said it was very important news and I had to open it now. I just laughed and said I'd open it when I got home because I needed to be somewhere. The next thing I knew, he had a knife to my side, telling me I'd better 'fucking open it right now.' I had no choice. I slit it open with my nail and the next thing I remember there was an almighty flash, and everything went black." She shivered. "I'd had a split second to wonder when I was opening it why he moved away so fast, but I had no idea anyone would do that to me."

She swallowed, her eyes full of tears. "The next I knew, I woke up lying in that doorway covered in blood with the police and everyone bent over me. My bag was gone so no one had any contact numbers to call Thomas. They took me to the hospital and I asked one of nurses to call the studio."

Sage leaned forward, clasping her icy hands in his warm ones. "It seems like a very elaborate hoax and the police still don't know much about it. I'm just glad you weren't hurt even more. It was a terrible thing to put someone through and if I ever find out who did it, I'll bloody thrash them myself."

His voice was fierce and Dianne smiled as she shivered, drawing her cardigan closer around her shoulders. Her voice trembled. "It must be a bloody psycho. What if they do it again? If they are trying to copy the scenes in the book, like Alex mentioned, the next big scene is the one where Carter's brother is injured in a hit-and-run. What the hell will that mean to this crazy person?"

Sage leaned forward. "Dianne, the police don't seem to think that they're following the book. The ones Thomas spoke to seemed to think this was an isolated incident drummed up by someone who wanted publicity for the series. It's a sick way of going about it but it's definitely had the result they expected. The papers are full of it. And we have extra security for you now to keep the reporters and anyone else out."

Dianne looked at him hopefully. "Do you think so? I hope you're right. I don't want to have to look over my shoulder all the time in case someone's trying to blow me up again." She smiled wanly. "Once is enough."

"Thomas has enough security laid on for you to stop a whole phalanx of would-be attackers." Sage smiled as he stood up. "Come on, your taxi will be here any minute. You'd better go wait in front or they'll be getting all uppity with you."

Dianne reached over and hugged him. "You're a darling. I really don't know why some lucky man hasn't snapped you up by now. More fool them." She picked up her shawl, making her way to the foyer.

Exhausted by the long day of filming, Sage was the last one leaving the television studio, exhausted after a long day of filming. Seeing a light on in the office, he went over to turn it off. As he got nearer, he saw Alex slumped over the desk, arms above his head as if sleeping. Alex's coffee cup was overturned and there was liquid all over the desk and papers.

Alex. One of the most beautiful men he'd ever seen.

Sage carefully moved the empty coffee cup to the bin and mopped up the spill with tissues he found. He felt just enough charity that he couldn't leave Alex like he was, despite the man's recent less than amicable mood. These past two weeks Alex had kept very much to himself. Sage had asked what was wrong, but Alex looked at him stonily, saying it was none of his business and that he wanted to be left alone. Since then, things had become a little frosty.

"Alex? Come on, this is no place to sleep. You need to get home." He frowned at the lack of response when he gently shook Alex's shoulder. "Alex?"

The man's shirt was loose, out of his jeans and rucked up around his ribs against the chair back. As Sage reached to pull it down, he drew a breath, noticing purpling bruises across the man's lower back. Sage stared at the marks, not wanting to accept them. He lifted Alex's shirt slightly, wincing in horror at the livid weals and the deep bruising disappearing under the waistband of the man's pants. Slowly Sage drew the shirt back down, feeling sick to his stomach.

Feeling the first wisps of real fear start deep in his stomach, he leaned in to see if the man was still breathing, "Alex. Wake up."

Alex's face was ashen and drawn, his breathing shallow. Sage leaned over with more urgency and gently brushed his face with his fingertips. Alex stirred and moaned, and Sage felt relief as his eyes opened, unfocused and bloodshot, and stared at him in confusion.

Alex sat bolt upright, rocketing back in his chair, away from him in a motion of absolute panic and fear.

"Alex, it's Sage. You fell asleep."

Alex stared at him as his eyes focused. He passed a trembling hand across his face. "I fell asleep? What time is it?"

"It's seven thirty. Everyone's gone home already. I was just getting ready to lock up and saw the light still on. You need to go home. You don't look well."

Sage reached out a gentle hand to help him up, but Alex knocked it away. "Leave me alone! Just stop it, will you? I keep fucking telling you I'm fine." He spat the words.

"Jesus, Alex! What the fuck is wrong with you? You pass out on your desk, you push everyone away and you act like a bloody drama queen. What bug have you got up your arse that you can't accept someone's help?"

"I don't need help—especially from you, Christopher Sage, so just leave me the hell alone."

But Alex's voice quavered and he bit his lip, and Sage's anger dissipated. He knelt down beside the man. "Alex. Talk to me, please. Tell me what's wrong." He hesitated. He wasn't sure whether he should mention what he'd seen, a bit afraid of being branded a pervert or incurring a sexual harassment charge. But he wasn't the sort to hold his counsel. His mother always said that the phrase "Curiosity killed the cat" was tailor-made for him, even as a boy.

"I saw the marks on your back. Your shirt was up and I saw the bruising and the swelling. Who did that to you?"

Alex stared at him with such fear and desolation that Sage's heart finally broke.

"Is someone hurting you?" he asked. "Is that why you're so defensive? Why you don't let anyone close?"

When Alex spoke, his voice was that of a broken man. Small. Pitiful. "Just let it go, Sage. Please, just let it go. Don't make me tell you."

Sage reached up from where he crouched beside Alex's chair, cupping the man's face in his hands. It felt so right. And he was resolved to get an answer. "Who's doing this to you?"

"Me," Alex whispered. "I'm doing it to me."

Sage frowned, not understanding. "I don't follow. How do you mean you're doing it? To yourself?"

Alex nodded. "Please don't ask me any more. Please, Sage." He pulled away, but Sage stood, pulling him to his feet, holding him close to his chest, wrapping his arms around him. Alex melted into him.

Sage stroked his back with care, mindful of the injuries. For a while there was quiet before Alex finally pulled away. His face was pale, his eyes haunted. Sage again thought he was the most beautiful man he'd ever seen, especially vulnerable and without any barriers. Finally.

He spoke quietly. "Are you going to answer my question, then?"

The man scowled, and for a minute Sage saw the old Alex surface. "Christ, you never give up, do you? You're like an annoying pressure headache that just won't go away unless someone drills a hole in your brain."

"An apt analogy." Sage laughed. "It's been said before, just not in those exact words." He saw the faint hint of a smile on Alex's face, but the expression was gone before it even took proper shape.

"I can't tell you. If I do, you'll never want to speak to me again." Alex's voice was expressionless, and he didn't meet Sage's eyes. "As we have to work together, that wouldn't be a good thing."

"I'm an annoying headache, remember? One way or another I'll keep asking until I get an answer." Sage moved closer, unwilling to be deterred. "I want to know how those marks got on your back, who put them there, and why."

"Have you got a lifetime then?" Alex's voice was silky, taunting, suddenly more in charge. "Do you really want to hear all the sordid details of my little life? Remember, sometimes you get what you ask for."

"Yes. I want to hear."

Alex regarded him thoughtfully and then smiled—fairly nastily, Sage thought with a pang.

"All right then. I'll give you the short version first. Then you can decide whether you want to hear any more."

There was a note of satisfaction in Alex's voice, and Sage suddenly thought that perhaps this wasn't the right thing to do after all. The sudden change from vulnerable to "here goes whether you like it or fucking not" Alex was quite scary. What the hell had he gotten himself into?

Alex focused steadily on Sage's face. "When I was seventeen, I was introduced into a cult by an older man called Rudy. He kept me as his bitch for eight months. He used me for sex, whipped me, slapped me, raped me, burnt me with cigarettes and finally slashed my back four times with a sabre when I said something he didn't like. This all kept happening until I was rescued by an extraction team. They came to save someone else and found me as well."

The room spun for Sage. Alex carried on in apparent disregard. "I was repatriated and had counselling for the abuse for nine years with the same people who rescued me. Now I'm in formal therapy. Part of my therapy is that I see a man called Eric at least once a week—more of late—who whips me, slaps me, bites me and then fucks me. It makes me feel better.

"So tell me, Christopher Sage. Is that the kind of man you'd like to take home to meet family?"

Sage looked at Alex, feeling both a surge of overwhelming tenderness and horror at his story. Now Alex's past behaviour made perfect sense. Sage saw through the bravado, through the curt words, noticed Alex's trembling hands, the swallowing in his throat, the rapid breathing. But most of all, he saw the sheer anguish in his eyes as Alex expected him to turn tail and run.

He'd expected to shock Sage, to disgust him and turn him away, but all Sage could think of was the wonder that this man could have come through this horrific ordeal and still be able to face his demons in a relatively normal fashion to the outside world.

His happily ever after romance novels made perfect sense now.

Sage moved toward Alex swiftly and Alex flinched as if he expected him to hit him or worse. Instead, Sage pulled him close, kissing him with a hunger that he hadn't ever felt before for a man. Alex stiffened at first and then finally relaxed into him, his arms wrapping tightly around Sage's neck, his mouth devouring Sage's in a kiss that seemed to swallow him whole. Alex's hands wound themselves tightly into Sage's hair as he ground his mouth against his, pressing his body against Sage's, leaving no doubt how the man felt.

Alex seemed to want to meld them together as one. Eventually they needed to come up for air and when they did, they were gasping at the intensity of their passion for each other.

"Jesus, Sage, I wasn't expecting that. I didn't think you'd want me after that story," Alex breathed against Sage's mouth, driving him even crazier with desire.

Sage thought he might explode there and then. "Does this feel like a man who doesn't want to be with you?" His voice was low as he ran his hands over Alex's hips, pressing himself against him.

Both men moaned at feeling their hardness against each other's stomachs. Alex reached down to caress Sage's groin.

"God, don't do that," Sage groaned. "I'm barely holding it in as it is."

Alex's low chuckle made Sage's control even more difficult as Alex reached out first to turn out the light Sage had originally come to switch off, then to pull Sage over to the two-seater couch in the corner of the office. The room was now pitch dark with only the dim streets lights from outside shining through.

"It's not the Ritz but it'll have to do. I *so* want you to fuck me, Sage. It's all I've been thinking about for weeks," Alex murmured, unzipping his jeans, tugging them and his silk boxers down over his hips.

His erection sprung out, ready and glistening with moisture. Sage couldn't take his eyes off it as he yanked down his own pants. Alex reached out and pulled Sage's shirt over his head, then slid a hand through his chest hair and his shoulders.

Sage closed his eyes at Alex's touch, feeling himself stiffen even more, his breath ragged and deep.

"Christ, Alex," Sage murmured, knowing his limits and conscious that he'd reached most of them. "I'm not made of bloody steel, and you've been driving *me* crazy for weeks as well."

"I have to leave my shirt on, Sage." Alex's voice was filled with resolve. "I'm not ready to take it off yet."

Sage nodded. "If that's what you want." His hands stroked Alex's back through the fabric, feeling the play of the man's muscles beneath his eager fingers. He pushed Alex back onto the studio couch, covering him with his own body, so the men's cocks were sandwiched together, skin to skin, slickness to slickness.

"No foreplay needed," Alex whispered in his ear, his breath tickling the sensitive skin. "I just want to feel you inside me. It's all I want right now."

Sage groaned. "Alex, stop. We can't do this without protection. I have condoms in my jeans pocket. Let me get one." He could honestly say he'd never wanted to wear a condom less than with this man but he wasn't going to take any chances for either of them. He hated himself for thinking it, but with Alex's history it made sense.

Alex released him. "You *are* a good Boy Scout, Sage. Go on then."

Sage found his jeans on the floor and scrabbled for the pocket. He wasn't usually in the habit of carrying them around with him but since meeting Alex, he'd made sure he was prepared.

"I want to put it on you," Alex whispered. Sage grew another inch at the thought of him performing that intimate action for him. He nodded, breaking open the packet, handing over the latex balloon. Sage groaned loudly as Alex reached out and grasped him, sliding the sheath over his cock, his hands artfully caressing him at the same time.

"Jesus, Alex," Sage said through gritted teeth.

Alex laughed softly, releasing him, pulling him back down. His wet mouth found Sage's. "I want you to do it from the front. Is that okay? I want to see the man I'm making love to."

Sage nodded. It was his preference too, giving him access to his lover's mouth, nipples and all the other erogenous spots he liked to find with his lips, although Alex's shirt might prove a hindrance to that.

Alex lifted his legs, drawing his knees back as Sage positioned himself at the man's hole. His cock was burning with the need to be inside Alex. Sage felt a sudden spurt of panic.

"Shit, I have no lube," he groaned.

Alex laughed teasingly. "Then I guess we'll just have to use self-lubrication," he said huskily, spitting on his hands and then coating Sage's sheath-covered cock. "It'll be fine, honest. You won't hurt me. It's nothing new for me."

Sage was now ready for him and he slid into Alex, who gripped his hips, pulling him closer.

"Oh, God, that feels really good." Alex's moans in Sage's ear were an aphrodisiac as his greedy tongue nibbled his ear. Sage smelt the sandalwood essence on Alex's skin, felt the rasp of his stubble against Sage's own. Alex chuckled as he pushed his hips to meet Sage's thrusts. "I can really feel you. It *is* true what they say about men with big feet."

Sage grinned in the darkness, finding Alex's mouth, their tongues twisting and tasting each other. His thrusts were steady and deep and he heard Alex's moans in his mouth, sending him into an even deeper frenzy. He looked down at Alex's flushed face, his half-closed eyes as he moved beneath him. Alex's cock stood proud, bobbing against Sage's body as he thrust in and Sage wished he could wrap his mouth around it at the same time he was inside Alex.

"You are something else," Sage whispered as his mouth grazed Alex's, his tongue teasing his lips with small licks of wet heat. Alex tried to kiss him, but Sage resisted, pulling his head away, denying him the satisfaction.

"Hell, you are such a tease," Alex groaned and Sage took pity on him, grinding his mouth against his, tongues finding each other.

It was taking all Sage's self-control not to come as he strained to pace himself. Alex felt just as he thought he would—tight, hot and very willing. Sage felt his skin prickling with the intensity of his contact with Alex, felt the sweat between their lower bodies mingle and smelled the musky scent of his arousal as Sage's cock pushed deeper and deeper inside him.

"Touch yourself, Alex, I want to see you come," Sage whispered, and Alex nodded, reaching down to take his erection in desperate greedy hands, stroking himself with hard strokes that made him bite his lips. Alex tensed beneath Sage, his thighs tautening, his hips rising up like the bow of a ship in stormy seas.

Alex gasped loudly, a fierce exhalation of air as he climaxed, hot spurts of his semen coating both their bodies and Alex's shirt with slick stickiness and the scent of pure lust.

Sage felt Alex's orgasm in his channel, felt his muscles contract around him, driving Sage to cry out. He found his own release with a sense of satisfaction and as he came, emptying himself inside the condom, inside Alex in a rush of hot fluid as he ground his mouth against Alex's, little breaths of pleasure escaping as he collapsed on top, his heart beating crazily.

For a moment there was no sound other than their deep breathing and the noise of the traffic outside the windows. Alex's hands still tightly clasped Sage's hips. Sage kissed his lover's lips gently, tasting his sweat. Finally, with a sigh of reluctance Alex released him and Sage rolled off to lie beside him on his back on the narrow couch, half on, half off, one foot on the ground to steady himself. He took off the condom, tying a knot in the top and placing it on the floor. A clock ticked somewhere, a comforting steady sound. Sage reached out a hand and slowly traced the line of Alex's face in the darkness.

"That was incredible, even though it was over way too fast. I'm sorry about that," he murmured. "Look at what we've been missing all this time."

Alex reached up, his face soft, as he caressed the line of Sage's jaw tenderly. "If I'd known my story was going to turn you on like that, I'd have told you a long time ago."

Sage frowned and sat up. "That wasn't what 'turned me on.' I'm not a bloody ghoul who gets off on sexual abuse stories." He felt a deep stir of anger at Alex's words.

Alex sat up. "Sorry," he said guiltily. "That was a poor choice of words. I wasn't thinking. That wasn't what I meant."

Sage was slightly mollified by the words, although not completely. He lay for a while in the darkness whilst he thought how next to broach the subject that had led to the situation he was in now. "I can't even begin to imagine what you went through," he said quietly. "I've never heard of anything like that before, something so extreme. I can't imagine how anyone can do such a thing to another human being. The fact you're still sane means you must be a very strong person."

Alex laughed harshly. "That's one way of putting it." Alex sat up. "I'm sorry I sprung it on you like that. I've never told anyone but my therapist the story before."

"So how's that special therapy going for you?" Sage said quietly. "Is it working? Do you think you'll be able to get better completely or is it something you'll have to do for the rest of your life?"

"You mean Eric." Alex's voice was low.

"Yes. I mean Eric." The conversation had turned very surreal. He'd just made love to a man and now he was asking how long said man would have to see the other man in his life who was intimate with him. *If* intimate was the word for what seemed like more of a business arrangement.

Alex's voice was soft. "I don't know is the honest answer. I've been going to him once a week for the past two years. Before that I was an even worse mess. Now at least I can control my fears and urges a little."

Sage heard the pain in Alex's voice and closed his eyes at the images his words were conjuring up, images he really didn't want to see in his mind. "What kind of fears and urges are we talking about?" Sage asked quietly. He'd never had to face anything even remotely like what Alex had experienced and he didn't think he could even begin to understand what the man was going through. Sage's childhood had been happy, filled with love and caring. The thought of not having that in his life was alien to him.

"The fears? I wonder if I can ever have a normal relationship with a man," Alex said. "I just think I'm incapable, because each time I've tried to think I can start something, it doesn't work out. Then when I'm back to being alone again, the only way to feel better is to have someone like Eric take care of me in the only way I know how."

Sage stroked Alex's brush-cut hair gently as he listened, his heart full of compassion for this man who seemed so vulnerable now he was in Sage's arms.

"I'm so scared I'll never be able to have a proper relationship, that I'll always be on my own because no one wants damaged goods." Alex swallowed.

Sage pulled him closer. "That's not going to happen," he murmured. "You may have these 'demons' but look at us now. Here we are, together. And honestly? All I see is one amazingly strong and sexy man who just wants to make a life for himself. Look at what you've achieved so far. You've written best-selling books and you've just made love to a sexy film star."

He grinned and Alex chuckled. "I tried to tame my urge recently, to reduce my level of dependence on Eric. But then something bad happened and I found myself back where I started."

"Was it the thing with Dianne that made it worse?"

Sage sensed Alex's hesitation. "No, it was something else. It doesn't matter what it was."

"So this thing with him—is it a punishment you think you deserve or is it something you want to happen?" Sage wasn't a psychiatrist but it sounded a lot like self-punishment to him.

Alex was quiet for a long time before he spoke. "My therapist Melanie would tell you the root cause is self-loathing because I allowed my situation to happen, mixed with punishing myself *because* I allowed it and didn't fight back. It all sounds so simple but it's really not." His voice trembled. "She's right to a point but old habits die hard." Alex chuckled but Sage heard the despair in his voice.

Sage stood up, walking over to where he thought his clothes lay in the darkened room. He found his jeans and shirt on the floor and pulled them on. He'd find his underwear later. He made sure to pick up the used condom and put it in his pocket for disposal later. He didn't want that anywhere in the office, not even in the waste bin. Cleaners tended to talk and the last thing either of them needed was gossip about them fucking in the office. "So has anything ever worked out to the point that you feel you can give Eric up?"

Alex reached down for his jeans then frowned slightly, his eyes roving the room as if looking for something. Then he shrugged as he slid on his jeans. He turned to face Sage.

"No, Sage. A man wouldn't want to share me with some other man who hurts me and does things to me that they'll never be able to understand. I wouldn't expect them to. These are my demons and that's why I don't get involved."

"I can't accept that." Sage watched Alex in the darkness. "You've been doing this so long now perhaps it's just a self-fulfilling prophecy. Perhaps you haven't really had something or someone you care about enough to try and give up your other side and make it work."

Alex laughed harshly, the sound jarring in the quiet room. "On the self-fulfilling idea my therapist definitely agrees with you. But it would take a very special type of man to have the patience to do that. Are you offering, then, Sage? Are you going to be my *saviour*?" His voice was mocking.

Sage strode over the room, pulling Alex to him, holding him close, feeling the heightened beat of his lover's heart against his chest as he wrapped his arms around him, pinning Alex against him.

"Stop it," he said savagely. "Stop being such a bastard, pushing away anyone who wants to help you. It's not going to work on me because I see right through it."

Alex leaned his head against Sage's shoulder and Sage relaxed his grip. Alex's arms slid in around Sage's waist, burrowing in under his tee shirt, touching the warm skin beneath. Sage leaned down, kissing him fiercely. "You've gotten this far. We can take it a step further if you want. I want to help you, Alex."

Alex looked up at him. Sage saw the wonder in his eyes. "You're just a little too good to be true, even if you are banging other men. Not that I can complain of course. I'm banging another man."

Sage heard the wry tone of Alex's voice but he also heard the insecurity in it. "Alex," he started to explain about Brian, but Alex reached up, laying a finger against Sage's lips. "You don't have to explain anything. You have needs, you're not a bloody monk and you had no responsibility to me. I had no right to be upset."

Sage groaned. "Alex, I blame you anyway. You left me all hot and bothered. So I suppose you could say in a roundabout way it *was* your fault." He grinned, then Alex's last words sank in. "What do you mean, you had no right to be upset? When I spoke to you that night, you acted as if you couldn't give a damn."

Alex was quiet. "It doesn't matter. Just forget it," he said evasively.

Sage moved back, looking at Alex. "Is that what upset you that you had to go to see your 'therapist?' Was I the cause of the bruises and the welts you have on you now?" He felt sick at the thought that he might have driven Alex into Eric's domain.

Alex shifted in his arms. "Forget it. You aren't responsible for the fact that I'm all fucked up. You can never be responsible for anything I do."

Alex moved away as Sage ran a hand through his hair in consternation. Alex switched the light on and Sage could see his pale face and the bruised lips from his kisses. It made him want to start all over again. Sage moved around the room, hunting for his boxers, spotting them lying on the floor in a heap. He picked them up, stuffing them into his jeans pocket with a sigh of relief as Alex moved to the door, waiting for him. Sage felt a little out of sorts. This was a particularly unusual situation, he had to confess. "So what happens now?" he muttered.

Alex looked at him with sympathy. "Sage, I really like you. All we can do now is see where this goes. I'm not ready to tell you everything yet or answer any more questions. You have one very big advantage over anyone else I've been with. You're the only person I've ever told the full story to apart from my therapist. Even the few friends I hang out with know nothing about my past. And the other men I was with? I just did everything in the dark, skirted around all their questions and finally drove them away because I was a bastard. So for me this has all been a little liberating. But for you it will be the opposite. You might want to pursue this— thing—we have but you need to understand you're not the only one I'll be seeing. I have no idea whether you'll be able to do that without driving yourself crazy."

Alex reached up, touching Sage's face gently. "I don't want to hurt you. But you need to understand that's a risk you might have to take if you intend on being with me."

Sage swallowed. "I understand. I don't know if I can do it either. Seeing you hurt like that, in places I don't even want to think about…" He winced.

Alex reached up and kissed him tenderly. "I promise you I'll ask him to tone it down. I owe you that much if you're prepared to put up with me like this. But I can't make any promises. Not yet."

Sage nodded. "I suppose we can only try." He gave a twisted smile. "This isn't quite how I'd imagined this going. Normally we'd start with dinner, not agreeing on levels of S and M with another man." He swallowed, realising the full enormity of the situation he found himself in. "But if it means I can be with you just that little bit more, or help you get through this then I'm prepared to take a chance, at least for now." He smiled faintly. "I really like you too."

Alex grinned at him. "That's all I can ask of you. But we need to have a safe word."

Sage looked at him, his face darkening. "A 'safe word?' I don't intend on doing any of those bloody S-and-M activities to you—"

Alex shook his head emphatically. "A word that tells me you've had enough, that tells me you need to move on without lengthy conversations, guilt or recriminations. Think of one. Then tell me what it is and I'll tell you mine. It'll mean that any time we want, if it gets too much for either of us, we just need to leave a note for the other person or tell the other person once. We have to promise each other we won't try and make the other person stay and we don't have to explain ourselves. You have to promise me you'll follow the rules."

Sage looked at him and sighed. He supposed what Alex said made sense in what was likely to be a very unorthodox relationship.

"Tallulah," he muttered.

Alex frowned. "Is that your mother's name or something?"

"My horse," Sage remarked drily. "She's the safest animal I know. It makes sense to me."

Alex looked amused. "You and your horses. I hope to meet this other rival for your affections one day." He stared at Sage. "My safe word is Chrysippus."

Sage frowned. "That's a bit dark. I know that story. We did Greek tragedy in drama school. He was kidnapped and raped by his tutor, then apparently killed himself. You have a fairly black sense of humour. I'm not sure I like that word and all its implications."

"That's my word. You don't get to change it. Are we agreed then, with the words and the rules?"

Sage felt weary. "Yes, I agree. Chrysippus and Tallulah. God, they sound like women of disrepute in a whore house."

Alex chuckled, looking more relaxed than he'd ever seen him. Sage's heart lifted. Perhaps this would be all right after all.

"Come on, you." Alex took him by the hand, leading him out of the office. "I need to get home and I'm sure your friend has a spare man at home for you to bonk."

"No other men." Sage shook his head. "Only you."

Alex looked at him strangely. "Sage, I can't insist you be exclusive with me. That was never my intention whether I like the idea it or not. That wouldn't be fair on you under the circumstances. Just you knowing about me and being there occasionally for me is more than I've ever had before. I have no idea how this is going to work, when we'll get to see each other—"

"No other men for me." Sage was implacable. "That's my commitment to you if this is ever going to work. I'm not having you going off half-cocked again and getting hurt."

He saw relief in Alex's eyes as he reached up, cupping Sage's face in his hands then kissing him softly on the lips.

"Fine. Just me then." Alex grinned impishly. "I liked jumping your bones so you'd better be ready for more of the same."

Sage smiled. "Ditto. As long as you do it often. I'm very needy. Although perhaps next time we can manage it somewhere a little more comfortable and I certainly hope it takes longer."

They were outside on the pavement now, Sage locking the door behind them. "I'll walk you home and then get home myself," he said quietly.

Alex opened his mouth to protest and Sage shook his head firmly. "No argument. With everything that's happened to Dianne, I want to see you safely home first. Safety in numbers."

Alex considered, nodded then tucked his arm in Sage's. Sage marvelled at the transformation in him. Alex seemed a different person. His face was more relaxed, his walk more chipper and his overall demeanour seemed much brighter.

If Sage could do that for him in just one night, surely over time he could wean the man off Eric for good? Sage knew he had a challenge to face. He also knew they had a lot more to talk about. Alex's admissions of the evening had raised more questions for him than answers. He wanted to get to know Alex more and perhaps even get to see his whole body in the light. He'd no idea whether he was up to the task. But he'd give it a damned good try and if all else failed he could always say "Tallulah" no matter how much it broke his heart.

Chapter 14

The following morning Alex arrived at the studio early and made himself a pot of coffee. He'd slept better last night than he could ever remember doing. When he looked at the couch in the corner, he grinned in memory of what had happened there last night with Sage. He'd been incredible, really strong and sexy, and he could feel his groin tingle just thinking about him. He hummed to himself as he powered up his computer, taking his coffee over to the window and looking out into the street below. He turned when he heard a polite cough at the door to see Luke standing there, an apologetic smile on his face.

"Alex? Good morning. I wondered whether you'd had a chance to make those writing changes for me yet for today's schedule?"

Alex nodded, setting his coffee cup down on the desk. "I have them here. Let me print them you for you." As he sat down to print the documents he saw Sage at the door. Luke stepped into the room to make way for Sage.

Sage smiled at him. "Good morning," he said softly. "Morning, Luke. I'm glad to see you're cracking the whip so early. You have to keep the staff on their toes." He winked at Alex behind Luke's back and Alex's stomach lurched at the tender expression in Sage's eyes.

Luke frowned, a comical expression on his face as he reached down to pick up something wedged under the couch. "Well, what have we here?" he asked slyly as he held up the silk boxers Alex had been wearing the night before.

Alex's jaw dropped. He'd looked around for them last night. He'd made a mental note to look again. Then after he'd dressed, he'd forgotten. He glanced at Sage, whose face was currently pink and going pinker by the minute.

Hastily Alex stood up and deftly removed the offending item from Luke's fingers. He didn't know what to say and Sage wasn't helping.

Luke looked at him, then at Sage's blushing face. He'd got it all figured out.

Luke held up his hands in a gesture of pretended ignorance, all the time with a wide grin on his face. "I suppose they must have dropped out of your laundry basket, Alex," he said, nodding wisely. "You really should be more careful with your delicates." He picked up the papers from the printer, holding them aloft, and he sauntered out of the office.

Sage looked at Alex with horror. "Jesus Christ! I don't believe it. It'll be all over the studio grapevine in about a minute. Luke's terrible with gossip. That man's got the busiest mouth I know."

Alex spluttered in laughter as Sage looked at him in annoyance. "Alex, this is *not* funny. The whole bloody world is going to know you and I slept together in this office last night."

Alex chuckled. "Sage, it's your blushing that gave it all away in the first place. I might have been able to blag it out had it not been for that. But won't it be better than keeping it secret and sneaking around?"

He stopped as a thought occurred to him and he looked at Sage. "Are you saying you're ashamed of it? Is it something you don't want out in the open for that reason?"

Sage looked at him. "Don't be silly. I want to shout it from the bloody rooftops. I'm more worried about the fact that it will get out to the newspapers. The papers will spare no effort at finding out everything they can about any relationship in my experience, which might mean looking at you and your background. I know you must already have considered that when you decided to become a author and then got famous. But this will add another facet to the press's insatiable desire to drill down into all the sordid details no matter how it hurts. Is that something you want?"

Alex felt ill, realising Sage's words were true. He'd overlooked that part in his amusement at being caught shagging the sexy film star in the studio. He looked worriedly out at the corridor.

Sage sighed. "It's too late. It'll be viral by now. Get ready for the hoo-hah when you go out of this room. They won't let us live it down." He took Alex's hands and held them. "This is just something we'll have to watch. I can only take the 'no comment' thing so far if I'm collared. You need to be prepared for it too." He beckoned to Alex. "Come on. I need to get to makeup. We may as well go out and face whatever's coming together."

Alex followed him into the corridor, walking away behind him. Already he saw the sly glances and thumbs-up he was getting from a lot of the crew. Bloody hell, Luke had only a five-minute head start. Sage had the same attention, people walking past him, slapping him on the shoulders as if he'd just completed something extremely important rather than diddled the in-residence writer in his office. Sage waved them off good naturedly and Alex marvelled at his ability to simply take it in his stride.

Alex saw Sage stop suddenly as Sarah Brose stepped in front of him. The woman stood regarding him for a moment with a sneer on her face. She said something to him and he stepped back, almost as if she'd threatened him. Sage replied but Alex was too far away to make out what was being said. Finally Sarah moved out of his path and Sage walked on, whilst Sarah watched him, her eyes boring into his back. He disappeared into the makeup room.

Ally, one of the lighting crew, sauntered up to Alex with a grin. "Alex, you lucky man. I've heard all about your night of passion with our resident Mr. Dark and Sexy. I won't be all nosy and ask how it was, because that would be rude." She laughed. "But if you want to tell me, I'm all ears." She leered at Alex. "We've all noticed the size of his feet and we'd appreciate knowing whether there's any truth in the old urban legend."

She chuckled, touching Alex lightly on his arm before moving on. Alex made it to the other side of the studio and sank down thankfully into a large easy chair whilst he settled in to watch the filming. A heavy hand fell on his shoulder. He looked up into the set face of Sarah.

"Sarah, can I help you with something?" Alex was puzzled by the look on the cleaning lady's face. Her attitude and attention toward Sage were beginning to bother him.

"I just wanted you to know I'm here for you, that's all. You know where I am if you need me." Sarah turned and strode away, leaving Alex bemused.

What the hell was all that about?

Alex shrugged, watching as Carter West and Gillian Blake made love in front of the cameras, all the time wishing he was the one up there with Sage.

Alex had a session with Eric in a few days' time. He gave a thought to cancelling and immediately felt a wave of distress. He knew he wasn't ready to give it up yet. He'd need to take this new relationship one day at a time.

Chapter 15

Sage finished changing back into casual clothes, giving a sigh of relief. It had been a long day. Despite the fact that a few days had passed since Luke had outed him and Alex, everyone was still giving him sideways glances and pokes in the ribs every time they saw him. It was still apparently a hot topic of conversation amongst the film crew. It was getting annoying and he thought he might deck the next person who made any rude gestures or expressed their approval of his and Alex's night of passion.

He wondered how Alex was managing all of it. Sage's time had been very busy with filming and other promotional events and they'd only managed to make love again once since that night, in Alex's office again. He was looking forward to perhaps convincing Alex to go out for a bite to eat tonight. He looked at his watch. Five p.m. It was a nice early finish to the day for a change. He went to find Alex but he was nowhere to be found. Sage frowned. It seemed a bit early for him to leave. Seeing Janine standing over by the coffee machine, he made his way over. "Janine? Have you seen Alex?"

"He left a little while ago. Said he had an appointment."

Sage's stomach dropped. "Did he say where?"

Janine shrugged and then winked. "Nope, sorry. You'll have to give the hanky-panky a miss tonight, it looks like."

Janine grinned at Sage's ferocious expression, waving her finger in his face. "Sunshine! You can't expect to do what you two did and not get the stick that goes with being caught. Don't worry, it'll all be over soon unless someone finds some more underwear lying around." She chuckled as Sage shook his head in exasperation and walked off.

Sage took out his mobile, thinking perhaps Alex had left him a message. Sure enough, he saw a short text message from him and his face darkened when he read it.

Sage. 2nite is an E nite. wanted u 2 know. i'll call u l8r A.

He shoved his phone back in his pocket savagely.

Christ, I don't want to know about Alex's plans for the night with bloody Eric! I especially don't want to have to talk to him after he's had another man inside him either. God, this is going to be hard. It's only been a few days and I don't know if I can do this.

He saw Sarah Brose on the other side of the studio and frowned.

That woman was *psycho*. She'd gotten in his face just after the news about he and Alex had been leaked and told him to leave Alex alone, that he was worth more than Sage's attention. Sage had told her in no uncertain terms to fucking mind her own business and for a moment he'd thought she was going to hit him. She'd then trundled off and he'd not spoken to her since. She seemed to have a real problem with him and he had no idea why. What he did know was that he wanted her off the set. She was trouble, he could sense it. He made a mental note to speak to Luke about it later. He sat down on the easy chair in the studio and clasped his hands in front of him as he tried to control his thoughts about what Alex might be doing right now. There was a gentle hand on his shoulder and he looked up to see Dianne smiling down at him.

"Sweetheart. You look so glum! What's the matter?" Dianne nudged him over and sat down on the chair arm next to him.

He smiled tiredly. "Just tired, I suppose. Having everyone think you're the office Romeo hasn't helped either. Dodging the puns has been bloody exhausting."

She chuckled. "I for one am glad you two got it on. I always thought there was an attraction there and I'm glad to see my instinct wasn't wrong. Alex is such a gem, a little self-contained perhaps, but he's absolutely gorgeous and the two of you make a lovely couple." She raised two immaculately plucked eyebrows. "You are a couple, aren't you?"

Sage couldn't really tell her they were a threesome. "It's a little complicated. It's still very early days so don't go assuming too much yet."

She patted his arm as she stood up. "You hang in there. Things will work out, you'll see. I'm going out to dinner with Thomas. Do you want to join us?"

Sage shook his head. "Chinese takeaway and a night in, I think. I need to catch up on some 'me' time."

Dianne ruffled his hair as she walked away. "Tell Alex I say hi."

He grinned and stood up, ready to leave. His mobile rang as he did so and he answered it. "Chris Sage."

The voice on the other side was matter-of-fact and terse. "Mr. Sage? This is Nurse Sarah White from Broomfield Hospital. I've been given your number as a contact for Mr. Miles Conway. I'm afraid he's been in a car accident. He's here at the hospital."

The news caused Sage to sit back down in shock, feeling as if a pile driver had been driven through his chest. "How is he?" he managed to say.

"He's holding his own. He's in surgery at the moment," the woman said quietly.

"I'll be over as soon as I can. You have my number so will you call me if anything changes?"

"I don't think anything will. But of course I will, Mr. Sage."

"Thanks. I'll be there as soon as I can." He put his phone back into his pocket with shaking hands.

Luke noticed him and came over. "Sage? You look terrible. Is everything all right?"

Sage shook his head blindly. "No. My godfather has just been rushed to hospital. He was in a car accident. I have to get to Broomfield Hospital. I have no car here, has anyone got one I can borrow?"

Luke nodded decisively. "You're in no shape to drive, getting news like that. Come on, I'll take you in. This seems to becoming a habit for us, driving people to hospitals."

He ushered Sage out of the studio and into the underground car park. It took them nearly two hours to get to Chelmsford to the hospital. The London traffic was a nightmare. Sage was almost eating his fingers after biting off his nails in his agitation to get to Miles.

Luke pulled up into the hospital and gestured to Sage to get out. "Go. I'll find somewhere to park and I'll find you."

Sage needed no urging. He legged it out of the car and into the A&E department. The young receptionist took one look at him and gave him her full attention.

"Mr. Sage. I saw you on TV in *Dalton's Hospital*. You were amazing, really. Are you here to see someone?"

"My godfather, Miles Conway, was admitted here earlier. He was in a car accident. I need to see him."

The receptionist looked at her computer screen and nodded. "Yes, Mr. Conway was admitted a few hours ago. But I think he's still in surgery."

Sage felt faint. "Where do I find the doctor?"

"If you take a seat in the waiting room, Mr. Sage, I'll tell the surgical team you're here and they'll come and speak to you when they can."

She motioned to the room at the far side of the emergency entrance and Sage nodded and made his way over. He sat down on one of the plastic chairs, heaving a shuddering sigh.

About ten minutes later Luke came in and sat down beside him. "Have you heard anything yet?" he said. Sage shook his head mutely.

Luke reached over, grasping the younger man's shoulder. "Don't think the worst, Sage. Be patient." He stood up. "I'm going to get us coffee from that machine over there. Be back in a minute."

Sage's mobile rang. He looked at it distractedly, ignoring the glares from everyone in the waiting room and the cheery soul in the corner who tut-tutted and pointed to a sign that said "Switch off all mobiles." It was Alex.

Sage closed his eyes and answered. "Hi. I'm at the hospital in Broomfield. My godfather was in an accident. He's in surgery at the moment."

"I'll come down now to be with you." Alex sounded horrified.

"No, you don't need to come down here. Just go home. I'll be fine. I'll call you when I can and let you know what's happening. Thanks for the call."

He disconnected his call, switching off his phone. He didn't want to see Alex tonight after he'd been to see Eric. He needed to be focused for Miles' sake. It was more than an hour later when the doctor came out to give them the news on Miles.

"He's stable now but it was a tough one. He's sustained breakages to his ankle, his tibia, an arm and various internal injuries and cuts and bruises, which luckily aren't life-threatening. He's got a nasty gash on his head from where he fell but we think it will be fine. We'll have to wait and see when he wakes up, which I don't think will be for a while."

"Can I see him?" Sage looked at the doctor, his face bleak.

The surgeon nodded. "He's in recovery now. You can go in and visit for a short while. It's unlikely he'll know you're there though."

Luke nodded at Sage. "Go in and see him. I'll wait here in case you need me."

Sage nodded his thanks, following the doctor to the recovery room. He saw his godfather covered in various bandages and casts, pale and drawn, lying in the hospital bed. Sage felt an ache in his chest that threatened to overwhelm him. Miles was his rock, his surrogate father. If anything happened to him, he'd fall apart. He'd lost his parents and he couldn't lose another father figure. He sat down beside Miles, reaching over and taking the man's large, calloused hands in his.

"Miles? It's Sage. I'm right here." His voice caught as he leaned forward. "The doctor says you'll be all right. Tough old bugger like you, of course you'll be fine. I'm going to stay here with you for a while." Sage swallowed, close to tears. "I was going to come down this weekend and bring Alex to visit the cottage. You'll like him; he's pretty special. He's never ridden a horse before so I thought we could saddle up Tallulah and let her take Alex for a ride."

Sage rambled on a while longer, telling Miles about what had happened at work, the underwear incident—which he knew Miles would appreciate—and generally filling him in on his week. Eventually the nurse came in, quietly asking him to leave for a while whilst they transferred Miles to his private ward. Sage waited impatiently for them to do that whilst pacing up and down the corridor. He was bone tired, his eyes gritty.

Luke came over, placing a comforting hand on his shoulder. "Sage, the police are here. Because it was a hit-and-run they need to ask you some questions about Miles."

Sage nodded. "Stay with him as they transfer him, will you? Come and let me know if anything happens."

He walked out into the adjacent reception room where the police were waiting for him.

"Mr. Sage? Detective Sergeant Doyle and Detective Constable Merriweather from CID at Chelmsford Police Station. We wondered if we could ask you a little bit about Mr. Conway."

"You can, but I was filming in London when the accident happened. I'm afraid I don't even know what happened yet."

"We can perhaps fill in a couple of the blanks, sir. Can we sit down?" The three men sat down and DS Doyle looked at Sage with compassion. "First let me say I'm very sorry about your godfather. Hopefully we can get to the bottom of what happened and find the bastard that did it."

Sage nodded in agreement.

"An eyewitness said Mr. Conway was walking down the high street in Finchingfield when a car mounted the pavement and hit him at quite a speed. The car then backed up and drove off. All we can find out is that it was a white Ford Fiesta driven by someone in a hoodie —no one caught a better sight of the driver. We don't even know yet whether it was a man or a woman. The witness said it looked as if it was meant to ride him over."

Sage shook his head in bewilderment. "Who the hell would want to run Miles over? He's one of the most popular people in the village. Everyone loves him. I can't believe it would be anyone in the area. I don't know anyone who drives a white Fiesta either, in case you were wondering."

The policeman smiled. "Thank you, Mr. Sage. That would have been my next question. I'm afraid at this time we have very little to go on. We're checking all the CCTV footage in the area to see if we can spot anything."

He looked at Sage curiously. "Your godfather—he isn't your uncle by any chance is he? Your father or mother's brother?"

Sage shook his head in confusion. "No. Miles was my Dad's best friend. Why do you ask?"

"The witness said the person shouted something out of the car window as he or she drove away. She said it sounded like 'Carter's brother.' We thought perhaps your father's name was Carter. Does that mean anything to you?"

Sage felt as if he'd fallen down a long deep rabbit hole and that at any time he could expect to see the manic figure of the white rabbit scurrying in front of him. "'Carter's brother?'" he said faintly. "That can't be possible."

DS Doyle frowned. "What does that phrase mean, sir?"

Sage leaned back in the chair and closed his eyes. "It's going to sound crazy." He muttered. "I can't quite believe it myself."

The policeman sighed in long-suffering patience. "Do you think you can explain it to us, sir, no matter how fanciful you think it is?"

Sage saw him look at his colleague with a slight rising of the eyebrows as if to say, "Actors! Bloody drama queens." He scowled slightly. He'd do an Alex summary for them, see how they liked it.

"Just over a week ago, my co-star was involved in a letter-bomb incident on the outskirts of London. It so happens that this incident almost mirrors the first scene in the plot of a TV series we're currently filming, called *Double Exposure*. The Central Middlesex police thought the attack was staged to reflect this opening scene. I'm the main lead playing a character called Carter West. The second major incident in the book is a hit-and-run accident involving Carter West's brother. Except I don't have a brother so it looks like someone targeted poor Miles instead."

The policemen were staring at him in complete fascination as he finished.

DS Doyle narrowed his eyes as he observed Sage. "Let me get this straight," he said slowly. "You think someone is staging scenes from a TV series in real life?"

Give the man a bloody cigar!

Sage nodded. "If not, it seems a helluva coincidence. I'm not a believer in coincidences, DS Doyle. Talk to your colleagues at Middlesex. They'll tell you all about the first incident."

"Might I ask what the next incident might be so we're forewarned?" DC Merriweather leaned forward to ask his question.

Sage hadn't thought that far. He took a moment to remember. "The next violent scene, if it follows suit like these ones, would be the main character—that would be me—getting kidnapped and beaten to a pulp by an underworld gang boss." He smiled wryly. "Whilst I don't fancy that idea, I'm sure you won't let it get that far."

There was silence as the policemen digested this bit of information. DS Doyle stood up and Sage followed.

"I think we have what we need for now, sir." DS Doyle said, holding out his hand to Sage to shake. "I'll speak to my colleagues at Middlesex as you suggest and see what they have to say. If we hear anything, we'll be in touch. If you are correct and this is someone staging scenes from your film, can I ask you to be especially vigilant, sir? You never know with psychos."

Sage nodded. "I'll do my civic duty to be psycho-aware, Detective Sergeant."

The policemen chuckled and departed. Sage went into Mile's room to see Luke reading a magazine in the visitor's chair. He filled him in on the conversation with the police.

Luke gazed at him in disbelief. "Sage, you need to be careful. If this is what you think, you could be in danger. We need to get you some sort of bodyguard or something."

Sage laughed. "Jesus, don't be so melodramatic! I don't think anyone's going to kidnap me, for God's sake. I'll keep an eye out for potential candidates though."

He looked at Miles. "How's he been?"

"No change. He seems comfortable enough though." Luke looked at his watch. "Do you want me to take you home? I need to get off."

Sage shook his head. "No, I'm staying here. I'll see how he is in the morning before I go home. At least it's the weekend. I'll get a taxi if I need transport. Thanks for bringing me. I really appreciate it."

"Try and get some sleep. You look knackered. I'll call you tomorrow and see how you're getting on." Luke disappeared into the corridor.

Sage flopped down in the visitor chair, leaning back and closing his eyes.

A nurse came in with a smile and a blanket. "Here you go, Mr. Sage. That'll keep you a little warmer. It can get a bit cool in these wards."

He murmured his thanks, draping the blanket over his legs. The stress of the day slowly disappeared as he fell asleep.

* * *

It was six o'clock in the morning and the ward where Sage was still sleeping was dark with the only noise the hum of the machines attached to Miles. Alex watched Sage sleep as he sat in the other visitor chair. He'd arrived about an hour ago via taxi.

Sage had sounded so stressed on the phone and Alex wanted to be with him. He'd tucked the blanket up around Sage's body, thinking the man looked so vulnerable when he slept, his black curly hair all tousled and his very kissable mouth relaxed in sleep. He was snoring softly.

Alex hoped he'd gotten his text about the visit to Eric. He was quite proud of himself. He'd only let him use the chamois flogger with no biting, and whilst the actual sex was still rough, as it always was with Eric, Alex had felt more detached last night. He'd kept thinking about Sage, about his smile and his strong, warm body that had enveloped him in his passion. Eric would never know it was Sage Alex had been thinking about when Eric had been busy with his fingers driving him to orgasm.

Alex knew Eric hadn't been pleased with the new development. Melanie had been right in her original feeling that his principal was somehow more emotionally invested in their sessions that Alex had thought. That could be a big problem for Alex. Alex looked up as the nurse bustled in, then eased back into his chair.

"Good morning, dear." The nurse smiled at him as she went over to Miles to take the obligatory readings.

At her voice, Sage woke up, peering blearily around the room, seeing Alex sitting in the chair across from him. His face lit up. "Alex. When did you get here?"

Sage stretched, grimacing at the sounds his bones made as did so and then stood up. Alex smiled at him, glad to see that he seemed pleased he was there. The nurse moved around the bed, checking equipment. Finally with a soft smile at the couple, she disappeared out of the room.

Sage went over to Miles, looking down on the sleeping man. "He's got more colour than he had last night. I suppose that's a good sign." He reached down and tenderly stroked his godfather's cheek before turning to Alex again.

"I got your message," Sage said quietly, observing him with a brooding expression. "You don't have to tell me when you're seeing him. In fact, I'd rather *not* know if you don't mind. At least that way I can bury my head in the sand and pretend you were simply out doing something else."

Alex's hands tightened at his words. "Of course," he said quietly. "If that's what you want."

Sage nodded and Alex felt his eyes keenly watching him. He had the uncomfortable feeling Sage was trying to see if any evidence remained from last night.

"It wasn't too rough, Sage." Alex shifted in the chair. "I told you I'd try and tone it down and I did. Melanie would say it is a good sign."

Alex saw Sage frown at the name and hurried to explain. "Melanie is my therapist."

Sage nodded again, yawning then covering his mouth with his hand. "Sorry. That chair isn't particularly comfortable and I don't think I slept that well." He looked at Alex wryly. "I'm not going to say I'm glad you're pleased about the way last night's 'toning down' went, because honestly, I don't think I want to process it all right now. But I am glad you're here. Did you go home first then?" he asked casually.

Alex wondered if he was really asking whether he'd gone home first to clean Eric off him. "I had a shower before I came here, Sage." Alex gazed at him evenly.

Sage looked uncomfortable at him seeing through his question, wandering out into the doorway. "I'm going to try and hunt down some coffee. Do you want some?"

Alex nodded and Sage went to in search of his morning wake-up fix. Alex felt trepidation. Sage seemed a little different this morning. He hoped it was just because of his godfather and that he wasn't having second thoughts about their arrangement. Miles stirred and Alex stood up, moving over to his bedside. Miles's eyes opened and he looked at him with dark brown eyes that seemed fairly focused considering what he'd been through. For a moment he stared into Alex's eyes and then Alex saw a faint smile float across the injured man's face.

"Am I in heaven?" His voice was throaty from the tube they'd used in surgery. "With those eyes you sure belong there."

Alex grinned at him, reaching a warm hand to hold Miles's cold one. "No. You're in the hospital. Sage is here, he just went to get coffee. I'm Alex."

Miles tried to nod his head and winced in pain. "You're Sage's fellow," he said.

A warm feeling spread from Alex's head to his toes at the fact that Sage had told his godfather about him in some form or another. He smiled. "Well, perhaps not quite, but I wouldn't mind being. You did a good job with him, Miles. He's a wonderful man. You should be proud of him."

Miles smiled as he closed his eyes. "He is at that. A good man."

Alex heard a noise behind him as Sage came in bearing two cups of something steaming in polystyrene cups. He smiled widely, seeing Miles lying there with open eyes. He put the cups down on the side table and hurried over to his side.

"Miles. Jesus, you old bastard, you scared me to death. How do you feel?"

"Like I fell off a horse and got dragged down a hill feet first. What the hell happened to me?"

Sage sat down in the chair, taking Mile's hands in his. "You had a confrontation with a car and the car won. The doctors say you'll be fine. You just need a lot of rest and time to heal. I'll be coming home to do that for you so don't worry."

Miles frowned, trying to sit up. He gave a gasp of pain. "Christ, I can hardly move. How fast was that bloody car going?"

Sage grinned. "Fast enough to break and arm, your leg in a couple of places, and to make sure you got that noggin of yours reconfigured. You're now the proud owner of a couple of dents."

Miles brow furrowed. "I don't remember much."

Sage frowned. "It'll come back you in time. Anyway, the important thing is you're okay. I really thought I might have lost you." His voice broke slightly.

Miles reached out a hand to take his godson's. "You don't get rid of me that easily, son. I'm here for the long haul."

Sage grinned, leaning forward to kiss his godfather's forehead. Alex marvelled at the fact he could show emotion so easily and be so comfortable with it. He supposed the fact Sage was an actor helped as emotions were part of his trade. Alex had made it his life's mission to suppress his.

Miles gestured toward Alex. "I've met your boyfriend. He seems a nice enough chap. You'll want to hold onto him."

Alex held his breath, wondering what Sage's response would be.

"It's a work in progress," Sage said softly, looking at Alex. "But I have every intention of doing just that."

Miles closed his eyes in fatigue and Sage pulled the blanket around him. "I don't want you overdoing it. I need to get home and make sure everything's all right and bring some clothes and stuff back for you. Tell me you'll do as you're told and you won't go getting all macho with the nurses trying to get out of bed too soon. I'll have a word with the doctors as well and find out how long you need to be here so I can get the time off to come home."

Miles frowned. "Sage, you have a filming schedule to meet. You can't be taking care of me."

"The filming schedule can wait." Sage's face was unyielding. "You're more important."

Miles reached out, grabbing his hand. "Son, listen to me. This TV series is important to you. I'll get Lanie to come in and look in on me. She'll do it, I know."

Sage looked at Miles quizzically. "Lanie? I thought the two of you couldn't stand the sight of each other. Since when have you and Lanie been talking?"

Miles looked very uncomfortable. "We've sort of ironed out our differences and actually she's quite a nice woman. We've had dinner together a couple of times..." His voice tailed as he saw Sage's wide grin.

"I don't believe it. You dog! Lanie is the woman you've been—"

"Sage, there's someone else present. Don't embarrass him." Miles raised pleading eyes at the younger man who chuckled and shook his head.

"You mean embarrass *you*, you lecher. Fine. We'll leave it there. But I still think I should be there—"

"Jesus! Do as you're bloody told for once instead of giving me chapter and verse. Lanie can keep an eye on me. Alex, please tell your man that he has a career to think of and leaving it now won't do him any good."

He looked pleadingly at Alex, who didn't quite know which side to take. He glanced at Sage, who was regarding him with an air of anticipation.

"Um, I suppose if you think that's what should happen then Sage should listen to you. You know what's best for you after all."

Sage sighed and shook his head. "Betrayed by one of my own troops. I never thought I'd see the day." But his voice was amused. He looked at Miles. "OK then. I'll speak to Lanie when I get home and ask her to be your nurse." He smiled nastily. "Though from what I've heard, you two might have done—"

"Sage!" Miles voice was a warning despite his weakened condition.

Sage laughed loudly. "Keep your pants on, old man." He snorted in laughter, causing Miles to scowl. "I'll be very genteel and the soul of discretion."

He looked at Alex. "Do you want to come home with me, back to the cottage? Or do you have somewhere else you need to be?"

Alex looked at Sage sharply at his words but Sage's face was simply enquiring. "I'll come with you and give you a hand if you like. I've nothing else planned."

Sage nodded. "Fine. Miles, remember what I said. Behave. I'll be back later to see you."

He made his way out into the corridor. Alex followed him as he once again ordered a taxi. The man must spend a fortune on taxis, he thought. Alex didn't even know whether Sage owned a car. He smiled to himself.

It looked like he might get the time to find out, though, and perhaps find out more about the uber-sexy Christopher Sage, his very own dream come true.

* * *

Outside in the car park, DS Doyle's face was dark and threatening as he spoke on his mobile. "Sir, I hear what you're saying. But I assure you, my taking this case on is nothing personal."

Detective Inspector Barry Fenwick's voice was dry. "But this is a little out of your jurisdiction, isn't it, Reg? I know you have permission from the Met to pursue this case and you know I'm in agreement with it, but why do you care about it so much?" His boss's voice was quiet but Reg sensed the reprimand in it. His hackles rose.

"I know what everyone thinks, Barry. I've heard the water-cooler scuttlebutt. But I can assure you this has nothing to do with my son. I'm invested in this case because this is a young woman who was viciously attacked and a pensioner who got run down in a cowardly attack. The fact Christopher Sage is involved and he looks like my dead son has nothing to do with it, and I resent the implication."

Reg's son Luke had died at age thirty of leukaemia. Reg could not deny that the resemblance between Sage and Luke was substantial. Both also had the same spirit and tenacity too. He felt a little guilty disavowing it. He knew that it was in some part true but he wasn't about to let his boss know that. He wanted this case.

He stalked the corridors, his feet making small slaps against the shiny linoleum as he did so. "Something very strange is going on here. This is not an isolated incident. And to be told I'm getting emotionally invested when I'm not is an insult. So just let me do my bloody job and find out what's going on before something else happens. If you want me to pass this across to the team in London and butt out, I'll do it gladly."

He stood stock still, his frown receding as Barry spoke. He and Barry had a long-standing relationship—they'd come up through the police ranks together. There was no better man or friend than Barry Fenwick.

Barry sighed. "Reg, you know I think you're one of the best policemen we have. I'm sorry if you feel that was a criticism. I just don't want to see you get sidetracked."

"There'll be no detours, I assure you. I'll stay on this one then and give you a briefing tomorrow when I'm back in the office. I'll interview everyone again, get my team turning over every bloody stone. Something strange is going on here and it smells rancid. I'm on top of this one, you have my assurance on that one."

Reg rang off and strode off to the hospital exit, ignoring the clamour of press and photographers as they surged toward him like a line of battle troops.

Chapter 16

It was close to nine A.M. when the taxi finally arrived at Sage's home. The trip home had been a quiet one. Occasionally Sage had glanced over at Alex, smiling, reaching out and stroking Alex's hand absentmindedly as he gazed out the window at the fields beyond. Sage had dozed on and off, his head nodding down in sleep. Alex watched in amusement as Sage's curly head dropped then jerked awake again. As they reached the picturesque village of Finchingfield Alex could see why Sage liked it. But it was Sage's cottage that took his breath away. It looked like something out of a fairy tale, all white walls and thatch, with a fairly overgrown garden filled with large trees. Alex heard the steady hum of bees as they busied themselves in the blossoms.

The taxi deposited them in front and Sage paid the driver, who drove off with a cheery wave. Sage unlocked the front door, heaving a sigh of relief as he walked into the cool, dark entrance hall that smelt of oranges.

He turned to Alex. "The kitchen's through there if you want to put the kettle on."

He waved vaguely to his left as he disappeared. Alex walked into a huge open-plan kitchen, kitted out with oak units and a huge centre island table with stools randomly placed around it. He found the kettle, filling it and switching it on, then hunted for coffee cups. As the kettle boiled he gazed out of the kitchen window onto a field, with stables about forty feet away. There was a sense of peace here that he'd never felt in London. Ten minutes later, Sage walked into the kitchen with a grin.

"Well, Lanie's happy to look after the old sod. She says just to let her know when he gets home and she'll come over. She's most put out that she didn't know about the accident yet. I tried to explain that he'd been bloody unconscious and I didn't know about their relationship but she was having none of it. He's got some explaining to do to her when he gets home."

"Your home is lovely." Alex walked around the island and stood beside him. "It's a real retreat, isn't it?"

Sage looked around his house with fondness. "It's been a haven for me. I had the opportunity to move to London and live with Dan permanently but I love it here too much. Good memories here, plus of course I have the horses. Talking of which, they probably need feeding and they'll certainly need exercising." He grinned. "Hopefully my little helper will be around soon. She has ears like a bat and eyes that can spot movement a mile away and by now she'll probably know I'm home."

Sage opened the back door, walking down toward the stables. Alex followed him, enjoying the early morning sunshine on his face. Sage disappeared into one of the stalls and Alex peered in nervously to see him standing beside a huge grey horse that nuzzled his neck as he spoke softly to it.

Sage looked up, grinning. "Alex, meet Tallulah. This is the favourite woman in my life." He murmured to the horse. "No apples at the moment, old girl, but I'll bring you some later."

Reaching over a short fence on the other side of the stable, he hauled out a huge sack. He picked some sort of implement off the wall of the stable and deftly slit the sack open before lifting it effortlessly to his shoulder and pouring the contents of the feed into a trough in the stable. Alex watched open mouthed and more than a little turned on. Sage made the whole thing look so sexy and Alex wanted nothing more than to do him right there in the stable.

He watched the play of muscles in Sage's back and arms under his cotton tee shirt, saw the taut backside in the jeans he wore tense and move under the fabric. Alex had a sudden vision of ripping the clothes off Sage's body, pushing him down onto the straw in the corner and mounting him like a cowboy on a horse. Sage was unaware of Alex's scrutiny and lascivious thoughts as he whistled softly, moving around the animal as she munched on her feed.

Sage heaved a sigh of satisfaction. "That looks good, Lulah. It's healing nicely. Now for the other bloody animal. I hope he's in a better mood than last time."

He winked at Alex, making his way out of the grey's stall and into the one next door. Alex took the opportunity to try and adjust his growing erection to a more comfortable level. He'd never quite had this kind of visceral reaction just by watching someone do a mundane chore.

There was a loud snort. Alex heard Sage shout loudly. "Jesus, Jack. Take it easy!"

Alex hurried to the other stall, glancing inside in trepidation. Sage was trying to calm an even bigger beast, one who was jet black, had rolling eyes and at the moment was generally cavorting around the stall in frenzy. Sage held onto his reins, pulling them as he tried to calm the horse down. Alex watched nervously, but Sage knew what he was doing. The horse finally quietened down as Sage spoke to him gently, rubbing his flanks and stroking his nose. After a while the horse stood still, snorting and whickering.

Sage looked at Alex with an amused expression. "You can come in now. He won't bite, I promise. Just stay in front where he can see you."

Alex sidled in, still nervous. Horses had never been something he'd had much exposure to. He reached out a hand to stroke the horse's nose and smiled when he whinnied softly.

"He seems to like you," Sage said softly. "This one is the bane of my life. I've been thrown and bitten by him more times than I care to remember." Sage looked at the horse fondly. "But I haven't made the decision to turn him into glue yet. You're lucky, Mixed Jack. I'm too bloody soft with you." He looked at Alex. "Jack was my dad's horse. Lulah was my mum's. We've all grown up together—haven't we, old boy?"

He moved away to the corner of the stall and again opened a large sack, lifted it to his shoulder and poured it into Jack's feeding trough. As he did so, there was a loud call from the entrance to the stable.

"Sage! You're back! Can I take the horses for a ride now?" A young girl who looked about thirteen ran past, launching herself at Sage.

He dropped the bag, picking her up effortlessly and swinging her around as he laughed. "Jesus, Annie! Watch who you nearly knock over, you hooligan!" He put the girl back down and she grinned at him, her brown hair unruly, her green eyes sparkling.

She was a tiny thing, barely four foot and slim. "I'm really glad you're back, Sage. I missed you. Where were you? Where's Miles?"

"Whoa, Annie. Hold on with all the questions!" Sage laughed as he looked at Alex. "First let me introduce you to a friend of mine. Alex, this is Annie, my next-door neighbour and general pain in the arse. Annie helps me out with the horses."

Alex smiled. "Hi, Annie. Pleased to meet you."

Annie stood back, regarding Alex closely. He felt as if he was being sized up for a coffin, so intent was the girl's look.

"Are you Sage's boyfriend?" Annie peered at him warily. "Are you going to be staying here sometimes like Mason? He was nice. I liked him. Why do you have different colour eyes?"

Sage moved over to Alex and rolled his eyes. "Annie, Alex and I are just friends. We work together. His eyes are different because he was born like that. It's a genetic thing."

He touched the girl gently on the shoulder. "Miles was in a bit of a car accident in town but he's fine. I'm going to see him later. So I need some help from you."

Annie gasped in shock. "Is Miles all right? Is he in the hospital? Can I go see him?"

Sage reached out a finger and laid it against the teenager's lips. "God, Annie. One at a bloody time, please! Yes, he's fine, he's in the hospital and I'm hoping he'll be home soon anyway. That's why I'm going to need your help with the horses."

Annie looked at him solemnly. "Okay. Tell Miles I hope he gets better soon and I'll bake him some brownies when he gets back."

Sage smiled. "I'll tell him. Now, if you're quite finished with the hundred-and-one questions, you can saddle Lulah up for me and take her for some exercise. Then you can take Jack if you like. I might need you to do that every day for the next few days. Can you manage that?"

The young girl looked at him scornfully. "Of course I can, silly. I'll look after them for you every day if you want." She cast one more appraising glance in Alex's direction and went out of the stall, no doubt to attend to Lulah.

Sage grinned at Alex. "Sorry about that. Annie's like a little sister. She's an absolute godsend when it comes to the horses. She'll do anything for them. She wants to be a jockey when she's older."

Alex nodded. He was still a bit put out as being described as Sage's friend. He knew who Mason was, Sage's ex-boyfriend, having seen it on Google. But no one apparently had any idea why the two had broken up. Sage didn't seem to notice his slight disquiet as he left the stall, beckoning to Alex to follow him. He went back into the house, switching the kettle on again as he busied himself making the coffee.

"Are you hungry?" He looked at Alex. "I can make scrambled eggs if you like." He frowned. "That's assuming there's eggs which"—he looked in the fridge and sighed—"there aren't. Sorry, I retract that offer. What with being in London most of the time I haven't really managed to stock up."

"Who's Mason?" Alex couldn't help asking the question to see what Sage would say.

Sage scowled as he looked at him. "My ex-boyfriend."

He didn't offer any more information so Alex probed. "Were you together long? How 'ex' is he?"

Sage shrugged. "We were together eighteen months but he's been gone about eight months now." He sounded fed up.

"What happened?"

"Jesus, Alex, I don't really want to talk about it. He's out of my life now, so let's just leave it there." Alex realised he'd hit a nerve. Sage was getting very testy.

"Did he live here?" Alex knew he was pushing the envelope but he had to know. Sage turned to him suddenly and he felt a pang when he saw Sage's expression. The man had obviously meant a lot to him.

"Yes, he lived here off and on. But he doesn't anymore. There, happy now?"

Sage stormed out of the kitchen, back down to the stables. Alex sighed. He'd just had to push it, hadn't he? And now he'd upset Sage. He finished making coffee and sipped it as he watched Sage in the courtyard with Annie and Tallulah.

Sage helped Annie saddle Lulah, tightening the big strap that ran under the horse's belly. He turned and marched back up the house. Alex silently handed him his coffee as he came in and Sage took it and drank it as he walked into the lounge. Alex followed him then gasped in surprise.

The lounge was a large, airy room, with huge picture windows running the whole length of one wall. The decor was very masculine with a long black couch, a similar armchair and a magnificent centre table of glass and steel.

There were various pieces of artwork dotted around the walls, a huge bookcase in one corner filled with books and a huge wall-mounted Plasma TV on one of the walls with other gadgets surrounding it. It was all very modern and definitely not what he'd expected from what he'd seen of the rest of the house. He hadn't really expected this sort of setup from Sage either. Sage caught Alex looking around in amazement and he smiled slightly. He'd seemed to have forgiven Alex the indiscretion about his ex. "I'm not a farm boy, contrary to popular belief. If you think this is fancy, you should see my bedroom."

His tone was suggestive and Alex's insides churned at his words. Sage plonked himself down on the sofa, motioning to Alex to sit beside him. He followed and immediately Sage pulled him over, finding his mouth, kissing him deeply as Alex leaned into him. His tongue met Sage's in a fierce kiss. Alex ran his hands through Sage's hair and when he pulled away, he left Alex with a sense of loss.

Sage regarded him with curious eyes. "What's with the fascination about my ex anyway? I've moved on."

"Why did you break up?" Alex heard himself asking the question and winced.

Sage sat up, annoyed. "Jesus, leave it alone, will you?" He looked at Alex out of the corner of his eye. "I tell you what though. I'll answer your question about that if you then answer one of mine about you. I think that's fair. We can make it a sort of 'getting to know you' process."

Alex grew cold. Even with what he'd told Sage about himself already, there were still more secrets in his closet, packed away deep on hangers inside the recesses of his subconscious wardrobe, hopefully never coming out. He regarded Sage thoughtfully. "I think you owe me one anyway. With what I told you the other night, I actually think you owe *me* a few answers of your own before we're even."

Sage looked at him in contemplation then nodded. "Fair enough, I'd agree with that." He leaned back against the couch, his feet once again perched on his glass table, and looked at Alex. "Mason cheated on me with his so-called assistant, some young guy I found with his mouth around his dick when I paid him a surprise visit at his office. Given what I'd been through before with my fiancé fucking his friend at our home in London, I wasn't disposed to letting Mason get away with it no matter how much he told me it was just a temporary 'fling.'" Sage gave a harsh laugh as he gave a twisted smile. "I'm not a polyamorous guy. I don't like sharing. That seems to be a problem for the men I've picked in the past." His face shadowed as he regarded Alex. "Well, no agreed sharing, except in your case."

Alex's heart lurched. "I'm sorry, Sage. That must have been tough."

Sage nodded. "It was for a while. We had a flat rented in London and I moved back here full time. I was missing the house anyway but Mason thought this was out in the sticks so he preferred the place in the city. Dan made sure I had enough distractions to take my mind off things." He grinned. "He's good at that. Eventually I accepted it was just not meant to be."

Alex saw the hurt in Sage's eyes and moved his mouth onto his, soft lips pressing down as if trying to draw out all the pain. Alex pressed himself against him, hands slipping beneath Sage's shirt, touching the warm skin beneath. His hard-on was ready to launch out of his pants.

Sage groaned. "God, you drive me crazy, you know that? All I want to do is take everything off you and drag you through to the bedroom. You turn me into some sort of caveman."

"Then what are you waiting for?" Alex murmured in his ear, as his lips nibbled his earlobe. He loved that he could do this to Sage, cause this level of reaction in him.

Sage chuckled huskily. "Much as I'd love to do that, I have to get back to the hospital to see Miles. I've still got a load of stuff to do here too, so stop tempting me. I'm getting all hot and bothered."

Alex huffed then grinned, moving away with a wicked smile. Sage reached up and cupped Alex's face with a gesture of tenderness he'd never had from a man before. A lump formed in his throat.

"Keep those thoughts ready for later." Sage looked at him with darkened eyes. "If you're a good boy, we can come back here tonight and you show me what you're thinking."

Alex murmured, "They're very naughty thoughts, so you'd better save all your strength for later." He moved away from Sage, trying to ignore the heat in his groin, walking over to a set of photographs mounted on one of the walls, peering at them at he moved past. He frowned when one caught his eyes and he turned to Sage. "Is this you here with this guitar? You look as if you're playing in band!"

Sage laughed as he stood up. "I'm afraid it is. It was one of my dad's favourite pictures of me. I was eighteen then and played guitar for a rock band."

Alex stared at him in amazement. "Wow! That is such a turn-on. I'm diddling a rock God."

Sage laughed. "Hardly. Although we were pretty good. We were called the Vykings, with a y, and we did a couple of gigs around the country supporting some of the bigger acts. We were all huge Oasis fans and we sort of modelled ourselves on them."

Alex stared at him open-mouthed. "What made you give up a rock career and go into acting then?"

Sage's face darkened. "One of the band members died and it wasn't the same after that. We carried on with another vocalist but then my folks were killed and that was really it for me. I had other responsibilities what with this place and starting university. Finally we all went our own ways."

"Who died? Was he a friend?"

"Jerry was the lead vocalist and fellow guitar player." Sage sounded grim. "I found him OD'ed in his apartment one night when I went back to pick him up for a gig. We all knew he was into drugs. We all tried but none of us could talk him out of it. I tried to do CPR and called 999 but he was dead by the time they arrived."

"Oh, Sage. That's terrible. I'm so sorry."

He shrugged but Alex could see it was still painful. "It was a waste, he was only nineteen. I just don't understand how anyone can do that to themselves, why people have to get high to enjoy life. It just seems so pointless."

The hangers in Alex's wardrobe started to vibrate madly and he quelled their movement with a fierce thought. "Sometimes people get caught up in it. It might be the only way they have of escaping their reality."

Sage looked at him sharply. Alex met his gaze unflinchingly.

"Have you ever done drugs then?" Sage asked, eyes searching his face.

Alex nodded. "Yes, I did. Both whilst at Bohemia and after when I was trying to come to terms with it all. I was very lucky. I had someone to help me get through it. But I know what's it's like to be lost in them." Alex watched Sage's face carefully. "Are you disappointed in me?"

Sage shook his head. "I'm not going to judge you. Not after what you went through." He hesitated. "Are you into anything now I should know about?"

Alex shook his head fiercely. "No. You don't have to worry about that."

Sage looked relieved. "I'm glad." He chuckled in disbelief. "I can't believe half the conversations we have. It's all very surreal. S and M, sex, drugs and rock and roll." He smiled. "It's definitely an unusual relationship."

Alex smiled. "Oh, so it's a relationship now is it? I seem to recall you just wanted to discuss business the last time that word was used. I thought I was just a friend?"

Sage looked exasperated. "You don't know Annie. If I'd told her we were seeing each other, she'd be an absolute pest about it. She drove Mason crazy, so 'friend' seemed the safest thing to say for the moment." He looked at Alex with amusement. "I didn't realise you felt so strongly about it." Sage ignored his own rule about getting hot and bothered, pulling Alex over for a long kiss which left him reeling. They were both breathing fairly hard by the time Sage let him go.

"I need to go over to Miles's place and pick up some of his things," he said, glancing back at Alex. "Make yourself comfortable here. It's just down the road so I won't be long."

Alex watched as Sage meandered to an outdoor building, probably a garage of some sort, disappearing inside. Before long, the garage door opened and Alex watched in awe as a helmeted Sage appeared on a shiny black motorbike—he couldn't see the make—and roared down the road in a snarl of engine and dust.

Jesus, the man had a motorbike! Actor, great-looking, sexy, demi-rock god in his opinion and he drove a bike. Alex's cock grew even harder and he hoped like hell there'd be a plan to relieve the tension when Sage got back. He moved curiously toward the rest of the house, telling himself he was looking for the bathroom but in reality he wanted to see just what Sage's bedroom looked after his earlier cryptic comment.

Chapter 17

The cottage looked smaller from the road and was definitely deceptive. In addition to the lounge and the kitchen, there was a dining room to the side which Sage obviously used as an office. There was a computer and other electronic equipment on the solid wooden table set in the middle of the room. Papers and documents were spread around the table and there was yet another large plasma screen on the wall opposite his chair.

This man loved his gadgets. Alex was a bit of a geek himself.

Moving out of the dining room, he found a small guest bedroom with a single bed and a small wardrobe. Next to it was yet another room, which was used as storage with boxes, filing cabinets and other clutter. Alex pottered around it curiously for some time, picking up photo frames and old newspapers, smiling at the pictures of what he thought was Sage as a boy, standing with a man and woman he imagined to be his parents. There was a large box filled with newspaper articles about horses and races and a lot of photographs with a tall, rather large man with pitch-black hair and a weather-beaten face standing with various horses. From the resemblance, he imagined this was Sage's father.

Alex felt no guilt as he moved around the room, taking a peek into Sage's past. It was an incredible insight into this man's life and Alex had so few memories of his own like these ones that he relished the ones others gave him. Finally he left this room and approached what looked like the "man lair." He pushed the door open in anticipation, wondering what he might find. He wasn't disappointed.

God, the man really likes his black. Alex remembered reading an article recently about what colours meant for you as a person. From what he could recall, positive black traits were those of protection, comfort, someone strong and contained, someone seductive. Alex chuckled. He could believe that based on his current sexual state. Negative attributes were those of secrecy, holding back and conservatism. Alex wasn't so sure they fit the man he knew, who seemed to be for the most part an open book. He supposed wryly everyone had hidden depths.

Sage's bedroom was huge, with large picture windows looking out onto the fields beyond. There were black curtains at either side of them, made of a heavy, luxurious fabric which shone in the morning sun. The room was decorated in shades of black and amber and a huge metal king-size bed with an ornate metal headboard formed the centrepiece of the room. He saw another door on a far wall leading off to what he assumed was an en-suite bathroom. Black lacquered wardrobes lined one wall and in the corner of the room there was a small three-legged table and two armchairs. There was again the requisite plasma TV screen in viewing distance from the bed.

Sage definitely has a fixation with TVs.

Alex wondered wickedly whether he'd ever filmed himself in bed with anyone—the TV and bed were certainly in the perfect place. There was an ottoman at the end of bed, covered with richly coloured cushions of black and cream silk. There was no overhead lighting, only strips of silver lining the walls. Alex assumed it was lighting of some sort. On a far wall there was a large geometric print in shades of black, cream and amber, lighting up the room like a lick of fire. It exuded male sensuality like the man himself. Alex reached down, running a hand over the bedspread, feeling its cool smoothness beneath his fingers. He felt a spurt of jealousy as he wondered just how many men had enjoyed the comfort of both Sage and his bed.

Alex heard a low laugh behind him and he turned guiltily to find Sage standing at the door to his room, eyes narrowed with a very intense look on his face.

"Doing some exploring, are we?" Sage brushed past him to the opposite side of the bed. Alex smelt sweat and the fragrance of what Alex thought was Davidoff's Cool Water. It was one of his favourites.

Alex nodded. "I'm sorry. I was looking around the house and after what you said earlier, I had to see the bedroom. It's incredible."

"I'm glad you like it, seeing as I intend you being in here fairly often." Alex hitched a breath at that comment. Sage picked a watch up from the bedside table, putting it on. His hair was mussed up from the bike helmet, unruly and falling over his forehead in a swathe of black curls. His dark eyes shone and Alex saw the rise and fall of his chest through the thin tee shirt he wore. He swallowed, trying to quell the rising desire in his body.

This man was driving him crazy.

"You didn't tell me you had a motor bike." Alex waved toward the general direction of the garage.

Crap. Talking about a roaring beast that sat beneath Sage's legs and had intimate contact with what Alex wanted was definitely not the right topic now.

"You didn't ask," Sage said, making his way to the wardrobe, taking out a clean tee shirt. "I find it a much easier way of getting around, especially when I have to drive into London, which is fairly often. Have you been on a bike before?" He turned around, taking off his sweat-stained tee shirt in one supple movement.

Alex would have liked to answer in the affirmative but his breath left his body at the sight of Sage's naked, hairy torso, the clean lines of the muscles on his stomach and that sexy hairline leading down toward his groin. The deep crevice created by Sage's hip bones beckoned Alex to run his hands over them then trace the warm skin down into their depths with his tongue. He wanted desperately to taste what lay beneath those low-slung jeans. Alex decided he'd had enough of being a gentleman and he moved swiftly toward Sage. He pressed his lower body against Sage's front, feeling the other man's arousal as Alex ran needy hands down Sage's chest.

Sage took a deep breath. "Alex, I was going to change. I thought we agreed..."

"I don't remember agreeing anything. And seeing you like that just makes me really fucking horny. I want you so badly."

Alex lowered his mouth to Sage's chest, running his tongue from Sage's left nipple to the pulse that was throbbing madly in his throat. Alex heard his lover's hiss of pleasure and felt a sense of satisfaction. Sage's hands wrapped around his waist, pulling him toward him as he dropped the tee shirt he'd been about to wear on the floor. Alex's mind worked frantically as Sage continued driving him to distraction.

Those curtains look very heavy. I'm sure they'd be able to block out the light. I'll keep my shirt on anyway so he doesn't see the scars on my stomach and back. I'm not ready to share those with him yet. I don't want to put him off. He won't want a bloody Frankenstein in his bed. Fuck it, I want him so badly I can't wait.

"I don't intend letting you out of here until I've had you in my mouth." Alex whispered in Sage's ear. "So perhaps you could close those curtains and we should shut the door so no one can disturb us. I'm sure Miles can wait just a little bit longer."

Sage needed no further encouragement, moving over to the window, pulling on a silver rod that activated the curtains as they glided together effortlessly. The room went dark instantly as he moved over to the bedroom door, shutting it firmly before turning to Alex again, pulling him into his body, kissing him, his mouth urgent.

Alex's hands were already undoing Sage's jeans zipper. "I need to keep my shirt on," he whispered into Sage's ear. "I'm not ready yet to take it off."

Sage looked at him, his face etched with compassion. "I'm going to want to see you fully naked at some stage. You don't need to be ashamed of anything in front of me."

Alex shook his head vehemently. "Not yet. Please just do this for me."

Sage nodded and Alex ground his mouth into his, wanting to taste and feel everything about this man that he could. He couldn't remember ever feeling this needy. Sage's hands travelled to the waistband of his chinos then he pulled Alex's shirt free, running his hands over the skin underneath. Alex shuddered in sheer pleasure at Sage's touch. Desperately he tugged Sage's jeans and underwear off his lean hips to fall to the floor. His eyes widened at what he found.

"Wow, Sage. I hadn't realised you were circumcised. You're not Jewish, are you?"

Sage shook his head. "I had an infection when I was a baby and as a result, the doctor thought a circumcision was the answer. It's been a talking point in gym lockers ever since."

"I like it," Alex whispered." But then again, I'd daresay I'd like anything this big. I am truly blessed." He chuckled. "Not to mention fucked."

Sage's eyes darkened. "Take off your pants," he said huskily and Alex obeyed with alacrity. Soon he was naked except for his long-sleeved, button-down blue shirt. Sage reached down, caressing the tip of him gently with his thumb, and Alex gasped.

Sage's hands moved over Alex's groin, then stopped as he realised Alex was shaven. His eyes danced.

"I didn't get the chance last time to inspect much of you." He grinned. "I've never had a man who was totally nude there before. It's quite a turn-on." He raised a sexy eyebrow. "Is that a personal preference then?"

Alex blanched. He wasn't about to tell Sage it was an instruction from his Principal because Eric got off on seeing the marks he left when he whipped and bit him there.

"Yes," he whispered finally. "I prefer it this way."

Sage nodded as he leaned down for a kiss. "I like it."

He pushed Alex back onto the bed, taking his mouth again, his hands stroking every bit of bare skin of Alex's that he could find as their kisses grew more passionate. Alex had never felt so free. All those years of abuse seemed to have faded as he made love with this man, a man who knew his secrets yet still wanted him. He removed his mouth from Sage's, staring up into his smoky eyes, which were darkened with desire.

"You make me feel whole again, Sage," he whispered. "You make me forget the dark times."

Sage reached up, tenderly running his hands over Alex's short hair. "I'm glad," he murmured huskily. "You're an incredible man. You deserve some happiness after what you went through."

"And you, my friend, deserve my mouth." Alex moved down on Sage's body, licked him from shaft to tip with one long, slavering movement, then took him in his mouth. Sage's hips arched upward, pushing his cock further into Alex's greedy, wet, hot mouth. His hands gripped the covers tightly as Alex enjoyed him, teasing, licking, slurping and generally finding anything of Sage's he could fit in his mouth. Shaft, balls anything was fair game. Sage wriggled, cursed and thrust as Alex worked him.

"Alex, enough," the strangled entreaty from Sage made Alex lift his head to look at his lover. Sage's eyes regarded him with avarice. "I need to be inside you. Now."

Alex laughed and moved up over Sage's body, straddling his waist. "Fine. Does this way work for you? I'll ride you and you can jack me off."

Sage nodded. "Lube is in the bedside drawer," he managed to get out. "Condoms too." Alex leaned over and got the much-needed items. He opened the condom packet, teasingly fitting it over Sage, then squirted lube into his hands and onto Sage's covered cock. Then he lowered himself onto Sage, watching his face as he took him in. It was a challenge. Alex was filled to capacity and he hissed as Sage pushed upward into him.

"Easy, tiger," he panted. "I don't need you coming out of my bloody throat. That'll do neither of us any good."

Sage gave a hoarse chuckle, his eyes never leaving Alex's. Alex found his stride and he bobbed up and down on Sage's straining erection. He closed his eyes, revelling in the sensation of Sage inside him then gave a startled jump as a strong hand gripped his cock and with light feathering movements up and down his heated, slick skin, began stroking and rubbing him in a way Alex had never been touched before.

It was as if...

"Are you playing a bloody guitar on my dick?" Alex managed to gasp out. Sage laughed, continuing his movements, his fingers moving as if he were playing guitar chords. It was a most unsettling but incredible sensation. Sage's fingers alternately increased then reduced the pressure, causing exquisite torture until Alex ground his teeth together in frustration.

"Enough with the guitar playing," he said between clenched teeth. "I want to come, Sage. God, playing a guitar has given you certain skills. You're definitely strumming my bloody strings."

"Christ, Alex, you're too much," Sage chuckled but began to move his hips with Alex's up-and-down assault of his body. The two men watched each other's faces as Sage worked Alex's dick with hard, firm strokes until Alex groaned loudly, his backside muscles tensing and his breaths getting deeper until he gave a loud shout and climaxed, his come coating them both with its musky, warm smell. Sage moaned loudly, tensing and straining against him as he too emptied himself inside the condom buried in Alex's channel.

Alex collapsed on top of Sage, kissing his eyes, his mouth, his nose until finally their bodies stopped shaking. Sage held Alex tight on top of him, Alex feeling warm breath against his neck. Finally Alex moved, trying to ease Sage out of his body. He rolled off, lying beside Sage, his chest heaving. Alex reached over and removed the filled condom, tying it and placing it on the bedroom table. He heard his lover take a deep breath as he nudged his cock, still sensitive from the activity. There was silence in the dark room until Sage turned to him, running his hand under Alex's shirt, across his tight, flat stomach.

"When are you going to let me see what you look like under this shirt?"

Alex shifted in frustration. "I'm not ready, I told you."

"Eric gets to see more of you than I do." Sage's voice was low.

Alex heard the faint hurt in his voice. He took a deep breath. "It's not the same thing. To Eric, I'm a customer, someone with no emotional investment. With you—I care about you."

Sage turned to lie on his side on his elbow, regarding him. "All the more reason to show me. I care about you too and I want to learn more about you. I want to know the man better."

Alex needed to breathe into a paper bag, his apprehension was so great. "But what if you don't like what you see? What if you think I'm"—he swallowed heavily—"a monster? The scars are bad. They remind me of another time and I'm not sure I want you to be reminded too."

Sage leaned in, kissing his lips softly. "I've kissed your mouth and other body parts and been inside you. Don't you think I like you regardless of what's underneath your shirt? That I can cope with anything you throw at me?"

His gentle words make perfect sense but Alex was still wary.

Sage sighed. "You don't need to put the lights on or anything. I ate plenty of carrots when I was a kid and my eyesight is pretty good even in this light. I just need to see all of you."

The yearning in his voice was evident and Alex took a deep breath. Sage deserved that much. He sat up and with trembling hands started to unbutton his shirt.

Sage reached up, stopping him. "Here, let me do that." His hands deftly opened the buttons one by one until finally the front of Alex's body was revealed to him. Sage started to slide the shirt off his shoulders and Alex pulled back in apprehension. Sage reached over and touched his cheek gently. "Alex, babe, it's fine. Lie down. Just let me look at you."

Alex lay back against the pillows, comforted by the endearment, his eyes closed as Sage slowly traced the contours of his collarbone and chest, trailing his fingers down his chest and stomach. Alex sensed him studying his body and when he spoke again Sage's voice was rough with anger. But he knew it wasn't directed at him.

"Are these cigarette burns?" Sage softly stroked his stomach where there were ten deep circular holes where Rudy had burnt him. Alex's face flushed with shame and he nodded tightly. Sage bent forward, his breath warm against Alex's stomach as he kissed each one of the marks, small fluttering kisses that made Alex's heart ache. Sage's hands caressed his hip gently and then he looked up at him, his eyes questioning in the dim light.

"And this?" He touched the deep, two-inch-long slash on Alex's right hip bone, puckered and still sensitive after all this time.

"A hunting knife. He got drunk one night and wanted something to do." Alex's voice was a whisper. He heard Sage's deep indrawn breath as he leaned down and kissed it, trailing his mouth along his scar with reverence. Alex could hardly breathe. No one had ever touched it before let alone kissed it.

"Turn over on your side. Let me see your back."

It was an order from his lover and Alex obeyed wordlessly, hearing Sage's sharp breath on seeing the four long parallel scars on his shoulder blade and the small circular marks of yet more cigarette burns and careless knife slashes across his back and buttocks.

"Hell, Alex," Sage said, his voice raw with pain. "The man was a fucking animal."

Sage caressed the scars slowly with his fingers and his warm mouth kissed them one by one. He spent time on the ridges on Alex's shoulder, running his warm, wet mouth down each one. Alex's whole being was filled with such indescribable joy at this acceptance of his past that he was breathless with it. His eyes filled with tears, as he wept hot, salty tears silently into the pillow, tasting them in his mouth. Sage's worried voice echoed in the heaviness of the air in the room which was soaked with feeling and sheer emotion.

"Alex, are you okay? I'm sorry, I didn't mean to make you cry…"

Alex nodded his head, turning over and wrapping his arms around Sage's neck, burying his face in Sage's shoulder. Sage held him, stroking his back as Alex cried, years of pent-up fury, guilt and shame exposed as well as an awe of this man who was the first outside of Eric to see the badges of pain and courage that he bore from one of the worst periods of his life. Eventually all that he had left inside were soft hiccups as he stopped crying, trying to catch his breath.

Sage waited as Alex sniffled, finally pulling away from him. His lover got up and padded naked into the bathroom, returning with a wad of tissues, handing it to him, lying back on the bed as Alex blew his nose and wiped his face.

"Are you all right now?" Sage asked softly.

Alex nodded, feeling embarrassed. "Jesus, I'm so sorry, Sage. I'm like some silly bloody teenage girl whose date just dumped her."

Sage reached out, pulling Alex into his arms, his warm hands caressing his cheek as he snuggled in. "God, Alex," he murmured. "You'd have thought you were the hunchback of Notre Dame the way you carried on. Instead, there's just this sexy, gorgeous man with a few scars. The rest of you was perfect from what I could see. And feel."

Alex smiled softly. "You are the most amazing man I've ever met. I don't know what I did to deserve you."

Sage chuckled. "I didn't have a choice, did I? There I was with my shirt off and there you were all over me like a bloody hungry octopus, all greedy hands and lips. Not that I'm complaining, mind you."

Alex stared into Sage's eyes intently. "No one else has ever seen me like this before. This is the second time you've liberated me. Thank you."

Sage pulled him into his arms, holding Alex tight against his chest. "You're welcome." He sighed. "I suppose I should try and get in that shower now and then we can go see Miles if that's okay with you? Then if you like, you either come back here or I'll take you home. I think I asked you if you've ever been on a bike before, but I don't recall getting an answer in all the excitement of being assaulted." He grinned.

Alex chuckled, his heart feeling lighter than it had in years. "Yes, I've been on a bike, even rode one myself for a while. Not as sexy as that beast you have outside, though."

Sage stood up, looking at him with a glint in his eyes. "As we've come this far, do you want join me in the shower? Or is that too much too soon? I promise to behave myself."

Alex considered his offer. The bathroom was fairly dim. "Can you leave the light off when you shower? I'd feel more comfortable that way."

Sage nodded. "I'm sure I can find the soap by touch and feel— as well as anything else that takes my fancy."

"You said you'd behave." Alex grinned as he got off the bed and they walked together into the bathroom.

Chapter 18

Sage and Alex arrived back at the hospital around midday. Sage grinned as Alex got off the back of his bike. The man had held so tightly to him on the way over he'd thought he'd had a boa constrictor round his waist. It hadn't been fear but sheer possessiveness. Alex took off the helmet, unzipping the leathers Sage had given him, which had been Mason's.

God, the man looked good in leather. It definitely made Sage want to buy him more clothing in that particular fabric.

They fitted well enough, perhaps a little on the big side. Sage had kept them, unable to throw them away yet.

Three weeks ago Dan had told him the new man Mason was apparently seeing had no motorbike but instead had a Porsche and a yacht moored out in the Ipswich Marina. Sage had been surprised at his lack of care for the situation. He was truly over Mason.

He unzipped his own leathers, loading them both into the panniers on the side of the bike.

Alex smiled at him. "Wow. What a ride. That was incredible. You're quite the animal on that bike, you know."

Sage laughed. "She's an amazing beast to drive. I kept to the speed limits most of the time." Together they walked into the hospital. Sage frowned when he saw the policemen standing outside Miles's room. He increased his pace in his hurry to get to the room. He was aware of Alex trying to keep up with him.

"DS Doyle. What are you doing here? Is anything wrong?"

The policeman regarded him calmly. "Mr. Sage. Nothing's wrong. We were just here to ask Mr. Conway some questions about the hit-and-run."

Alex stiffened beside him and Sage groaned inwardly. He hadn't had a chance to tell him much yet. "Has he remembered anything else?" he asked. The policeman shook his head.

"Nothing really new, but we had to check. We'll keep looking. I have someone looking at the CCTV footage as we speak." He nodded at Sage. "I'll be in touch. Good afternoon, sir."

Alex turned to Sage, his face grey. "Sage, your godfather was injured in a hit-and-run? I thought he'd just walked in front of a car by mistake."

"It's been a bit hectic. I just hadn't gotten around to it yet."

"It's just like my book. The next incident was a hit-and-run. This must be the same person that hurt Dianne."

Sage nodded. "I've already been over that with the police. They know about it all and they're looking out for whoever it might be."

Alex paled. "The next incident is the one where Carter is kidnapped and beaten up by the mob. What if that's the plan for the next scene? You could be in danger."

Sage sighed. "I've already been over that with the police too. I really don't think anyone will try anything with everyone watching."

He walked into Mile's room to see him sitting up, propped up with pillows.

Miles smiled widely. "Sage, my lad. Glad you came back. And you brought Alex with you as well. Did you see the police outside?"

Sage nodded. "I spoke to DS Doyle. They're still checking CCTV footage to see if they can find the car that hit you. Hopefully they'll come up with something." He grinned at his godfather. "You're looking better. I'm glad to see you more up and about."

A weight lifted off his shoulders as he sat beside Miles. Not only had Miles come through a horrible ordeal, so had Alex. Sage still felt the burn of fury and hatred at the man who had brutalised him. In the shower Alex had been nervous, but Sage had actually been able to wash him, lathering soapy suds across his body, enjoying every minute he had the man beneath his hands.

Of course one thing had led to another and Sage had ended up giving Alex a blow job that had made him gasp and flatten his hands desperately against the wall tiles.

Then Alex had returned the favour. Sage was feeling a little overwhelmed. He was starting to care about this man very much. He'd tried to forget about Alex's other needs. He wasn't looking forward to having to face them again. He looked at Alex now, talking animatedly to Miles, telling him about his books and the filming. Sage felt a swell of pride for his lover's courage. When visiting hours were over and it was time to leave, Sage kissed his godfather goodbye with the promise to see him the next day.

Outside he looked at Alex. "Do you want me to take you back home to London?"

Alex shook his head. "No. I'll come home with you if you don't mind. Then you can take me home tomorrow if that's okay."

Sage smiled in relief at having Alex for longer. "That's fine with me. We'll need to stop and get some food though. I'm starving. I don't actually think we've eaten all day and all that exercise has definitely given me an appetite." He leered at Alex as he zipped up his leathers, getting up on the bike behind him.

They finally reached the house about seven p.m. armed with bags of Chinese food and various other household provisions. They watched the news together, seated at the kitchen island. Sage was almost through his second helping of spicy beef when Alex's mobile rang.

Alex looked at it, grinning as he answered. "Cully! This is a surprise. I thought you were in Argentina."

Sage could tell this person, a man from the sound of it, was very special to Alex. He felt a surge of jealousy as he concentrated on the TV, trying not to appear to pay attention whilst he listened to every word.

Finally Alex rang off, turning to him with a huge smile. "Cully is a very good friend of mine. I'm seeing him tomorrow. He's the one who rescued me out of Bohemia."

Sage frowned, feeling a sense of relief at finding out who Cully was. "You mentioned both names earlier. Was Bohemia the name of the cult you were imprisoned in?"

Alex looked down at his food, a strange expression on his face. "You have to understand that when I first joined, I wasn't a prisoner. I chose to go there with Rudy. I was seventeen and confused, and after a load of foster homes all I wanted was one place I could call home."

Sage stopped chewing, looking at him in dismay. "You were a foster kid?"

Alex nodded. "My parents died when I was two. They were killed in a fire. I was in and out of foster homes all my life. Some good, some bad. When I was seventeen, I'd had enough. I came to London to try and find work, make some money. I met Rudy in a bar. He was older than me, twenty-five, and he seemed friendly and very concerned. I went home with him."

He shrugged and Sage watched Alex's face as once again he laid his soul bare to him.

"One thing led to another and eventually I was staying at his place. A few days later he said he knew this group we could go to who would look after us, feed us, give us somewhere to stay and ask very little in return." Alex grimaced. "I said, why not. We went to this huge compound out in Surrey, out in the middle of nowhere." He swallowed.

Sage laid a hand over his. "Don't you think you've made enough breakthroughs today? You don't have to tell me anymore just yet." Sage's innate curiosity was burning questions on his own soul but he felt he needed to make the offer.

Alex nodded, linking his fingers with his. "It's all right. I think I can do this." He looked down at their combined hands. "The first few days were okay. The people seemed decent, they really looked after us. Then things changed and Rudy…"

He cleared his throat. "Rudy started to turn nasty. I found out he was the leader of the cult. He'd go to London, find stray boys and men who had nowhere else to go, sweet-talk them and then take them back to Bohemia. We were mostly men but there were some women there, cooking, cleaning, doing the whole stereotypical thing."

"What kind of cult was it?" Sage asked. "Did they have any specific rules and beliefs?"

Alex nodded. "Very much Third Reich teachings. White supremacy, the whole Nazi thing. Apart from one difference. Bohemia had to stay a fringe organisation because as a lot of them were homosexual. The really right-wing Third Reich guys didn't like them for obvious reasons. But Rudy was bisexual, and he didn't care what the extremists thought about him fucking men. He had a huge following and was pretty powerful."

Alex took another large gulp of his wine, his hands trembling. "Most of the guys there were blond, fair skinned. But I was his favourite. I dyed my hair blond back then. And I had something special. I had two different colour eyes and in his twisted imagination that made me special. He saw it as a sign from God. He kept me for eight months. I found myself locked up in the compound most of the time and let out when I was good to him. And I was good a lot, Sage." Alex's voice was husky. "It was the only way I could get out and see daylight, walk around other people and have a conversation with someone that wasn't hurting me."

"Jesus, stop." Sage couldn't stand to hear the pain in Alex's voice. "That's enough. You don't have to go on."

Alex ignored him, drinking the rest of his wine then pouring another glass. "I was so broken I'd do anything. I knew it was wrong, I knew deep down inside he was a monster but he was all I had. I thought if he cared enough to be with me all that time he must feel something for me. I was lucky though; some of his 'consorts' as he called us—male and female—were given to the other men in the compound, but he never did that with me. I was only his."

Alex looked at Sage and he saw the desolation in his lover's eyes. "So I put up with anything he wanted. I learnt more about sex and bondage and pain than anyone ever should know. It became a way of life and I thought he would only do what he did if he loved me. So I let him." He heaved a shuddering sigh, looking down at his hands circling the glass.

"One day I lost my temper over something—I don't even remember what. I was young and stupid and I taunted him about being a fudge-packer, a queer. Told him he'd never count in the big scheme of things. He hated being reminded of that. I knew sometimes that he felt it was a weakness, holding him back from joining the big boys in play, the real heterosexual ones. He wanted their respect but they wouldn't give it. He beat the shit out of me, broke a rib, raped me with a beer bottle." Alex's voice was quiet. "He tore me quite badly." He smiled twistedly. "I hoped he'd kill me. I think subconsciously that's why I started the whole conversation in the first place. Then at least it would be over."

Sage felt a blackness descend, a despair so deep that he lost his breath. His eyes prickled with tears, his throat aching at the thought of what had been done to his man.

"Christ, honey," he whispered as his hands tightened around Alex's. "I don't even know what to say to that."

Alex smiled sadly. "Then he smiled and told me he needed to teach me another lesson in manners. He took his sabre and cut me on my back." He swallowed. "He said it would remind me who I belonged to and that he was saving me from myself, that he wanted me to be the best I could be for him and only him. He apologised to me the whole time he was cutting me, he even cried at one point. But he didn't stop and no one came to help me even though I was screaming."

Alex's horrific story made Sage's stomach churn and still he couldn't speak.

Alex looked up at him, his eyes flat. "Then one night about a week later, I heard a commotion above. Rudy was…sleeping." His voice sounded guarded as he said this and Sage noticed the hesitation. "Rudy hadn't got me any medical attention for the last beating or the knife wounds, so I was a fucking mess. I'd never been in so much pain before. I could hardly move."

A slow, anguished tear dribbled its way down Sage's cheek and Alex reached over, wiping it away tenderly with his thumb. "I heard shouts and screams and gunshots and when it all stopped I heard the door open and I saw Cully." Alex's face brightened at the memory. "Cully is this huge West Indian black man with shoulders like a barge and the softest eyes I'd ever seen on a man. Apart from yours, of course."

He smiled softly and Sage's heart skipped a beat at the fact that this man was telling a horrific story about his abuse yet still found time to make a random comment about his eyes.

"He picked us up—I mean picked me up like I weighed nothing and carried me up the stairs out into the light."

"You said 'us.'" Sage regarded Alex curiously. "Was someone else there with you?"

"No. Just a slip of the tongue. I was alone. It was just me."

Sage thought the reply was evasive but he didn't push it.

"Cully got me into this repatriation group. I lived with them for almost three years, undergoing therapy. I had to work whilst I was there, contribute to the community. Cully got me a job as an administrator in an educational publishing firm in London. He found me a place to stay."

Alex's face darkened. "But I gave him such a hard time. I'd go out drinking until I was senseless. I'd just started taking cocaine and other stuff when Cully found out. He put me right back into the repat group and more therapy. Their tough love worked and I cleaned up my act and went back to work. I stayed sane for a little while but it was an uphill battle. I chose men off and on who hurt me and finally Cully said he'd had enough. He told me I had to see a professional therapist again and sort myself out. I started seeing Melanie three years ago on his recommendation when I was twenty-seven. She suggested writing as therapy and I soon found out I had a talent for it."

Alex's face darkened. "I still found myself trawling bars and clubs at the time looking for men who would meet my needs." His voice wavered. "Melanie was worried I'd get really hurt. Finally she suggested instead of doing that, I try going to somewhere where I could indulge my needs in a safer way. She helped me look for the right place, made some calls and I ended up with Eric at Study in Scarlet. I started seeing Eric just over two years ago to keep me sane. It formed another part of my therapy, one Melanie didn't like, but she knew she couldn't stop me. She's been the best thing that happened to me since Cully and now you."

He shrugged. "The rest you know. My maternal grandmother died and left me some money. She'd never really been close to me, had never wanted to know me at all so I was surprised at that. I supposed there was no one else and I was still family. I bought the place I have now. I kept writing, found a publisher, sold some novels and am currently making a film series and having sex with this amazing man I know who is sweet, compassionate, sexy and extremely dishy."

Alex finished the rest of his wine, his face shadowed. "Of course, I still have these needs I'm working on with said man's help. That's something that's going to take a little more time. But I think it might work out. I hope it does. I owe him that much."

Sage stood up, walking over to Alex. "Come here." He pulled him off the stool, pulling Alex to him, his arms encircling him tightly. Sage's chest was tight and he was choked up. "You are an amazingly brave man. You have more strength than anyone I have known. If anyone can overcome their demons, it'll be you. And I promise to do anything I can to help you do that."

Alex slid his arms around Sage's waist, leaning in for a soft kiss. "You've already done more for me that you can ever know just by being here." He leaned over, turning off the kitchen light. The room plunged into darkness. "Let's go to bed," he murmured. "I promised to share some naughty thoughts with a certain someone and right now I feel like being a cowboy. Pity I don't have the hat." Alex grinned wickedly as Sage chuckled.

"I guess that make me the horse then. I think Tallulah might have something to say about that."

Chapter 19

The next morning Sage's phone rang as he was shaving. He saw who it was and answered it with a smile. "Jenny. It's good to hear from you. How are things?"

"Sage, have you seen the news this morning?" Jenny's voice was strained. "I'm trying to control the situation but you need to be aware things are going to get a little hectic. Some reporter's made the connection between the Dianne incident and the hit-and-run of your godfather."

Sage's face darkened. "Shit, I was hoping they wouldn't do that. Alex is here with me, I'll let him know."

"The two of you are an item now?" Jenny's voice was wry. "Thanks for telling me. Yet another thing I'll need to manage if anyone finds out."

Sage sighed. "Sorry. I would have told you about it but it's all been a bit hectic this side. I don't think our relationship is common knowledge to the press yet, but I suppose it will be. It certainly is in the studio. I'll give you a ring later. Thanks for the heads up."

He rang off, walking through to the lounge with a towel around his waist and switched on the television. He flicked through channels until he found Channel 6 and watched in grim dismay as he saw pictures of himself and Alex flicking across the TV screen. The onscreen reporter was standing in front of Moorcroft Studios.

"There appears to be a connection between the recent letter-bomb attack on Dianne Cunningham, the actress who plays the part of Gillian Blake, and the recent hit-and-run of Miles Conway, a relative of Christopher Sage, who of course is the well-known up-and-coming actor taking the leading role of Carter West in the new *Double Exposure* series. Is it a coincidence that these two incidents closely reflect the actual fictional events depicted in Alexander Montgomery's novel? This reporter doesn't think so. Whilst there may be differences, it certainly appears that in this case life is imitating art. Mr. Montgomery has been unavailable as yet for comment and Mr. Sage's publicist has advised us that at this stage, there will definitely be a response of 'No comment.' This has also been the police response. I'd suggest you all keep watching Channel 6 as we bring you regular updates on the situation. This is Grace Evans for Channel 6 Entertainment Today."

"It's a circus," Alex said quietly as he came up behind Sage, his hair wet from the shower. "I've got half a dozen messages on my phone. Your phone hasn't stopped either."

He waved over to the kitchen table where Sage's phone was charging. "They seem to have made the assumption that there's a connection. I can't blame them. I think the same."

Sage sighed. "Alex, it was just a matter of time before they put two and two together."

"My book sales have soared." Alex shook his head. "My publisher phoned earlier in a very good mood to tell me their site crashed earlier this morning and they've had to rent more server space to accommodate the book sales. If that was this person's intention, they've certainly got their wish." His voice was bitter.

Sage frowned. "I know it sounds like a stupid question but how sure are we that they *aren't* doing all this to generate the publicity? Stranger things have happened."

"My editor, Gaynor, tells me the police have already approached them with the same question. The company told them categorically that it isn't them doing this and the police appear to believe them." Alex looked at him with a bitter smile. "In fact, apparently they want to ask me the same questions to make sure I'm not the one doing this to increase my own book sales. I've been asked to go Chelmsford police station later today to 'answer their enquiries.'"

Sage looked at him in frustration. "Surely they can't believe you'd have anything to do with this?"

Alex shrugged. "It appears they do. I suppose I'll need to go down there and see what they have to say. Will you come with me? They said I can come down anytime and to ask for DS Doyle."

Sage nodded. "Absolutely. Let me get changed and we can go there this morning and get it over with. I can't believe they think you have anything to do with this. We'd better get it sorted out quickly. We'll need to try and avoid the reporters though until we figure out what we tell everyone. I think we'll be okay for now. No one knows about this place yet, I hope, so we should be safe enough."

Sage disappeared to finish dressing. It was close to lunchtime when Sage delivered Alex back to his London home. Alex was relieved to see the sidewalk was paparazzi free but he knew it wouldn't be for too long. Once they got wind of where he lived, they'd be camped out on his doorstep. He dismounted the bike with a relieved sigh. "I'm not used to this. My butt is aching from the bike. I'll be glad to get in and sit down on something soft and cushiony."

Sage grinned, taking off his helmet and leathers. "It takes a bit of getting used to. I can always rub your butt for you later if you like." He waggled his eyebrows. "I can think of a few other things I could do with your backside too."

Alex laughed. "Christ, you are a randy sod." But he was pleased. "I'm glad we got all that interrogation done. Do you think they believed me when I told them I really did have nothing to do with it all?"

Sage nodded. "I don't think they really thought you did in the first place. They were just covering all the bases. DS Doyle seems like a very fair man."

Alex unlocked his door, beckoning for Sage to follow him into the cool recess of his apartment. He breathed a sigh of satisfaction at being home.

"Cully will be here pretty soon. Do you want to stay and meet him? I know he'd like to meet you. He's always been a big fan of yours. He thought it was a great idea when I used you as my inspiration for—" he stopped short uncomfortably, wanting to kick himself for blurting out the words.

"Inspiration for what?" Sage said suspiciously.

Alex shuffled uncomfortably. "I sort of developed the character of Carter with you in mind."

"What do you mean?" Sage asked curiously.

Alex sighed, knowing he'd have to tell him the truth now. Sage was insatiable when it came to getting answers and he was no fool.

"I'd seen you in *Dalton Hospital* and in *Loving Katie* and then *King Solomon's Mines* and I thought you were really amazing. I had the vague idea for the story but no idea of the character yet and I thought you'd be a great template to use for Carter. Then the story just wrote itself. It was so much easier."

Sage's eyes grew wider.

Alex sighed at the expression on his face. "So I wrote the character of Carter using you as my visual. *You* are Carter, not the other way around, Sage."

Sage's eyes narrowed. "Let me get this straight. You saw me and decided to write a book so you could include a character that looked like me?"

Alex nodded, feeling very embarrassed. "Not just looked. I used some of your movements and your body language to develop Carter."

Sage chuckled softly. "I see. So when you were writing your fairly raunchy sex scenes, in your mind you saw me? And you've been seeing me ever since you started writing over a year ago?" He was smiling suggestively now and Alex flushed.

"I suppose so. It's a way of visualising what I'm writing, it makes things so much more real…"

"So, Alex Montgomery, to put it bluntly, you've been having fantasies about me in your 'writing inspiration' long before you even met me?"

Alex scowled. "Don't get so bloody full of yourself."

Sage laughed, a great chortling belly laugh that made Alex's insides churn and his hands want to rip his clothes off and take him right there and then.

"Is that why you recommended I get this part, because you actually wrote it for me?"

Sage was very quick, Alex had to admit. He'd hoped he wouldn't figure that one out. His hesitation told Sage all he needed to know. Sage pulled Alex over to him, lifting his chin and gazing into his eyes. Alex swallowed, feeling the surge at his groin, feeling Sage's hardness pressed against him.

"So…when were you going to tell me all this?" Sage's eyes widened in mock surprise. "Oh, I get it, you weren't. That would mean admitting you wanted my body long before I met you. That you longed for me and thought about me every night you were in your bed, alone, jacking off—" his self-satisfied voice was suddenly muffled as Alex moved his mouth on his, kissing him voraciously, his hands twisting violently in Sage's curly hair, pulling his head down to his own with a sense of urgency. Sage's arms wrapped around Alex's waist and Alex's growing hardness pushed through his jeans as he groaned softly.

"This is the only bloody way I can shut you up, you egomaniac," Alex whispered as he softly ran his tongue over

Sage's top lip. Sage laughed softly, his hands sliding down to Alex's backside, caressing it, finally sliding up under his polo shirt to tease his nipple. Alex thought he would burst there and then.

An amused voice broke into their make-out session. "I'm sorry to interrupt you both as it looks like you're really busy but I did knock."

Alex broke away, his face flushed. Sage's face also flooded with colour at being caught in the act by a stranger. Alex grinned in delight, reaching out to a black giant of a man who stood in the entrance to the open door.

"Cully! God, it's good to see you." He hugged the man, an expression of true affection on his face.

"Alex. Hell, you are looking good. Better than I've seen you look in a little while. You've put on a bit of weight. Been working out?" He reached out a hand to the still pink-faced Sage, giving him a huge grin. "Mr. Christopher Sage. It's a great pleasure to meet you. I'm a huge fan of yours."

Sage smiled, shaking the man's hand, and Alex chuckled at seeing it dwarfed in Cully's huge one.

Cully grinned even wider. "I take it from the action on the doorstep that you've been taking care of my man? That's really good. He needs some tender loving care. But if you hurt a hair on his head, I'll have to hunt you down and kill you, you know that?" His face was expressionless as he looked at Sage.

Sage looked at the big man in horror and both Alex and Cully collapsed in peals of laughter. The big man shook his head. "My God, your face, you should have seen it, brother. I'm not the violent sort, I was joshing you. I shoulda been an actor too."

Alex pulled Cully into the lounge. "Come in, Cully. Come and tell me what you've been up to other than giving poor Sage a heart attack."

The big man followed Alex, still chortling. Sage followed a little warily. He wasn't quite sure how to take the other man. He wondered with a flick of jealousy whether they'd been lovers as they seemed really comfortable together. They finally sat down in the lounge, drinks in hands.

Alex turned to Cully. "So, spill the beans. What have you been doing?"

Cully sat back, regarding them both. "Just the usual. Travelling around, rescuing people, some who want to be rescued, some who don't." He shrugged. "Not much to tell, Alex. You know how it is." He leaned forward, gazing at Alex intently. "I'm more interested in how you're doing. I meant what I said. You look really well."

Alex looked at Sage fondly. "It's all down to Sage. I've told him most of the story." His tone was warning and the pair shared a glance, a secret glance that had Sage not been watching closely, he probably would have missed. "He knows about Eric and Scarlet and he's seen the scars."

Cully whistled. "Look at you, Alex. That's a real step forward. I'd say that's even a miracle."

He observed Sage, his deep brown eyes affectionate. "If you've done this for him, Mr. Sage, I'd say you definitely deserve my gratitude."

"Call me Sage," said Sage uncomfortably. "And to be honest, considering what he went through, Alex is one of the bravest people I know. He's the incredible one."

Cully reached out with his huge paw, clasping Sage's hand warmly. "I'd agree with you on that one. Alex is a real trooper."

The conversation turned to common friends and remembrances of past times and Sage sat back and listened to them speak. He enjoyed watching Alex so vibrant and sparkling, looking so relaxed. The two of them seemed so at ease with one another. He felt a slight pang at the fact that he might struggle to get the same sense of familiarity with this man, someone he was definitely getting attached to. He did manage to find out that Cully had a wife, a doctor at a hospital in London, which made him feel better.

It was fairly late when Cully put his empty drink glass down with an air of finality and stood up. "I need to get off. I have an early start in the morning. Off to Somerset for a gig." He grinned but it wasn't a particularly nice one. Sage wondered what type of gig it was, sure it wasn't rock and roll. Sage stood up as Alex hugged his friend.

"It was good to see you, Cully. Come back soon. I don't see you often enough."

Sage shook the man's hand. Cully held onto him longer than normal. "Thanks for helping my boy, Sage. It can't be easy on you." He handed Sage a small business card. "You find things getting rough, you need to someone talk to, then you call me. Anytime you want. We'll have a drink together." He grinned. "You seem like a good man. But it's going to be tough. Make no mistake about it. This guy has a lot of demons." Alex regarded them both with watchful eyes.

Sage nodded. "Thanks. I might take you up on that."

Cully nodded and went out into the darkness of the street. He waved goodbye and started walking down the road. Alex closed the door.

Sage sighed. "I suppose I should be going too. It's back to work as normal tomorrow."

Alex caressed his face gently. "You're welcome to stay over rather than travel home, Sage. You look tired. I don't like thinking of you on the bike when you're tired. I'll quickly wash your stuff and put in the tumble dryer. It'll be fine for you in the morning."

Sage considered his offer then nodded. "That sounds like a better plan. I know it's not far to Dan's but I'm knackered."

Sage reached out, drawing his shirt up, taking it off in one fluid movement. He handed it to Alex then slowly unzipped his jeans, pulling them down over his hips. He stepped out of them and stood naked before him.

Alex's eyes drank him in hungrily. "Why don't you jump into bed and I'll be there as soon as I've sorted this out. It's the room on the right."

Sage disappeared and Alex watched the taut cheeks of his backside. Fifteen minutes later, after a quick wash cycle, he loaded the wet clothing into the tumble dryer, switching off the lights and making his way into the bedroom. Sage lay half-in, half-out of the covers, his long legs stretched out, his arms above his head. He was fast asleep, his mouth relaxed, his black hair falling over his face.

Alex reached down, stroking his jawline tenderly. "So much for my bad intentions. Sleep tight." He'd have to live with his hard-on a little longer, perhaps until early morning sex.

Alex kissed him on his lips and Sage shifted slightly and muttered. Alex stood up, slipping out of his clothes, then crept into bed beside him, feeling the warmth of his body and hearing his steady breathing. His hands rested lightly on Sage's stomach as he snuggled in. He'd never felt so safe or at home.

Chapter 20

A week later Sage brought Miles home. He'd borrowed Lanie's car, driven to the hospital and subsequently deposited his godfather in his own house and into what Miles called the "voracious" clutches of "that" woman.

Miles had grumbled good-naturedly about being fussed about like some sort of invalid but Sage saw he was relieved not to be alone. Miles still struggled to walk on his damaged leg. Lanie Whitcombe was a widow of about sixty years old, tall, nicely padded, with grey hair that was coloured auburn, and a face that looked as if you could confide anything in her and she'd fix your problem. Sage and Miles had known her for many years and Sage had always thought his godfather and Lanie would finally hit it off. Now it appeared they'd hit it off more than once and Sage was still amused at the fact they'd tried to keep it a secret—until now.

He dropped Lanie's car off at her home down the lane, walking back down the darkening lane to his own cottage to shower before he picked Alex up later for dinner. Sage had struggled a little this last week to commute between his cottage and the film set and his shared apartment with Dan, as well as make time for Alex. Miles was now safely ensconced at home with Lanie.

Annie and her mother had promised to look after the horses and the upkeep on his cottage between them. Sage hoped he could now focus on the job in hand: to complete filming on *Double Exposure* without further distraction. The police had still made no inroads into either Dianne's letter bombing or Miles's hit-and-run but DS Doyle had promised to keep him informed if there were any developments.

Sage had been right about the reporters. They were now permanently loitering on Alex's street. Alex was extremely twitchy about the media attention. He simply ignored them and they had backed off, sensing they were not going to get much out of the reclusive writer. Unfortunately Sage and Alex's relationship was now public knowledge and the fact that the writer and his leading man were together had made the front page of all the tabloids. Sage was used to the attention but Alex was finding the invasion into his privacy difficult.

Sage been lucky. His home was still fairly reporter free although his local publican had told him a couple of men had been sniffing around trying to find out more about where he lived. Barry, the pub owner, had sent them away with a flea in their ear and warned them not to hassle his village residents. Martin Cooper, an ex-military man who lived three houses away from Sage, had taken it upon himself to be his unofficial body guard and paparazzi watcher, and his huge six-foot-five frame was a menace to anyone intending any nefarious purpose or getting too curious. It was one of the great advantages of living in a small village where everyone knew and watched out for one another.

Later that evening Sage drew up outside Alex's apartment. He waved at the few waiting paparazzi as their cameras snapped, thinking he may as well be gracious with pictures and maybe they'd leave them alone on the interview front.

Alex opened the door to his knock, scowling fiercely at the photographers. He pulled Sage inside, closing the door behind him and getting busy with his hungry hands and lips. When he finally released Sage and drew him into the living room, Sage was breathless.

"Well, that's a great welcome," he said in amusement as he took off his leathers. Alex busied himself with pouring him a whisky and handing it to him.

Alex grinned, eying out Sage's thin grey silk shirt and black chinos. "You look so hot in that shirt and those pants, that all I want to do is take them off you. But I'm hungry and I need to be fed so I'll leave you alone—for now." He looked at him enquiringly. "Did you get Miles settled?"

Sage nodded. "Yes, he's at home. Lanie's staying over at his place for a while, moving between her home and his. She's a resilient lady and she'll keep him under control."

Alex laughed, and not for the first time Sage marvelled at the change in this man from the one he'd met that first day at his agent's. He felt a sense of pride that he'd had a helping hand in his continuing transformation.

They were really a couple now, sleeping over at each other's places, grabbing their lovemaking anywhere they could, even in Alex's office, which was one of their favourite places after hours and the source of a lot of post-coital conversation. But to be honest, no place was sacred including the stable, where Sage had indulged a fantasy of Alex's. Sage grinned at the memory of lying naked in the straw while Alex rode him, under what he was sure was an approving gaze from Tallulah.

He watched Alex now, dressed to stun in tight black dress pants and a wine-coloured dress shirt that clung to his tight abs. A slight sense of unease overlay Sage's pride.

Surely the worst was over? Alex was bonding with him and Sage knew damn well he had fallen head over heels, heart-stoppingly and crazily in love with him. How that was going to work out for him, he had no idea.

Sage became aware that Alex was staring at him curiously and he brought himself back to reality with a jolt as he spoke.

"Sage, is everything all right? You were miles away there."

Sage nodded, forcing a smile. "Yes, all fine. Sorry, I was just trying to remember if I gave Miles everything from the car. I had a sudden feeling I'd forgotten something." He heard the lie, seeing Alex's face soften.

"Well, then, lover, finish that whisky up and let's get walking to the restaurant." Alex smiled slyly. "The sooner we get me fed, the sooner we can get back here and I can jump your bones." He frowned. "We'll have to try and avoid those bloody vultures outside. I might punch the next one that approaches me with those smarmy smiles they have."

Sage chuckled loudly. "I'm not sure that will help, probably get you arrested. I'll sort them out for you." He smiled as he set his empty glass down on the side table. "Come on then, tiger, let's get off. I can't have you sitting beside me all sexually frustrated knowing I can alleviate your symptoms." Alex locked up and they started walking down the busy London street toward Le Chat, the French restaurant not too far away. True to Sage's word, he managed to stave off the reporters with a few choice words and a promise of a picture together for the morning paper. Alex wasn't impressed but it was a small price to pay to be left alone for the evening.

For Sage, the next few months passed in a blur of constant filming, trips between his home in Finchingfield to check on Miles and the horses, and spending time with Alex at his apartment. There had been no more incidents of violence against cast members and the whole film crew was breathing a sigh of relief. The police still had no fresh leads although apparently they were continuing their investigation.

The one area that was eating away at Sage's insides was his lover's Study in Scarlet sessions. They had definitely decreased as

Alex had promised but Sage was getting resentful that Alex still needed even one of them.

He knew he'd promised to be patient but it was becoming increasingly difficult to share his lover. The flogging wasn't the issue; the sex was. The thought of another man inside Alex made Sage's blood boil. Eric's name alone was enough to make his breath hitch and the deep ache in the pit of his stomach to grow deeper. Sage's feelings of frustration were starting to spill over into something else—an overwhelming desire to give Alex an ultimatum. Sage or Eric.

The ramifications of that urge scared him, so until now he'd bitten his tongue.

Sage watched now as Alex got ready for work. They'd spent the night at Alex's apartment and Sage wasn't due on set until later that afternoon. He lay in bed with the covers around his waist watching as Alex did up his tie. The man had a style all of his own, making a simple thing like tying a Windsor knot seem sensual and erotic. Sage was already semi-hard and he wondered if he could convince his boyfriend to come back to bed so he could stake some more ownership of the man. Perhaps that might assuage the deep-seated fear that Alex might never be able to give up his other lover for good.

"So," Sage murmured, shifting so that the covers dropped away and Alex could see his hardening erection. "You have to be where at what time?"

Alex glanced down at the state of Sage's groin then looked at him in amusement. "I need to be with Alan and the team in an hour. So no, there's not enough time for even a quickie." He finished tying his tie and looked around the room. "Have you seen my wallet? I could swear I left it on the bedside table."

"Sorry, no. You probably left it on the kitchen table when we came in and I took off all your clothes." Sage's voice was husky.

Alex grinned. "Oh, yes. When you *ripped* them off, you mean. That Ralph Lauren shirt is never going to be the same again. You tore the damn thing in your haste to get to my body."

"Well, it's a great body." Sage's hand reached down and stroked his cock through the sheet and Alex swallowed.

Sage grinned. "Are you sure you don't want to join me? It seems a shame to waste this." He wiggled his hips suggestively and Alex's eyes smouldered. Sage never grew tired of that look, the one that said Alex wanted to devour him bit by bit and lick up what was left.

"I can't, Sage," Alex whispered, mesmerised as he watched Sage's slow palming of his groin above the sheet. "This is a pretty important meeting, about the next series of books and the marketing strategy. I have to be there."

Sage shrugged, even as he reached down under the covers and closed his eyes as he grasped his dick in his hand and began tugging on it. Alex hitched a breath and moved slightly toward Sage. Then he stopped. "You are not going to do this to me today, you randy sod. Much as I'd like to." He grinned and turned to leave the room.

Sage scowled. He so desperately needed to possess Alex again. "Do you say no to Eric as easily?"

Alex stopped dead in his tracks and turned to face Sage. His face had paled. "Where the fuck did that come from?" His voice was tight and the eyes that just a minute ago had been flooded with heat were now ice cold.

Sage knew he was making things worse but his Black Irish was surfacing and he had a need to prolong the sense of frustration and fear he felt. "I just wondered if he was accommodating as me in being turned down."

Alex gazed at Sage his face tense. "You're being a spoilt brat, Sage. Christ, we made love this morning, now I have a business meeting and you're feeling unloved? Is that what this is all about?"

"No, it's not," Sage spat out. "It's about the fact I have to share you with someone else and it's driving me fucking crazy. It's all I can think about lately. Eric with his hands on you, touching you, being inside you." His voice choked. "I hate it. I fucking hate it."

Alex moved forward and sat on the bed beside Sage. Alex's eyes were wet, his face stricken.

"Baby, I'm sorry," he whispered. "I know this is difficult for you." His voice was anguished and Sage felt a surge of guilt at his insecurities rising up now, when his lover had somewhere important to be. Alex reached over and took Sage's hands, holding them both tight. "You have been the most patient man in the world. I couldn't ask for more from you. All I'm asking is that you give me a little bit more time. Please." He stood up prowling around the room like a caged animal. "I'm doing so well, it's getting longer and longer between sessions, and I"—Alex swallowed—"At my next session I was even going to tell Eric no more sex, it was no longer required. I thought I'd be able to do that. I was going to see whether I could do it before I told you about it and got your hopes up."

His face lit up. "I really think I can do this, Sage. What you and I have is so special, I can't lose it. I can't lose you, Sage." Alex's voice dropped to a whisper as a tear rolled down his cheek and at that, Sage's anger melted like a popsicle in the sun. His need for an ultimatum vanished.

Sage stood up, naked, and moved over to Alex, drawing his tense body into his and burying his face in the side of Alex's neck.

"Babe, I'm sorry. I shouldn't have done this right now, I'm a selfish son of a bitch." He drew Alex's trembling lips to his and kissed him deeply, tasting the salt on his skin. "You aren't going to lose me. I'm here for you, that was my promise." He huffed in frustration. "It's just I really care for you and I want you for myself. Every last, sexy, beautiful bit of you."

Sage felt Alex smile against his neck as he hugged him. "And I want that too, Sage. More than you'll ever know. Just please bear with me a little longer."

Sage nodded, held Alex tight and closed his eyes.

God, I love this man. I can't lose him either.

The dawning realisation of that fact made Sage all warm and fuzzy inside. He hadn't ever told Alex that and Alex hadn't said the words either. But Sage knew them to be true. At least for him. He stepped back and wiped the tear tracks gently from Alex's skin. "You'd better get off then before I ravish you."

Alex's beautiful eyes watched him in apprehension. "Are we okay?"

Sage sighed. "Yes, honey, we're okay. More than okay. But if I stand here naked against you for much longer, all damn bets are off. As it is I'll be wanking off in the shower, thinking of you." Sage grinned and moved away from Alex's warm body.

Alex leaned in and kissed his lips softly. "Good, Then I'll see you later and when I get home, I'll think of a way to make it up to you." He flashed a wicked smile. "I have a few creative ideas involving pineapple rings and cream that I think will make you happy." He chuckled softly at the look on Sage's face. "So I'll leave you with that thought and get on my way."

His lips found Sage's in a fierce kiss and then Alex was gone, his warmth and fragrance leaving the room. With Alex's departure, Sage felt a sense of loss. He decided to get in the shower and see what he could do to alleviate his current woody and in doing so, perhaps, bring Alex's presence back into the room.

Chapter 21

Later that week Sage and Alex sat cuddled together on the couch. They'd just had dinner and were now watching a late-night movie. Alex was cuddled into Sage's shoulder as Sage lazily stroked his back and the soft curls of his head. Alex was growing his hair slightly longer and it looked good. Alex looked up at Sage with lazy eyes.

"I have a surprise for you in my bedside drawer," he murmured. "Think of something red and furry."

Sage chuckled. "Unless it's a squirrel, I'm guessing it must be handcuffs." He leered. Alex laughed loudly. "Why the hell would I have a squirrel in my bedroom? No, it's a lot more fun than that." Alex licked Sage's ear suggestively. "I mean to have my way with you tonight and have you at my mercy. But only if you want to, of course."

Sage's groin stirred at the idea of being tied up. It was a game they played occasionally and one he'd found he really enjoyed, as did Alex. He seemed to take great pleasure in controlling the situation and Sage imagined it was because of his past situation. Alex was the one who now had the power. It only worked one way though. There was no way that Alex would ever consent to being tied up by him.

Sage was angry and resentful about that, wondering if Eric did it to Alex and whether he enjoyed it. Despite their spat earlier in the week and his promise to be patient, Sage hadn't quite managed to stop his badgering Alex to tell Sage what his Eric sessions entailed. He'd learnt a little about what happened with Alex in the sessions at Study at Scarlet, mostly as a result of idle post-coital conversation, but it was not enough for him.

Alex had told him that at his last session he'd told Madame Duchaine there was no more requirement for the rough sex, something Sage was grateful for. But it made his temper flare when Sage realised he was actually being told that another man was not going to be enjoying his boyfriend in that way.

As if that should ever be a scenario between two people in a relationship like ours. It was laughable and if anyone knew about it, they'd think he was insane to do it. It was why he hadn't told anyone, even Dan.

Sage stood up, beckoning Alex to join him. "You can't tease me with that and expect me to wait," he murmured, his eyes dark. "I think you should make good on your promise."

Alex stood up, taking his hand, drawing him into the bedroom. Out of habit, he switched the lights off as he moved through the apartment. Despite their intimacy together over the past few months, Sage knew Alex still wasn't fond of light showcasing his body. The bedroom was dark with only a glimmer of light showing from the streetlight outside. Alex led him over to the bed, king-sized with a latticed metal headboard, perfect for bondage games. He pushed Sage back onto the covers, kneeling beside him. Sage could see the hard ridge of his erection under the trousers he wore. He wanted to suck it into his mouth, feel that smoothness between his lips. But first he needed to be tied up. He was getting hard just thinking about it and what Alex was about to do him.

"Take your shirt off," Alex commanded huskily. "Slowly." He rocked back on his haunches, greedy eyes already undressing Sage, who sat up, keeping his eyes on Alex's. Sage unfastened his long-sleeved cotton shirt button by button, taking his time, watching Alex's face. He shrugged his shoulders out of the shirt, dropping it to the floor beside the bed and Alex drank him in, his eyes lingering on his torso. His hand moved down to his groin as he caressed himself, palming his cock with slow, deliberate strokes. Sage's mouth went dry at that erotic gesture and Alex grinned. Sage took a deep breath. Alex knew exactly what he was doing to him.

"Lie back and put your arms above your head," Alex instructed. Sage obliged, feeling his cock swell in his jeans and hearing his breathing quicken even as Alex reached over and opened the bedside drawer. Alex took out two pairs of red handcuffs, furry just as he'd promised, and Sage grinned in the darkness.

"I hope the poor squirrel that fur belonged to isn't too cold," he drawled lazily.

Alex laughed, a low, sexy sound which simply turned Sage's blood hot and intensified the friction in his trousers.

"I thought I needed it more than he did," his lover whispered, as he took Sage's outstretched hands, fastening the one handcuff around his wrist then locking it to the headboard. Sage reached out with his free hand to pull him closer and Alex shook his head, pushing Sage's arm back behind him again with more than a little force.

"Uh-uh. You're my prisoner, Sage. You need to do as you're told." He secured Sage's other wrist, then leaned back to inspect his handiwork. Alex gave a low growl of satisfaction, a sound that had Sage wanting nothing more than to pounce on him and make him beg for mercy of his own. But he was now powerless. Alex stood up, slowly pulling his long-sleeved sweatshirt over his head, revealing his firm torso with its sprinkling of hair down to his groin. He unzipped his trousers, letting them fall to the floor, sliding his dark blue briefs down his legs. His cock jutted out, red and inviting and Sage swallowed as Alex climbed onto the bed, straddling him and teasingly brushing his cock against Sage's lips.

Sage lunged forward to claim it with his mouth but Alex was quicker and moved away.

"Not yet. Have some patience, lover." He stroked himself, his eyes hooded, watching Sage's face intently.

Sage looked at him in frustration. "Christ, you are such a bloody tease. I know that's the whole point of this game but you're really driving me nuts."

He heard the yearning in his voice. Alex's shaved groin had always been a turn-on for Sage and seeing it just inches from his face, smelling his musky scent and feeling the heat emanating from Alex's body, he had a need for the man so extreme he felt his heart hiccup in his chest, a sensation of it beating two beats at one time.

Alex caressed Sage's groin through the fabric of his trousers. He groaned loudly, the exquisite sensation flooding his senses as Alex unzipped him, pulling his trousers down as Sage raised his body to let him tug them off his hips. They were flung onto the floor, leaving him in just his silk boxers, Pierre Cardin ones Alex had bought him a few days ago. Alex's hands slid over the silk on Sage's hips, his touch inflaming him as he smoothed the fabric against his heated and sensitive skin. Alex leaned down and slowly licked the tip of his cock through the silk. Sage moaned loudly at the incredible feeling. Alex's tongue slowly licked his shaft, top to bottom slowly, once, then twice, and Sage's backside left the bed, his hips twisting and pressing urgently upward against Alex's mouth.

"Fuck, you love seeing me at your mercy, don't you?"

Alex's eyes were black with desire. "It gives me great pleasure to see you squirm."

Alex took pity on him, reaching for the waistband of his boxers, sliding them off as once again Sage desperately raised his hips in the need to be naked. He sprung completely free, the warm air of the bedroom caressing his hardness as Alex gave a sigh of satisfaction. Slowly he leaned down, trailing his tongue up Sage's inner thigh, his hand stroking his chest, rubbing his palms against his nipples, until Sage thought they could get no harder. He moaned softly as Alex's mouth made its inexorable way toward his groin.

"God, that feels so good," Sage whispered huskily, his every fibre screaming for Alex to take him in his mouth and bring him some respite. He wanted to feel a warm, wet mouth taking him in, a tongue going to that most sensitive of places, lapping him until he could take no more. He finally got his wish as Alex's mouth wrapped itself around his cock, his lips sliding down his shaft, tongue probing and stroking him as Sage's body shuddered, arching up toward his lover, pleading for more. He heard his own breathing, heavy and laboured as Alex sucked and nibbled, sliding his mouth up and down him until he was dizzy with the feelings he was causing.

"Alex, babe, don't stop what you're doing, I think I've died and gone to heaven," he whispered, his body straining and his groin flooding with heat. Alex's fingers moved down deeper between his legs, reaching around to his backside, gently stroking him between his butt cheeks, running his fingers along from his back to the front, even as his mouth got busier. Alex's finger rubbed at his entrance, taking the moisture from his own cock, gently pushing his finger inside Sage, followed by another. Sage cried out loudly, unable to help himself and Alex stopped what he was doing.

"Do you trust me, Sage?" Alex whispered, and Sage nodded. "Do you trust me when I tell you we have no more need for condoms? I had a test, Sage. And there's nothing for you to worry about. I know you might have been worried about my past. I want to feel you skin to skin inside me. And I trust you. So if you're all right with it, I'd like to give them a miss."

"Christ, yes, Alex," Sage groaned. "I want that too." They'd talked about it but made no decision yet, and given what he was feeling now Sage knew he'd agree to anything Alex wanted.

In one fluid movement, Alex's warm, wet mouth was replaced by the silk of his body as he settled himself on Sage, taking him deep inside. Eyes closed, head thrown back, Alex enveloped Sage, and without the condom it was a sensation even more welcome than before. Their bodies blended in skin and heat, and Alex leaned back, placing his hands on Sage's thighs, rocking back and forth on his shaft. Sage moved his hips in time with Alex's bobbing.

"Sage, you always feel incredible, but fuck, this is definitely better." Alex gasped and opened his eyes, and the intense focus of those beautiful, catlike irises was like magic for Sage. He heard Alex exhale a deep sigh and felt Alex press himself down, bending further backward to get more friction.

Sage watched Alex rocking on him and strained to keep up his momentum. Alex's other hand drifted to his own cock and stroked. Sage felt a sense of sheer contentment at the sight, the fact that this man had claimed his heart and flesh. The scars on Alex's body made him realise just how much Alex trusted him, making Sage feel honoured. The scars were beautiful, just like his man.

Alex suddenly moaned loudly, his hips bucking as he came, his semen shooting out in hot, sticky spurts, covering them both with the salty scent of sex. At the sight of Alex's climax, his pleasure, Sage's groin flooded with a familiar prickling, the intense pressure giving him a pleasure he thought he might die of, happy and satiated. His own mini-explosion travelled all the way from his balls up his shaft to deep inside Alex. Alex's muscles contracted around his cock, and Sage arched his back, his semen flooding Alex's hot channel.

They both lay spent and satiated. The sweat on their bodies cooled as Alex panted and moved forward to take Sage's mouth, and the occasional tremors passing through both of their bodies subsided to shivers. Finally, when Alex had finished ravaging his mouth, Sage spoke.

"As fun as that was, these bloody cuffs are chafing me. Do you think you could take them off?"

Alex laughed softly, rolling off Sage to take the small key from the bedside table then unlock the cuffs.

Sage winced, rubbing his wrists. "Squirrel or no squirrel, these are more uncomfortable than the last ones we used. What happened to those, anyway? I thought they were specially made for comfort and were a damn sight better than these."

The smile disappeared from Alex's face.

Sage looked at him in puzzlement. "Did I say something wrong?"

Alex's voice was slightly wary when he replied. "I left them at Study in Scarlet. I haven't had a chance to pick them up yet."

Sage grew chilled despite the activity he'd recently been participating in. "You used those ones with Eric? I thought they were ours alone, not bloody communal ones." He heard the disgust in his voice even as he said the words and his mood instantly darkened. It was a rising flood of blackness that swum up through the mire of his emotions. The resentment he'd thought *he* was controlling took control of him instead.

Fucking Eric and Alex's damned sessions.

Alex spoke softly. "It was a couple of sessions ago, Sage. With me only going once or twice a month now, I haven't had the chance to collect them."

Sage sat up, his body tense as he leaned back against the cold metal of the headboard. "Eric used those on you or you on him?

Exactly how does that work? The same way you've just done with me?"

"Sage, please. Let's not go there. You know how I feel about it." Alex's voice was defeated.

Sage was no longer listening. His Black Irish was up and there was no stopping it until it had been totally spent.

"Is there anything else, other than your body and the handcuffs we've used in the bedroom, that Eric uses? The cock rings perhaps, or the silk ties?"

Sage knew he was being unfair but he was now on a roll and all the resentment he'd ever had in sharing the man he loved with another came seeping out of his pores like toxic waste leaking upward in a stream. "I already know about not being able to take you from behind because that's how he does it, that's 'your thing' and you'd rather I not, but is there anything else I really should know?" The mere words he spoke aloud made him imagine the other man behind Alex, driving into him. He swallowed, feeling sick to his stomach.

"Sage, please. Let's not do this." Alex's voice was choked as he sat up, wrapping his arms around his knees.

"I think I have the right to know the answers, don't you?" Sage said bitterly. "Just how exactly this other man uses you and you him, even if it's not with sex anymore. So you say."

Even as he said the words, Sage regretted them. But the heavy feeling in his chest still remained and the image was seared on his brain of Eric fucking or whipping Alex.

Alex shook his head fiercely. "No. There's nothing else we use that he uses with me. There, are you fucking satisfied now?"

Alex leapt to his feet, his face white. He disappeared into the bathroom. Sage sat there, listening to the sounds of Alex moving around. He took a few deep breaths, trying to calm his tortured soul. He lay back against the bed, closing his eyes, feeling the ache in the pit of his stomach and the taste of bile at the back of his throat.

The room was dark and quiet. He tried to get his mind back to where it needed be, to the place where he was supportive and understanding, just as he'd promised he'd be. Finally, with a deep sigh, he sat up, swinging his legs over the side of the bed. He pulled on his boxers, feeling like a complete heel. All the good he'd thought he'd ever done for Alex he'd just undone with a few cruel words and a spat of a sudden bad mood that had made what started out as a promising night into one tainted by his selfishness and impatience. He took a deep, shuddering sigh. He tried the bathroom door but it was locked.

"Alex. Can you let me in please?"

"Fuck off," was the muffled reply in between what sounded like fists punching the wall.

Sage hoped he wouldn't have to do any first aid. He sighed. "Please open the door. I know I was a bastard again, and I really need to apologise to you. But I want to do it face to face not through a bloody locked door."

He waited patiently for a few minutes. Then he heard the tap running. Sage stood by the door, his arms folded, his chest aching at the trauma he'd just caused for someone that really didn't deserve it. Alex had warned him that this state of affairs was something he'd have to face eventually. He'd sort of known what he was getting into even though in his wildest dreams he'd never thought he'd be so accepting of any of it.

Finally he heard the lock turn and the door opened slightly. He pushed it open, walking inside. Alex stood to one side, a towel around his waist, his face taut. Sage saw the streaks of blood in the bathroom basin. His stomach lurched.

"What the hell did you do, Alex?" The anguish in his voice was unmistakeable and Alex blinked. Sage strode over to him, gripping his wrists, seeing the bruised knuckles and blood on Alex's hands. Alex regarded him without expression. His eyes flicked briefly to the tiles on the far side of the bathroom next to the shower and Sage saw the red flecks staining the cream surface.

"Christ, baby. Please don't go hurting yourself like that because of me. I'm sorry. I shouldn't have said those things. You know I can get these moods and the thing with the handcuffs just tipped me over the edge." He moved toward Alex but his lover stepped back. When he spoke, instead of the anger Sage expected, Alex's voice was resigned.

"It's fine, Sage. You've been so patient with me so far and you have the right to go a little mental. No one has ever done what you're doing for me and frankly, I'm surprised you've lasted this long. Three and a half months is longer than anyone else lasted. I've been counting the days wondering just how much longer the good times are going to last."

Sage moved closer to him, pinning Alex between the sink and his body. Alex stared at him defiantly and Sage reached out, cupping his face in his hands, his thumbs caressing the strong curve of Alex's jaw. He saw something flicker in Alex's eyes, a fierce hope that disappeared almost as it arrived.

"You don't have to keep going with this, Sage. I don't expect you to." Alex swallowed, his face filled with pain. "You can leave me," he whispered and Sage's heart broke at the defeated tone in Alex's voice.

He had to fix this. No matter what it took. He wasn't going to be the cause of Alex's pain again.

Sage kept him close to him. "I need to tell you something. Something I haven't said to you yet, but I need to." Sage's stomach lurched. He'd said these words to a man before but he truly didn't think he ever meant them as much as he did now. Everything seemed crystal clear, he'd realised as he sat outside on the bed, listening to Alex punch a wall.

"I know it's not been that long but I love you, Alex. Heart and soul. You're my soul mate, the one person I want around forever." Sage saw Alex's eyes widen, the glimmer of hope coming back into his eyes. "This whole sharing thing is hard for me, make no mistake. I've never even envisaged being in the place I am now, but I'd do it all again in a heartbeat if I thought it would make you better, help you get over these demons you have inside you. I think I'm helping and then I go and fuck it all up again like tonight. It's just so bloody difficult. And I will never fucking leave you. Never." His voice choked and he stopped, uncertain what Alex's reaction would be. He wasn't quite prepared for the look of amazement in Alex's eyes at his declaration of love.

"How can you love me, Sage?" Alex said wonderingly. "I'm so bloody damaged, and I have these needs and you hardly know me at all really."

Sage pulled Alex to him, holding him tightly. "Because you're brave and noble and an incredible human being. You have worked so hard at trying to overcome these needs you have. Look at where you are now, only seeing Eric once or twice a month. I promised you my help, Alexander Montgomery, and I really want to get you through this. If you'll still have me after I've been such an arsehole."

Alex's face looked up at him with such adoration that Sage's chest tightened. He hadn't been sure if he felt the same way about him but the look in Alex's eyes was saying what he hoped he'd hear.

"I love you too, Sage," he said simply. "You're my saviour. And you need to understand that whatever Eric does with me, he will never have what's in here. This belongs only to you."

Alex laid a hand on his heart and Sage's own swelled with emotion at that simple gesture. Alex reached up, taking Sage's mouth in a tender kiss that conveyed so much more than words. When they finally drew apart, both of them were a little tearful.

Sage knew he had to try harder. Alex had come so far. "Come on back to bed," Sage whispered in his ear. "I think I just want to hold you close and go to sleep and forget all this craziness for a while."

He took Alex by the hand, leading him out of the bathroom, switching the light off as they walked into the dim light of the bedroom. They crawled under the covers, Alex spooning into his back as he wrapped his arms around Sage's waist. Sage put his hands over Alex's as Sage drifted off into a calming sleep.

Chapter 22

Alex sat in Melanie van Pelt's office as he waited for the psychologist to finish her discussion with her secretary. He stared down at the busy London street below, watching as people scurried on the pavements in the late September morning rush hour. Moments later, Melanie was seated opposite him.

"You're looking very relaxed. Alex. I take it everything's still okay between you and Sage?"

Alex chuckled as he sat back, his hands casually lying on the couch arms, his long legs stretched out in front. "Having an incredible man in my life and a lot of really good sex is definitely recommended."

"It's still good then?" Melanie leaned back, making a notation on her pad.

Alex nodded. "Sage has been the best thing ever for me, Mel. Whilst he hates what I do with Eric, he's trying to deal with it. It has been difficult but he's been so patient. We've had one or two little episodes of stress but we're both trying to deal with it. We've been spending a lot of time together and we have a real relationship." He smiled quietly. "He told me he loves me and I said it right back."

Melanie nodded her head in approval. "That's incredible news. It sounds like you're moving along. You aren't even coming to therapy as often as you were. I last saw you two weeks ago."

"And I'm not seeing Eric that often either. My next session is in four days' time—Friday. It'll be about three weeks since I last saw him. I just don't seem to be as needy as I was."

Alex sounded very pleased with his progress and Melanie smiled. This man had every right to be proud.

"I've really toned it down; no heavy stuff. I don't want Sage to have to see any bite or whip marks." Alex grinned at the absurdity of the words. "And I've told Madame Duchaine that I no longer need the sex bit now I'm getting it from someone else. And it's *so* much better." He grinned. "Eric just has to put up with that part of it."

Melanie smiled even though she thought Alex was being a little too hopeful about Eric's reaction. "You and Eric have had a very intense relationship for over two years now, Alex. Are you sure that this gradual downplaying of it to almost nothing is going to be acceptable to him? He may not like the new rules and he may want you to find someone else to partner with."

She didn't miss the shadow on Alex's face at her words.

"He has been very aggressive and rough when I do see him. I know he misses the full experience but that's just not where I want to be now." Alex's voice was resolute. "I'm the customer and he needs to do what I want, not what he wants. I don't want to lose Eric but if I have to, well, then he'll have to move on. I have Sage now."

This was the part that worried Melanie. Alex had certainly come a long way but Melanie was still concerned that if anything happened to affect his relationship with Sage, if the man decided he'd had enough, it would destroy Alex and put him back in a worse place than ever before.

"You sound as if you're placing a lot of reliance in Sage, Alex." Melanie's voice was quiet as she tried to think how best to approach this. "I hate to be a party pooper but have you thought about what might happen if he ever used his safe word?"

Alex paled. "Of course I have." He looked up at Melanie and the therapist could see the fear in his eyes. "I think about it all the time. I know what would happen if he did. I'd fall apart." He smiled faintly. "I am so in love with the man. I never thought I'd be able to have this emotion in my life. I suppose I'm lucky to get this far. So I guess I'll just have to hope he doesn't go anywhere." He looked at Melanie with a determined focus. "I was going to ask Sage if he wanted to move out of Dan's and come stay with me. He spends so much time at my place anyway it makes sense. I was going to talk to him about it soon."

Melanie nodded. "It sounds like that could work. As long as the two of you don't get crowded working and living together." Her tone was noncommittal but she wanted to make sure Alex knew what he was asking for.

Alex frowned. "I guess that's true. I'll mention it anyway. If he doesn't want to, that will be fine. I'll settle for whatever I can get from him."

"You're allowed to have expectations, Alex." Melanie looked at him carefully. "Just tell Sage how you feel and take it from there." She didn't want Alex believing he had to settle for anything less than what he wanted. He deserved much more. Alex's progress in counselling was nothing short of miraculous.

Alex nodded, and there was a comfortable silence while Melanie updated her notes.

"I didn't tell you before but I went to get tested." Alex fidgeted and looked at his hands. "I wanted to stop using condoms and put Sage's mind at rest. He never said anything but I knew it played on his mind."

"And what was the result?" Melanie asked quietly.

"I'm fine, I'm all clean, which I knew anyway, but I needed to prove it to Sage. Not for him but for me. Sage insisted on having a test too, which was clear, but I knew that. He told me he was."

"I'm really pleased for you, Alex. That's excellent news. What about Eric? Have you told him you're in love with Sage?" Melanie wasn't sure why she thought this was a bad idea but she had an instinct it wasn't the best thing to do. She'd been hearing about Alex and Eric for two years now and she thought she knew Eric as well as she could from afar. He sounded like a classic narcissist and that could be a problem.

"No. I won't tell him that. He might guess but I can't help that." Alex shrugged.

Melanie smiled. "That's pretty sensible, Alex. I'm really pleased things are good with Sage. That poor man has been exposed to more strange things since meeting you that I bet he's ever seen in his life. But he sounds incredibly supportive."

The session was soon over and Alex was on the tube on the way back to the studio. As he walked in he saw Sage standing talking to Luke. He waved and Alex smiled as he walked over. Sage leaned over and kissed Alex briefly, his hand brushing his cheek.

"Hey. Glad you decided to join us. Luke says the last scene shoots were incredible and he's trying to threaten me with certain death if I don't perform to the same standard today."

"You're always amazing, Sage." Alex tousled Sage's hair and the director groaned.

"God, Alex, don't do that or he'll have to go back and have it all fixed up. When will you two learn it's time and money to keep redoing makeup and hair when the two of you just kiss it all off and spend your time touching each other?" His eyes twinkled as he regarded the couple out of the corner of his eye.

Sage flushed and Alex laughed. He turned as someone came up behind him.

"Mr. Montgomery? Someone left this for you at the front desk." The young man handed Alex a brown envelope and he smiled his thanks as he took it.

"Sage, I'll leave you and Luke to get on. I have some work to do myself." Alex turned, going into his office, sitting down at the desk and picking up the letter opener to open the envelope. There were a number of newspaper clippings inside and he frowned as he picked them up. When he saw what they were, he dropped them onto the blotter as if they burning hot. He stood up and just made it to the bathroom outside before he was sick, vomiting into the toilet bowl with deep retches, bent over the bowl with eyes that streamed both from hot tears and the effort of being sick.

He heard a sound at the entrance and turned to see Sage standing there, his face anxious.

"Alex? What's wrong? Here, take this." He handed Alex a wad of tissue paper and Alex wiped his mouth, standing up unsteadily. He turned on the tap, running water over his face and drinking some to take the vile taste out of his mouth.

"What the hell happened?" Sage's voice was quiet but firm.

Alex heaved a shuddering sigh, turning to face him. "It's in my office," he said weakly. "In the envelope I got."

Sage turned tail and disappeared. Alex followed him into the room where Sage stood with the clippings in his hand.

He frowned as he came in. "These seem to be articles about some man called Evan Harding who went missing in 1999. What do they have to do with you?"

Alex looked at him, his eyes strained. "Look at the other clippings."

Sage picked up the other ones on the desk and his face paled as he read them. "These are about a man called Evan who was found at some cult in Surrey in 2000." His voice tailed off as he made the connection. "Is this about you, Alex?" His voice was flat.

Alex nodded. "My real name is Evan Harding. Alexander Montgomery is the name Cully's team got for me when I was repatriated. I needed a new start. If I hadn't changed my name the newspapers and the cult might have tried to find me and then it might all have started again. Cully thought it best."

Sage was reading the articles, his face ashen. Alex imagined he was reading the sordid details of what had been done to him, the situation he'd been found in, the details the newspapers had been only to eager to print for their sensationalism. Alex waited for him to finish and for the inevitable questions that would come.

Sage finally laid them down quietly, looking at Alex. "It says here Rudy was killed in the shoot-out when Cully and his team surrounded the compound to get back the little boy they'd come for, Sammy Hinton. He'd been kidnapped from his home by his stepfather and brought to the cult. It says his real father organised his extraction. You were lucky he did."

Alex nodded, his heart beating harder. "I saw them bring him in, this tiny six-year-old with the biggest eyes I've ever seen. He was petrified. Rudy was bragging about having another consort to train when he was a little older." His voice caught and he swayed. Sage came over and held him, his eyes watchful. "About a month later they invaded the compound and rescued us all. You know what happened from there."

"Well, I thought I did," Sage said softly and Alex heard the edge in his voice. "But I had no idea that the man I love had another name. Is there anything else you've not told me?"

Alex swallowed, hoping that he wouldn't be struck down by lightning at his next lie. "No. There's nothing else you need to know. I don't tell anyone about my real name. If it got out there's no telling who might recognise me and come after me. It's a remote possibility but I'd rather not force an issue."

Sage scowled. "Well, firstly, I didn't think I was just anyone and secondly someone obviously does know who you are—hence the clippings."

Alex could tell his boyfriend was upset at the fact he hadn't told him about this sooner

"Have you any idea who might have sent these?" Sage picked up the envelope, turning it over, trying to see where it had come from.

Alex shook his head. "I don't know. I suppose someone might have recognised me from the TV and decided to remind me who I used to be. I've changed my looks but I can't change my eye colour. In hindsight I should have worn contact lenses to hide my eyes."

"There's no postmark so someone must have dropped it off. Perhaps we can ask the desk to look at the CCTV footage." Sage pulled out his mobile, speaking to someone quietly before cutting the call. "George will see if he can see anything on the footage. That might give us a clue as to who brought it in."

"Do you think this is something to do with the person that hurt Dianne and hit Miles? Could it be the same person?"

Sage looked grim. "I don't know. We need to tell the police about this. I don't like it. What a bloody way to start a Monday morning."

His face grew softer as Alex went even paler. "This is all getting a bit out of hand. We have to tell DS Doyle so I'll give him a call and see if he can come over. Maybe they can do something with that." He waved at the clippings as he disappeared out of the office.

* * *

Later that evening Sage sat in Dan's apartment. DS Doyle had come to the film studio to take Alex's statement and take the clippings away in the hope there might be fingerprints so he could trace the sender. The detective had told them that this case was outside his jurisdiction but that the Met was happy for him to take the lead for the short term. No one was particularly hopeful. There'd been nothing on the CCTV footage either that shed any light.

The DS had promised Sage he'd try and keep Alex's identity a secret and not release any details about his past unless absolutely necessary and then only if he spoke to him first. He'd been very disturbed at the fact that the young man sitting in front of him called Alex Montgomery was actually Evan Harding, someone who had been the cause of a lot of newspaper and TV coverage all those years ago due his sensational rescue and horrifically abusive treatment.

Sage sat in front of his laptop with the words "Evan Harding+Bohemia" in the Google search box. He sat in indecision for a while as he deliberated whether to hit the search button. He'd been agonising over whether to do this search for days since finding out who Alex really was. Now his curiosity had finally gotten the better of him and with a determined gesture, he hit the button, sitting back as he waited for the results to be returned. He took a deep breath as he looked at the screen.

"Cult member finally released from living hell"

"Young man latest victim in self-professed 'Prophet of Bohemia's' harem"

"Evan Harding found living with cult leader in Surrey"

"Young man found chained and sexually abused in basement. Cult leader shot and killed in rescue."

"Too disturbing to publish in other newspapers—the pictures of young eighteen-year-old Evan Harding, recently rescued from cult in the South. Warning: these images are explicit and may offend sensitive viewers."

He clicked on the articles, reading them one by one, growing paler at each entry. Finally he opened the last one and after seeing the awful images and article, Sage sat back, slamming down the lid to the laptop violently. His hands were shaking.

God, I should never have done this.

He stood up, pacing around the lounge, staring out of the window into the Chelsea streets below. It was raining and the drizzle trickled down the windows, obscuring his vision and making the scenes outside fuzzy and distorted.

Dan came in behind him, two beers in hand. He passed one over to his friend. "Are you all right?" he asked quietly "You haven't been yourself lately."

Sage took the beer absently and opened it, taking a large gulp. "Not really. There's a lot going on at the moment."

"It's Alex isn't it? I've never seen you like this, Sage. That man has really gotten under your skin."

Dan sat down, propping his socked feet up on the centre table. He observed his best friend closely. "You are *so* in love with him, aren't you?" His face was serious.

Sage looked at him, his eyes hooded. "I do love him, Dan. A lot."

Dan nodded his head. "I knew it. You've been mooning around like a puppy since you met this guy. I don't know what it is about him, but there's definitely something. I like him though. I think you've been really good for each other."

Sage laughed harshly. "That's putting it mildly. If you knew the full story about our 'relationship' you'd put me in a loony bin."

"Then tell me. Share it. It's driving you crazy having no one to talk to and share a secret. I know you, you're a Sagittarius, curious as hell. I'm a Capricorn and we're good at keeping secrets."

Sage grinned despite how confused he was feeling. Dan's proclivity towards managing his life with astrological signs was well known. It would be nice to talk to someone. He couldn't talk to Miles about his relationship with Alex. He'd feel too sordid to do that. But Dan might understand and not judge. An hour later Dan was sitting in stunned silence as Sage finished his story and leant back in his chair with this third beer. He was feeling fairly mellow by this time and he knew sharing his burden had been a great idea.

Dan was still trying to get his head around it all. "So you have sex with Alex knowing he's going to go out and have it off with another man at some stage? That he's going to have this S-and-M episode and come back after being flogged and other stuff, and you're okay with that? Jesus, that's bloody harsh. How the hell do you do it?"

"With difficulty. But he's worth it, he's much better now than he was and he's really trying to stop it altogether. When you see what he went through, it's amazing he's normal in any way at all. Alex is one of the toughest people I know."

"You are definitely in love, my friend." Dan swigged the dregs of his beer down and grimaced as he reached over to pick up another one. "It's an incredible story. You must be a saint to do it. I couldn't." Dan peered at him. "What about all this malarkey at the studio, with Dianne and Miles and now Alex? What are you going to do about that? I thought it was all over but obviously not."

Sage shrugged. "I can't do anything. The police have all the facts. It's up to them to find this sicko. I just hope it stays quiet, like it has been. We don't need any more violent incidents." He looked at Dan in apprehension. "You have to keep this all to yourself. You can't tell anyone. I don't want Alex compromised at all."

Dan pretended to zip his lips. "They're sealed. It's between you and me. Thanks for telling me. I knew something was up but I never imagined anything like this." He looked at his friend wryly." You're more worried about what this getting out will do to Alex than you, aren't you? Typical Sage. You're a good bloke, my friend."

Sage shook his head grimly. "Not so good, Dan. I have this tendency to push him and I'm scared shitless I'll say something that makes him go off on a tangent again. We've already had one episode like that I can't face being the cause of another." He shrugged helplessly. "I sometimes can't help myself."

Dan sat back. "Sage, that's understandable. You're doing something incredibly difficult. All you can do is keep supporting him and hope things work out the way you both want."

Sage went to bed later that night feeling a sense of relief that someone else knew what he was going through. Alex's last session with Eric was over three weeks ago, and with the amount of lovemaking they were doing, Sage hoped he didn't need to see him again soon. Alex and he had talked about it only last night and he hadn't said he was seeing him again. Perhaps it was all finally over and it could just be the two of them. He smiled at the thought.

Chapter 23

The next few days passed with no further incidents and Alex found himself relaxing as each day went by. Alex had a session with Eric tonight. Eric had been particularly cruel lately and Alex knew now that Melanie had been right in thinking Eric felt Alex belonged to him. It was what had made him decide that after this session he was going to give it up for good and go cold turkey. His heart had pounded making the decision and he still felt nervous at the momentous decision he was making. But if it came to Sage or Eric, he knew which one he was choosing. He was also ready to broach the subject of Sage moving in with him.

Melanie had encouraged his decision about Eric too, saying she thought he was ready. Nothing could curb Alex's happiness in knowing that he'd give up Eric and his special brand of cruelty altogether. Alex hugged that fact to him like a blanket all day.

Unfortunately the day had been dogged with disaster from the moment filming had begun. Cameras had not worked properly; technicians had damaged some film, making Sage and Dianne have to redo a scene; and a special effects gig had gone wrong, leaving Sage with a large bruise on his back and a very bad temper. Alex had never seen him so tightly wound. He had a feeling Sage was still struggling with Alex's relationship with Eric and he was looking forward to telling him that it would be soon be over.

Alex looked up and smiled as Sage walked into his office. His lover's body language indicated he was still stressed and Alex's heart sunk.

"What are you up to tonight?" Sage asked quietly. "I've got a yen for Thai food and there's a really great place in Westminster that I know. It's been a bitch of a day and I just want to unwind."

Alex took a deep breath. "I'm not available tonight. I have an appointment."

Sage's face darkened as he looked at Alex out of eyes that were suddenly flinty. Alex saw the darkness creep up like a storm passing over a wintry sea, something he'd seen often lately.

"Are you going to see Eric?" Sage's tone was icy.

Alex looked at him, confused. "I thought you didn't want to know when I was going or I would have told you."

"I thought you were cutting down on your sessions?" Sage walked over to the window and looked out, his back rigid.

Alex sighed. "Sage, let's not rehash this again. You know I only see him about once a month now. That's a hell of an achievement." He didn't want to tell Sage he was leaving Eric until he was sure he could make it without him.

"I thought we were doing so well that you might not want to see him anymore. I thought perhaps *I* was starting to be enough." Sage turned and Alex quailed at the sudden expression of cold anger in his eyes.

"Sage, that is nearly the case." Alex thought he'd better bring his good news forward and try to appease his lover. "I know I'm close." He grinned but Sage's expression was implacable. Alex stood up and walked over to Sage, laying a hand on his arm. "You know I've stopped the biting, the hard whipping, and you know we're not having sex anymore—"

"Yes, that was certainly a step in the right direction, wasn't it?" Sage's words were savage. "Not having another man fucking you, coming inside you, that was a real coup for me, wasn't it?"

Alex dropped his hand, feeling sick. "I don't know what to say. I'm sorry I'm not meeting your expectations. I'm trying, believe me." His heart raced and he wished he could tell Sage he would stop right now. But the panic in his chest at considering that told him he couldn't. He needed to stick to his plan and psych himself to it. It was the only way he could let Eric go.

Sage nodded but Alex could see he wasn't placated at all. "Fine. Go have your session. Perhaps you should bring some of the equipment home and I'll take Eric's place and treat you like he does. Perhaps that way you'll get your rocks off—"

His words were brought to an abrupt end as Alex moved forward swiftly, punching Sage firmly in the mouth. Sage staggered back, against the wall, blood dribbling from his lip, which was already starting to swell. They stared at each other. Alex sensed the suppressed violence in his lover. He already regretted his hasty action but he was truly angry.

"Don't you ever fucking say that again. You mean too much to me for that to happen. I understand you're hurt and that perhaps things aren't moving fast enough for you. I am trying, I promise you. But these are my demons and I will never let you get tainted in that way by them."

Sage's jaw worked as he listened to the words and Alex felt a surge of guilt at what he'd just done. "I think it's a bit late to remain untainted, Alex." Sage finally said between gritted teeth. "I've been touched by it already. I'm sorry for that last comment. It was vicious and unfair. You bring out the worst as well as the best in me, lately more than ever." He moved over to the door. "Go see Eric. Do whatever you need to do. I'll call you tomorrow."

He disappeared into the corridor. Alex sat down in his chair, his legs giving way. He knew Sage was hurt and frustrated. Christ, Alex had thought he was doing so well to get this far but perhaps he wasn't trying hard enough. Maybe he'd never try hard enough.

* * *

Eric Rossi marched around the basement at Study in Scarlet in a real red-haired temper. His frustration with the last sessions he and Alex had experienced were really starting to tick him off. What the hell had happened to the man? It was that prick Christopher Sage he was seeing, he knew it. He'd seen the newspapers, the fact they were almost living together. Eric had even gone by the film studio a couple of times to see if he could see them together. The man had ruined his charge. Taken all that passion and sexiness Alex had inside him and turned him into a vanilla-flavoured lollipop. He turned as Alex came in the door and stood quietly. He had no shirt on, just his chinos which were already unzipped. He looked pale and ill. Even Alex's erection seemed to be flagging lately and Eric wasn't prepared for that eventuality. He took it as a personal insult. The man needed Eric, needed his special set of services and most of all needed his rough sex. That would make the man's cock stand up like a soldier again.

Well, we'll soon get that remedied. Wait until you see what I've got for you tonight. That'll put a smile on your face, just like it used to. All you need is someone to take charge then you'll realise just how much you missed it.

He walked over to Alex, feeling calmer now, his hands reaching out to slowly caress Alex's nipples and he leaned forward to take them in his mouth as he sucked them. Alex's eyes closed and he took a deep breath. Eric pulled Alex toward him, grabbing the band of his trousers and rolling them roughly down over the man's lean hips.

When Alex was naked, Eric pulled him roughly toward the cross, fastening Alex onto it, making sure the bonds were tighter than usual.

Alex was splayed out like a starfish, unable to move.

Eric licked his lips. "You seem sad, Alex. What's wrong? Is your boyfriend not giving you what you need? What you want?"

Alex's eyes flashed. "Leave him out of this. I don't want him mentioned here."

Eric nodded. "Fine, Alex." His voice was silky and dangerous. The sharp stirrings of anger in his belly made him focused. "I must confess I'm a little disappointed with the way our last sessions have been. I thought we had a good thing going here. Seeing as how I've been deprived of nearly *all* of my little pleasures, I have a slight change of my own to the schedule tonight."

He reached into his back jeans pocket, pulling out a red scarf, waving it in front of Alex's face. His eyes widened as Eric fastened it around his mouth and he shook his head frantically. Eric smiled. Alex had never liked being gagged.

Eric waggled his finger in front of Alex's face. "You took something away, I'm adding something. I guarantee you'll like it when you see what I've got planned."

He slipped out of his jeans, his cock at full mast. He gazed down at it in pride. "I'm feeling particularly virile tonight. You're a lucky man." He walked over to the corner of the room, picking up his rawhide whip. Alex shook his head, eyes wild. Eric smiled as he cracked it on the floor.

"Are you ready, Alex? Let's do it just like we used to do, just like you used to like it. I can promise you that you'll enjoy it. Remember how much fun it used to be and how much you enjoyed it. Then you'll realise what you've been missing. I'll tell Madame Duchaine you changed your mind." His voice grew hard. "If you decide to tell her anything else, I'll make sure that your actor fuck buddy gets his just deserts. One of my very large gay friends will politely invite him to a session just like this one. He might enjoy that, being in show business. My friends can be very inventive and your tame actor might like the sensation of being filled to capacity by an audience. A little like the seats in a theatre." He chuckled at his own wit then laughed nastily, hitting Alex with the whip across his stomach, slashing and wielding the whip like the professional he was.

Alex closed his eyes as Eric whipped, bit and slapped him exactly as he'd promised. He whispered his safe word through the gag half a dozen times but Eric ignored it. Finally the pain drove Alex further inside his head, his soul becoming darker and blacker with each abusive move Eric made. Tears trickled from Alex eyes. His mind was frantic with thoughts, whirling like dervishes in his brain. He had to protect Sage. Too many people seemed to be getting hurt because of him, because of who and what he was, what he'd written. Dianne, Miles, and now the threat against Sage. Eric could do what he wanted to Alex; he was used to people using him.

After what seemed like hours and when Alex was bloodied and bruised, Eric unfastened the ties from Alex's ankles, lifting his trembling legs around Eric's waist. Alex watched from eyes that were gritty and sore and a heart that had turned to stone. He didn't care about anything anymore; he just wanted this whole thing to be over. He thought dully that *everything* would be over after this.

Eric grinned at Alex, manoeuvring himself to the right position. "You'll enjoy this, Alex. God knows I've waited long enough. And maybe later I'll taste that lovely cock of yours too." The lust in his voice made Alex close his eyes. He didn't want to see Eric's face. It reminded him of Rudy's when he'd had him. Alex knew now deep in his soul that there was only one purpose for a man like him.

Eric rammed inside him, from the front, whilst Alex hung suspended. He didn't even stop to put on a condom or lube himself up. Alex's mind shut down as his body was violated without mercy, the pain he felt inside taking him into another dimension. Alex's body was brutalised and aching and all hope left him at this final act of betrayal. He finally gave in to the darkness that descended, covering him in its cold and cruel blackness.

The following day Sage frowned as he listened to Alex's voice mail message once again. He'd been trying to call him all day with no luck. Sage planned on going out to his apartment after he finished filming as he knew he had yet another apology to make. Once again he'd been a real prick, letting his emotions get the better of him, letting his disappointment and frustration rise to the surface. All his talk about him being there for his lover, being patient and waiting until he was ready—that had all been bullshit given his rant yesterday. Alex had every right to be mad at him. Sage had never seen someone try so hard to overcome his demons.

What the fuck was wrong with him? After their last spat, Sage had made his mind up to be more patient but then he'd gone off at a tangent yet again. He knew deep down inside that what he was expected to do to get Alex through this went above and beyond the call of duty that could be expected of any man, but he'd thought he'd be stronger than this. It was because he was so bloody crazy in love with the man.

He waded impatiently through the last scenes of the day, leaving the studio to walk briskly to Alex's apartment. It was close to seven p.m. when he got there and it was still fairly light. There didn't appear to be any lights on inside.

The street looked free of reporters. Lately the media attention had been wearing thin as there were no new developments or calamities to report on. Sage knocked and rang the bell but there was no response. He wondered if Alex had a spare key, hunting around in the various plant pots and flower troughs but finding nothing. He turned his attention to a small wrought iron squirrel standing by the door. Lifting it up, he saw a small silver key lying on the dirt. Smiling in triumph, he picked it up and set in the lock.

The door opened and he pushed it slowly, peering into the dim light of the entrance hall. "Alex? Are you in here? It's Sage."

He pushed the door fully open, walking in, shutting the door behind him. It was dark and the apartment smelt medicinal, as if someone had been using Dettol or some other antiseptic. He frowned as he slipped quietly through the apartment toward Alex's bedroom.

"Alex? Are you in here? I wanted to check you were okay. No one's heard from you all day."

He opened Alex's bedroom door slowly, his nostrils flaring as he smelt the source of the medicinal smell. Alex was in bed, covered with a blanket, his head turned toward the door, his eyes closed. He looked white in the darkness, his eyelids bruised and his lips bloodless. He was so still that for a heart-stopping minute, Sage thought he was dead.

Seeing the small bottle of pills on the side of the table and the empty vodka bottle, his mouth went dry with fear. Sage moved swiftly over to the bed, picking up the bottle. It was paracetamol. He bent down in panic, shaking Alex's shoulder gently, then more roughly, stepping back in fright when his boyfriend cried out in pain, shooting bolt upright in the bed, the covers falling to his waist, leaving his upper body bare.

Sage's heart thumped. "Jesus, I thought you were dead!" He held a hand to his chest.

Alex sat up, looking at him, his eyes and face emotionless. "How did you get in here, Sage?"

"I found the spare key. I was worried about you."

Alex held up a hand. "I'd like you to leave please. You shouldn't be here uninvited." His voice was toneless.

Sage stared at him in astonishment. "Jesus, Alex. I know I was a bastard yesterday and I need to apologise but I just wanted to see you were all right. It's me. I'm just not a bloody burglar or a rapist that's broken in."

Alex laughed harshly. "It really wouldn't matter to me if you were. I'd still like you to leave."

Sage heard the faint tone of something more vulnerable in Alex's voice despite the hardness he was now displaying. "What's that medicinal smell? Did you hurt yourself?"

Again Alex laughed but there was no amusement in the sound. "No. I leave that to other people. Haven't you learnt that about me by now?"

Sage was scared. "What the hell is going on, Alex?"

In one swift movement he leaned over, switching on the bedside light. Alex's eyes squinted with the sudden brightness. Sage saw the marks on his neck and throat, soft purple bruises left by sucking. He saw the bite and scratch marks on Alex's chest and the long, deep red weals across his chest and the front of his shoulders. Sage stepped back, his face darkening and there was silence as they looked at each other.

"Did Eric do that?" Sage's voice was hard, his jaw clenching. "You *let* him do that to you?" Bile rose in his throat and he thought he was going to throw up with his disappointment in this man he loved.

Alex regarded him expressionlessly. "What do you think? I was with him last night, wasn't I?" He shifted uncomfortably in the bed and at the movement, Sage felt sicker. That was the action of a man who was pretty tender down below. He'd seen it before with Alex after a rather marathon sex session where Sage had been pretty needy.

"I thought you said you'd toned it down." Sage glanced at Alex hopelessly, trying not to see the marks of betrayal on his boyfriend's body.

"We don't always get what we want. There is no happily ever after like in my novels."

The bitterness and hopelessness in Alex's voice drove nails of despair deep into Sage's heart. "What else did he do? Why did you change your mind? Was it because I was such a prick? Christ, Alex, if you do this to yourself every time we have a disagreement or an argument there's no hope…"

"There's no hope anyway. That's why I was going to give you this when I next saw you." Alex handed him a small slip of paper from the bedside table. Sage opened it and he felt the blood drain out of his head when he saw what was written there in Alex's neat cursive handwriting.

Chrysippus.

Sage looked up, nauseous. "You don't mean this. You're just upset."

"You promised to obey the rules. No arguments, no convincing to stay, just a parting of ways. I won't be coming into the studio anymore, I'm going to be working from home. I've sent Luke an email and set up conferencing facilities on my laptop. There's nothing more to discuss, Sage. So please leave." Alex looked implacable and Sage could see he was not going to be reasoned with.

The slow burn of anger and grief started to take over the incredible pain in his chest as he spat out his words. "I take back what I said about you. You're not brave at all, you're a damn coward. Things get tough and you go running off back to fucking Eric. If this is what you want, fine. I'm not going to argue. Life's too bloody short."

He turned, leaving the bedroom, his eyes blinded by tears, his breathing ragged and his being assailed by a dreadful sense of loss. He slammed the apartment door behind him, making sure he tucked the spare key back under the squirrel, walking blindly down the street toward the tube.

* * *

Back in his bedroom, Alex sat, tears etching trails down his pale cheeks, his heart-wrenching sobs echoing through the room. He felt as if life itself had just been wrenched out of his body.

I had to do it, Sage. I'm no good for you. I'll never be free to love you the way you deserve to be loved. I'm a fucked-up human being and I'll never be normal. Best to get it over before I'm even more in love with you than I am now. I don't want anyone hurting you because of me and Eric would. I couldn't bear that.

Chapter 24

Sage got back to his apartment hours later, after wandering aimlessly around the streets of London, stopping at any bar he could find to have a drink. By the time he got back to the apartment, he was drunk. He fumbled for his keys and when he couldn't find them, he started banging on the door, shouting for Dan to let him in.

Finally the door opened and Dan's blond, tousled head peered out into the corridor. "Shit, Sage. You're fucking wasted, mate. Come on. Get in here before we bloody well get evicted." He pulled his friend into the flat, locking the door. "I at least thought you'd ask me to the party." Dan grinned as he regarded his flatmate. "What made you go all one-man show? You don't normally."

Sage waved his hands around. "Celebration, old chum. I'm a free man. No more Alex. I can bang Brian again now." He squinted at Dan's closed bedroom door. "Is he here? Tell him to get his tight arse out here. I'm home and horny."

"There's no one here, just me and I'm sure as hell not doing you. Come on, mate, let's get you to bed." He led Sage into his bedroom, pulling back the covers and pushing him back on the bed.

Sage looked at him with raised eyebrows. "I thought you said you weren't doing me? This looks shuspishly"—he struggled with the word—"just like you intend giving me one, Dan." He chuckled drunkenly.

Dan shook his head in amusement. "Your backside's safe with me." He leaned down and took off Sage's trainers, lifting his legs onto the bed and pulling the covers over him. He sat down beside him, his eyes questioning. "What happened? Why aren't you with Alex anymore? I thought you two were solid."

"Chrysippus, Dan. Chrysippus. He said the word and I have to go. No arguments." His throat clogged up with pain.

Dan frowned, reaching out to clasp his shoulder. "I have no idea what you're talking about, buddy. We'll talk tomorrow. You need to sleep it off. I'll see you in the morning, Sage."

Sage awoke the next morning with a head that felt as if a train had been through it. He promptly raced to the bathroom, vomiting violently, spewing out the contents of his stomach as he retched uncontrollably. He stayed in there for about half an hour while his stomach settled. Finally he stood up, the room reeling, and went into the bathroom to shower. He stood in there for a while, letting the water wash over his body as he tried to dispel the feeling of emptiness inside him. The drink had taken it away for a short time but now it was back. He got dressed and went out to find Dan in the kitchen, sitting reading a newspaper.

Dan grinned as his friend came in. "Feeling all right there? Jesus, buddy, I've never seen you so plastered as you were last night."

Sage poured coffee from the cafetiere into a mug and sat down next to Dan. "I can't remember most of it. I don't even remember getting home." He drank the black coffee thirstily. "Thanks for getting me into bed."

"No problem. You've done the same for me before. Do you remember why you got drunk in the first place?"

Sage sighed heavily. "I remember. Alex gave me the boot. He used his safe word and that's it. We're history."

"Why did he do that? What the hell did you do?" Dan looked puzzled.

Sage stared broodily into his coffee cup. "He's scared. Confused. I was an arsehole. I stuffed it up and pushed him too hard. I can't even go and try and convince him otherwise. We made a promise that when one of us use the safe word that's it. I can't go back on that now so I need to live with it."

Dan shook his head. "Fuck that, Sage. You need to talk to him, reason with him. Don't give up, mate. That's not like you."

Sage shook his head helplessly. "I can't do this anymore, Dan. It's too bloody hard. Maybe I'm better off without Alex. This whole thing has made me into someone I barely recognise anymore. Some twat who gets jealous and angry and—" his voice choked up. "Someone who hurts people, Dan."

"Christ, Sage, of course you get jealous and angry!" Dan's voice was strident. "Alex has another lover, for God's sake. Maybe not in the truest sense of the word, but you're a fucking saint for getting this far." He stood up, walking around to his friend's side. Sage's hands clenched beside him in pain as Dan placed a hard hand on his shoulder.

"You, my friend, have done more than anyone could ever expect. I'll not have you thinking you've turned into some Dastardly Dan, Sage. That's just not true. Yes, you've become a bit of a moody git but then who wouldn't be, with what you're facing?"

Sage shook his head tiredly. "Dan, I know you mean well but this isn't Alex's fault either. It obviously just wasn't meant to be. He's a victim too. More so than you can ever imagine." He stood up. "I need to get to work. I need to keep my head busy, get back to normal. I'll see you later."

He reached out and pressed his friend's shoulder tightly. "Thanks for the support. I really appreciate it. I'll see you later."

That's a joke. Life getting back to normal. As normal as it can be without Alex. God, it hurts. Now we'll never know whether it could have got any better.

The next four weeks passed for Sage in a blur of hectic filming schedules and a whirlwind of promotional events. He'd taken everything Luke and Jenny could throw at him in an effort to forget Alex. Despite his promise not to push, Sage had given in to his need and called Alex a dozen times, leaving messages about getting together and talking. Dan had pushed him to reconnect to the extent that he'd felt like punching his friend in the face for his sheer optimism and goading.

None of it had made any difference. Alex hadn't returned one of his calls or texts. Sage had passed his flat on his bike a couple of times a day and even knocked on the door once to see if Alex was there. He either hadn't been in or hadn't answered the door—Sage suspected the latter. Finally he'd felt like some unwelcome stalker, deciding he'd better stop his incessant desire to communicate. He hadn't been with anyone since Alex had kicked him out, despite Dan's best efforts at getting the sexy Brian to visit him again. This time Sage had not availed himself of Bri's services and the man had left the apartment with a moody, displeased shake of his head. Sage met his own needs in the solitude of his bedroom, really not interested in being with anyone else just yet. His broken heart could take no more.

Alex had been true to his word, communicating with the film studio via conference call, email and video messaging. The few occasions he had come in person, he'd made sure Sage wasn't there, waiting until he was away at a modelling gig, an interview, a promotional dinner or lunch. The man seemed to have a direct line to Sage's social calendar and Sage thought wryly that its name might be Jenny. He didn't blame Jenny at all. Alex was her client too and there was still a TV series to be made. Personal issues needed to be put on hold.

Luke had been determined to raise Sage's profile before the launch of the *Double Exposure* series next year. Sage had generated enough publicity in the work he'd done to make this a fairly easy job. That meant travelling through Europe and the UK on a whirlwind, nonstop tour of events and opportunities. He and Luke were currently sitting in a pub in Munich, on yet another promotional tour, enjoying a large pint of beer each.

Luke looked at him quizzically. "How are you holding up with flying around the world attending events, premieres and awards ceremonies? Do you feel like a movie star yet?"

Sage sighed. "I'm enjoying it to some extent but I often find myself heaving a sigh of relief when I get back to my hotel room."

"How are you holding up really without Alex? I don't know the whole story behind your breakup, but it seemed a real shame." Luke's voice was full of concern for his young protégé.

"I haven't seen Alex in ages. I've seen him on your video conference calls but he hasn't really been to the studio whilst I'm there. He's definitely avoiding me." He'd even debated whether to send Alex a card on the twenty-fourth of October some time ago for his birthday but he'd decided against it.

He remembered seeing the face of Sarah Brose who'd smiled nastily when it was announced that Alex wasn't coming back full time. She'd glared at him in satisfaction. He was reminded now that he still hadn't talked to Luke about getting rid of her. To be honest, he didn't really care much now. The events of Dianne's letter bomb and Miles' hit-and-run had paled into insignificance as nothing further happened. The police were still investigating but nothing had surfaced. And his loss of Alex had just numbed him to anything. He was operating on autopilot, going through the motions without really thinking about anything. The ache in his chest had gotten no weaker.

Sage took a slurp of his beer, not sure whether he'd even get to the bottom of the enormous stein he was holding. "I'm concentrating on my career at the moment."

Luke smiled slyly. "Well, you are getting visible. Every time I see you you've got a different beautiful woman on your arm pleasing all the fans. I know those fashion shoots for the men's clothing chain were a hit. Women do love to see you in a suit."

Sage chuckled. "Don't remind me. The last time, one of them tried to grab the scarf I was wearing as a souvenir. I've never seen a fashion designer go so ballistic thinking one of her creations was being pinched. There was a lot of girl-fighting that night, I can tell you."

Luke looked at him with awe. "Crikey, you have the best life."

Sage laughed. "Jenny's also me got a whole load of voiceovers for various commercial radio ads when I get back. So she's really keeping me busy."

Later that night, alone in his hotel room, he sat, staring at the TV, watching an interview with Alex on national television with one of the entertainment channels. Alex looked a little thinner than usual but still as handsome as ever. His dark hair had grown longer, lying thick and straight on his head, making Sage wish he was with him to run his hands through it. Alex looked debonair and very sexy in his tight chinos and button-down cream shirt. Sage wondered with a pang in his chest whether he was still seeing Eric. The interviewer was asking him about the increased success of his books with the recent incidents. Alex was very professional, answering the questions and responding with a smile. It was only when the next question was asked that Sage saw him lose his composure.

"I know you were involved for a short time in a relationship with the delectable Christopher Sage. I'm not going to ask you anything about that, or why you're no longer together. I know you've both said it was an amicable breakup. But he is a man who's every gay man's fantasy. I'm sure our viewers would like to know what he's actually like as a person. Is he really as nice as seems to be on TV and in his interviews?"

Sage saw Alex swallow slightly, looking down at his hands. "He's a consummate professional and one of the nicest people I know. He's very charming and a complete gentleman. Yes, he's as nice as he appears to be."

The interviewer laughed, leaning forward, conveniently forgetting her earlier statement about not probing their breakup. "He was recently interviewed by *People* magazine and declined to answer any questions about the relationship the two of you had. He was decidedly cagey about it and at one time it even looked like he might deck the interviewer. Luckily they changed their tactic and went onto something less personal. He obviously feels less easy about it than you do. Can you perhaps tell us anything as to why he might feel that way?"

Sage held his breath. He remembered that interview vividly. The young reporter had definitely overstepped the boundaries of the agreed interview and he'd been lucky not to get punched on the nose on national television for his indiscretion. It had taken all Sage's self control to keep himself in check. He'd seen Jenny desperately trying to get the interviewer's attention, making throat-cutting gestures behind the scenes.

At the interviewer's blatant question, Alex looked like a rabbit caught in headlights. Sage watched his face intently, waiting for the reply.

"I'm afraid you'd have to ask him that and chance getting decked," Alex replied firmly with a tight smile. "I can't presume to know what he's thinking."

Sage watched the rest of the interview feeling numb. It appeared Alex definitely had *him* out of his system. He switched off the TV and lay back on the bed in the darkness.

Chapter 25

Alex watched Melanie as she sucked the end of her pen, reading something in her notes from their previous sessions since the Eric incident. When she looked up she frowned.

"So you've been seeing someone else since your last session with Eric. Somebody at Study in Scarlet?"

Alex swallowed. "No. I found another agency that specialises in it."

"How far do they take it with you?" Melanie's voice was soft.

A sense of shame washed over Alex. "Hard enough, the usual stuff. It's no worse than it was before, if that's what you mean. But it's not the same." He coloured. "I can't even orgasm when the sex act is going on."

Melanie regarded him with compassion. "Alex. This sounds to me as if it's become a habit as opposed to a real need. We've talked about this in therapy before. You're just going through the motions now. Being with Sage made you see there is another way of life."

"And losing him made me realise that there isn't," Alex spat back. "I still need this. I know I do."

Melanie sighed. "You're punishing yourself again. You think you can't be loved, ergo you need to prove someone needs you, even if it's just for the whipping and flogging."

Alex pressed his lips together mutinously. "I need to go. I just can't orgasm, it's no big deal."

Melanie regarded him thoughtfully. "Alex. Tell me more about why you used your safe word with Sage. We've talked about it since you split up but I still feel you're holding back."

Alex looked down at his hands. His lips tightened. "I needed to let him go."

"Why did you feel that?"

"He would have gotten hurt if I hadn't."

"Hurt by whom?"

Alex looked at the psychologist who was watching her intently. "Eric threatened to hurt him. And I knew that I would one day. Eric showed me that no matter how I try not to be, I'm still damaged."

"The same Eric that disregarded all the rules you put in place and used you for his own gratification? The man who assaulted and raped you?" Melanie's voice was hard.

"Eric didn't rape me." Alex's voice wavered. "He did what he normally did to me, what I normally pay him for." His body was cold and he trembled at the memory of that last vicious assault, the degradation and the pain he'd felt.

Melanie's voice was like steel as she leaned forward to look at Alex's face.

"But this time you didn't want that. You were in a relationship, with a man who loved you, whom you loved in return. You were trying to sort yourself out and you were getting better. And this man decided that wasn't enough for him, he needed more from you. So he bound you, gagged you—something you had requested he not do—did his S-and-M thing and then entered you from the front—again something you had been specifically against—and violated your body and your mind by not wearing a condom."

Alex heard from Melanie's tone and words that she wanted there to be no doubt that she didn't agree with Alex's assessment of the situation—his lie to himself.

Alex felt faint. He wondered why Melanie was being so harsh, so aggressive.

"Is that how it went down? Is that how you see it happened?" Melanie was unwavering.

Alex stared at the woman who stared back, deep into his eyes. "Alex. Is that right? Is that how you chose the evening to play out? Was it your choice to have it done that way to you? Or was it Eric's choice?"

Melanie's voice softened as she saw Alex's obvious distress. "I know you think I'm being cruel. But one thing I've always been with you is honest. I've worked with many people in your situation before and I have a lot of experience. I'm a specialist in this field— it's why Cully sent you to me. So I feel I can ask questions other people might not. And I'm asking you: Did you choose to have those things done to you or did you not?"

Her voice rose slightly. A wave of nausea washed over Alex and he jumped up, reaching the wastepaper bin and retching into it, whilst kneeling on the floor, his body shaking, head throbbing.

Melanie simply sat watching him. When Alex finally finished being sick, it was as if he'd been put through a mangle. His body and his ribs ached from the constant vomiting. The start of a red tide ebbed through his body, an anger that swelled up from the very depths of his being. He stood up slowly, turning to face Melanie slowly. Melanie still regarded him with an expression of expectation.

Alex's voice got louder as he spoke. "I didn't want it. I didn't want to be whipped, bitten and screwed like that. I wanted a basic need to be met and that's what I asked for. I was getting over all the violence, I was even over the sex because I had a really good man in my life who was good to me and gentle and provided me with everything I needed in that department. I was starting to feel like I had a future. Then I went to Eric. I was going to tell him that was the last session. He made me feel like I used to, dirty and used, like I was nothing. He hurt me so badly and I told myself it was me wanting him to do it subconsciously. But I hated every minute of it. It didn't feel right like it used to."

He broke off, his chest heaving. "I had to wait for more test results to prove I was still clean, that I wasn't infected with anything Eric gave me. That was so bloody hard, Melanie." His voice broke. "Thank God it was all right. I don't know what I would have done otherwise."

Melanie spoke quietly. "Alex, I was with you when you got the results. I know how difficult it was for you." Her voice softened. "I was so worried you might do something stupid."

Melanie didn't have to elaborate on this statement. Alex knew the therapist had been scared he'd try to self-harm or even worse, try and kill himself. This final betrayal by Eric may have well been the proverbial straw breaking the camel's back. But after what Alex had been through in his life, facing worse than what Eric had put him through, there was no way he'd ever give anyone the satisfaction of that action. Deep inside, he knew Melanie had known this too.

Melanie regarded him thoughtfully. "And now when you're at this new place? Does it feel right there either? How do you feel about it? Does it excite you, give you pleasure?"

Alex shook his head slowly. "No," he whispered brokenly.

Melanie spoke softly. "So you don't really want it any more. You were starting to cope without it and then someone came along and forced you to take it. Just like Rudy did. What does that make what Eric did to you, then? I need to hear you say it, I need you to be honest with yourself."

Alex stood there, white faced. He couldn't bring himself to verbalise what had happened with Eric any more than he'd been able to do it with Rudy.

Melanie sighed, closing her notebook. She stood up, coming over to Alex. She didn't touch him, simply stood close. Alex felt her warmth and smelt the fruity smell of whatever perfume she was wearing.

"Alex, look at me. Come on, look me in the eyes. Pretend I'm Sage. I know that's going to be hard but I need you to focus."

Alex raised his eyes slowly to meet Melanie's brown eyes. The woman gazed back at him, her look clear and unwavering.

"When you looked into Sage's eyes like this, what did you see, Alex? Describe it for me. Use any words you like, but tell me what he meant to you. What he made you feel."

"Safe. He made me feel safe. Loved and respected." Alex's whisper was hardly audible. Melanie nodded.

"What else, Alex? Think of your man. Tell me what he was like."

Alex thought back to the times he'd shared Sage's bed, snuggling up to his warm body in the aftermath of sex or just dozing on a lazy Sunday morning. He saw Sage's cheeky and surprised smile when Alex had pushed him down onto the hay in his barn, pulling off his clothes like a man possessed and mounting him like the stallion in the next stable. Alex heard Sage's deep chuckle echoing in his ears as they watched an episode of *The Big Bang Theory*, a show to which they'd both become addicted. In his mind's eye he saw Sage wrapping him into his strong embrace when Alex was troubled or in the grips of a nightmare, shushing him and saying that everything was going to be okay. And he remembered Sage's mouth, warm and loving on his skin as he kissed Alex's scars and told him that he loved him.

It was as if a dam broke inside him and all the feelings he'd been repressing since he'd sent Sage away welled up inside and threatened to overwhelm Alex like a tsunami rising up over a beach.

Alex gave a choked cry, shouting out a loud cry of sheer anger and pain. Melanie stepped away, out of reach, and stood silently watching as Alex turned, sweeping the objects on a nearby side table onto the floor with a vicious sweep of his hand. The green glass vase crashed to the floor, smashing into pieces. The magazines that had been so carefully organised fell to the ground like paper bricks. The tulips that had been in the vase lay strewn across the floor, petals of yellow and red having slowly floated to the ground like leaves of confetti. Alex's chest heaved, his breath coming in short, deep gasps as he looked at the destruction he'd caused. Melanie stood, still carefully watching, making no move to come to him.

Alex sank down to the floor, his arms wrapped around his knees, face buried in his chest as he sobbed. "Eric raped me. He abused me, Melanie. I thought I'd left it all behind and he went and dredged it all up again. Oh God, I lost Sage. I've lost him, Mel."

He was too busy sobbing to hear Melanie's sigh of relief as she came over to him, sitting down beside him, putting her arms around him and pulling him close. Alex leaned into her, his body heaving with sobs and the knowledge that he'd sent away the only man he'd ever really loved.

"Let it all out, sweetheart. You've been so brave to come this far. Now we can start the healing process all over again. We've done it together before. We'll do it this time as well. Maybe we can get Sage back for you, just in time for Christmas. You and me, Alex. We can do this."

Chapter 26

The end of the year was drawing close and Christmas was only a month away. Sage was in the midst of filming a particular gruelling action scene when he saw Alex come into the studio. His heart flipped and he missed a particularly crucial moment when he was supposed to raise his arm to defend himself. His co-star's hand smacked into his chin, knocking him to the ground in a blur of stars.

"Jesus, Sage! I'm sorry! Why the hell didn't you defend yourself, you silly blighter?"

Sage sat up rubbing his chin ruefully. "It's not your fault, Mike. I didn't follow the move through. I'll be fine. Just a little bit of wounded pride." He grinned but his eyes followed Alex as he disappeared into Luke's office.

What is he doing here? Perhaps he was coming back to work in the studio. The last six weeks had been sheer hell for Sage, knowing Alex wasn't far away but not seeing him.

He had butterflies in his chest, small, flying creatures that darted around, bumping the wall of his rib cage. He wandered over to Luke's office, his insatiable curiosity getting the better of him. The door was open and he looked into Luke's office, pretending to need a question answered, one which he'd already rehearsed in his head.

"Luke, sorry to disturb. Have you got the schedule yet for tomorrow's meeting with Manx Fashion?" He noticed Alex sitting on one side of the room and he acted surprised, hoping he was as good an acting talent as everyone said he was.

"Alex, hello. I didn't see you there. You're looking well."

Alex was looking well. He'd put on weight again and his face was rosier than normal.

He smiled slightly, looking nervous at seeing him. "Hello, Sage. It's good to see you. Although I see you often now on the TV. You're becoming quite the celebrity."

Sage nodded, turning back to Luke who was watching him with a faint grin. "So? Schedule. Times. You'll let me have them so I can organise my time tomorrow? I've got quite a bit on."

Luke nodded. "I'll give them to you. It's at eleven A.M. anyway. Put it in your Blackberry."

Sage nodded, turning to leave. He wanted to stay and talk but he wasn't sure what to do next without being too obvious.

Luke called out to him. "How's the chin? I saw Mike connect with it. Are you all right? I don't have to worry about any equity complaints for abuse of my actors?"

Sage chuckled. "I'm fine. I got distracted and didn't block him. It could have been worse."

Luke laughed. "I'm glad it's not bruised. You've got that black tie to-do tonight at the Dorchester. I understand you're taking Lance with you? He likes his men neat and tidy, does that one. He's a bit of a prig." Sage saw a glimmer of mischief in Luke's eyes.

Out of the corner of his eye, Sage saw Alex's eyes drop down to his hands at Luke's comment. "Lance likes me anyway, Luke. And not necessarily neat and tidy." He grinned and then saw the sudden play of emotion across Alex's face. He hadn't liked that last comment, Sage thought in surprise.

Luke waved him out. "Away with you, you randy sod."

Sage left the office, feeling very confused.

Why was Alex unhappy that he was going to a function with Lance?

In all truth he and Lance had nothing going, it was simply a plus-one arrangement the publicity company made to give him an escort at formal dinners. Sage sat in Alex's old office, a place he'd become partial to as it bought back good memories and kept Alex close. He was having a sandwich and a cup of coffee, keeping a beady eye on Luke's office and the activity inside. He watched Alex as he leaned over Luke, both of the sharing something on his desk, probably a script. Sage wondered again why he was here. At first he'd had the mounting hope that Alex was there to see him but that didn't seem to be the case. Sage was professional enough to leave his director and the writer alone to conduct their meeting but that didn't stop him wanting to rush in there and demand that Alex speak to him. He'd definitely try to see him before he left. There was a knock at the door. He looked up to see Dianne standing there.

"Sage, have you got a moment for Janine and I? There's some script changes we wanted to talk about for the shoot tomorrow."

Sage's eyes shot over to Luke's office. He and Alex still sat there.

He probably had a few minutes to spare, the way they were so deep in conversation.

Sage nodded. "Yes, of course. Let me bring my sandwich and we can talk while I eat."

But it was close to ten minutes later when he arrived back in the office after his discussion. He groaned in frustration. Luke's office was empty. Sage looked around the studio but saw neither of them. He searched the room, seeing no sign of Alex.

Shit. He must have left already. Just my crappy luck. That fucking meeting cost me my chance to speak to him.

Sage picked up his script, throwing his half-eaten sandwich into the bin in a temper. Darkness settled in his soul like a smog blanket. He was trying to concentrate on his lines when he heard a noise at the door.

Sage looked up and his heart leapt like a fish in a net. "Alex."

Alex moved into the room, his hands drawn tightly by his sides. He looked very nervous.

Sage stood up. "I thought you'd gone already. What are you doing in here? I looked for you; where were you?"

"I dashed out to get a new battery for my mobile. It's been giving me problems and there's that little mobile shop across the road." Alex moved into the room uncertainly.

Sage found his voice. "So how have you been? You're looking well."

Alex looked up at him. "I've been all right, Sage. I'm really glad I saw you though. I wanted to talk to you while I was here. It's the reason I came in today. If that's all right with you of course."

Sage nodded, Alex's words about his reason for coming in the last ones he'd heard. "We can stay in here and talk I suppose. At least it's private."

He perched on the end of the desk and waited. "What do you want to talk to me about?" Sage was determined to be polite and formal, not get his hopes up until he knew more about what he wanted.

Alex looked extremely uncomfortable. "I needed to see you to explain something. I'm going away on a book tour to the US tomorrow for the Christmas December Book Fest and I'm not sure how long I'll be there. It might be a little while."

Sage's stomach dropped at the implications of the words. He wondered how long 'long' was. It sounded like he might not be coming back. That must be what Alex wanted to tell him. His heart sank.

Alex swallowed. "The last time we met, when I gave you that piece of paper—I wasn't quite myself. I wanted to explain why I did that. I think I owe you an explanation after all."

Sage thought he had a right to be a little bloody-minded. "You don't need to explain anything. That's what we agreed, wasn't it?" Sage was uncompromising. "It was the whole idea of the safe word. No explanations. Just walk away. Your rules."

He'd been waiting for an explanation for weeks but now he had the chance, he felt difficult enough to challenge the fact. Bitterness welled in him again, unbidden but always just beneath the surface. Bitterness was something he wasn't used to, it was something Alex had created in him.

Alex nodded. "Yes, that's right. But can I please finish?"

Sage heard the steel in his voice. He gestured to Alex to continue.

Alex moved over to the window, looking out. His back was rigid. "I've been seeing Melanie a lot since that night. She's really been pushing me to confront my feelings. Whether it makes sense to you or not I wanted to tell you about the outcome. You deserve that much at least even if you never want to talk to me or see me again. I honestly wouldn't blame you."

Sage watched him carefully, not saying anything, not trusting himself to as hope flared in his beaten breast.

Alex turned to face him, his eyes bleak. "The night I went to see Eric at Study in Scarlet, I was ready to give it all up. I thought that would be the last session."

Sage's heart sank. His impatience and bloody-mindedness had been the catalyst for their breakup in his mind. Sage had never felt so wretched. He sat back in the office chair behind the desk, putting his feet up on the table as he watched Alex's face.

Alex took a shuddering breath. "Eric disobeyed all the instructions. He bound me, gagged me and then did what *he* wanted. Not what I wanted. He—"

He closed his eyes and Sage sat forward, seeing the pain on Alex's face. Sage's instinct was to reach forward and pull Alex to him but it was still far too early to do that. He still didn't trust Alex not to hurt him again.

"He hurt me badly that night." Alex's voice was flat. "He went berserk with his own selfish needs. He thought I'd betrayed our relationship. He just didn't stop. It was like Rudy all over again." His voice was husky. Sage winced at that image and at the pain in Alex's voice. But still he didn't move. He couldn't. If he did, he would never let Alex go. And he wasn't yet sure that was what Alex wanted.

"I was tied up and gagged and I couldn't do anything. Then"— his voice faltered but he looked at Sage defiantly—"Then Eric raped me. I know you might not think of it that way given what I did with him before but—"

Sage moved his feet off the desk violently and leaned forward, his face black. "Alex, no matter what you did before, if you didn't want sex, that's still rape." Sage wanted to put his hands around Eric's throat, choke the life out of him for making Alex wear the expression he did now. Shame, guilt and fear. "The man fucking raped you?" Sage wanted to beat Eric to a bloody pulp.

"Yes." It was a whisper and Sage stood up, striding over to Alex, pulling him close to his chest. He didn't care whether Alex wanted it or not. But from the soft sigh and the exhalation of warm breath he felt as Alex burrowed into his embrace, he thought he did. And Sage wanted it too, so very badly. There was silence then Sage pulled back to see Alex's face. "Tell me the rest," he murmured.

Alex closed his eyes, still nestled in Sage's arms. "I told myself it was all my fault, I must have caused it, but it wasn't. I didn't want the sex he wanted to give me, I was over that because"—he swallowed—"Because I had you and that was better than anything I'd ever had before. He threatened you, Sage. He said he'd get one of his gay S-and-M friends to show you a good time. I couldn't have anyone hurt you, Sage. The thought of someone doing that sort of thing to you just made me feel sick. I didn't want you to feel the same way I used to. Abused and violated. You're too good to go through that and you didn't deserve it, certainly not because of me. Too many bad things have happened to people you care about because of me and my bloody books."

At these words, Sage closed his eyes, a lump in his throat. He kissed the top of Alex's head. "Alex, why didn't you tell me all this then?" His voice was anguished.

Alex voice choked up and he looked up at Sage, his eyes bright. "I thought the best way to stop you getting hurt was to send you away because I knew you were upset with me already. I went back to that old place in my head. I thought I'd asked for what Eric did to me. I thought I deserved it. I knew I was just so fucked up and I couldn't drag you down with me. You deserve so much better than me, Sage."

Sage pulled Alex to him desperately, feeling the steady beat of his heart against his chest. "Jesus, Alex, babe. You might have been fucked up but you were *my* fuck-up." He felt the movement of Alex's mouth against his chest, as if he was smiling. "You could have told me all this instead of writing a stupid word on a piece of paper and breaking my bloody heart."

Alex's eyes drunk him in. "I'm so sorry, Sage. I had to tell you that before I went away. No matter what you think of me now."

Sage shook his head. "I never thought any less of you, Alex. I can't even begin to fathom what you've been through in your life. I can't pass judgement. And you are not responsible for what happened to Dianne or Miles. That's all the doing of the crazy person. You can't beat yourself up about that."

Alex's lips trembled and Sage groaned, taking them in a desperate kiss, his own mouth grinding against Alex's. Alex moaned and kissed him back, their tongues seeking each other's out as they pressed their bodies together. Sage knew then he was never going to let this man go ever again. Finally they drew apart but Sage didn't let Alex move too far away from him. His hands gripped Alex's waist tightly. Alex leaned his forehead against Sage's and gave a husky chuckle.

"You're going to give me bruises, Sage. I promise I'm not going anywhere."

Sage smiled against Alex's skin. "You're damn right about that. We've wasted too much bloody time already." He kissed Alex's cheek tenderly. "Not to mention the fact my sex life has been nonexistent since you went."

Alex leaned back, his face alight with mischief. "Dan didn't organise any pickups for you then? Brian didn't make a reappearance to avail himself of your marvellous oral skills?"

Sage's face flamed and Alex smiled. "No, Brian bloody well didn't. It wasn't for lack of trying though. Dan tried to get me to forget my woes by offering me every succulent morsel he could find." Sage grew serious. "But nothing seemed to assuage this need I had to have you back. You spoilt me for everyone else."

Alex kissed him gently. "Thank you for saying that."

Sage wanted to ask if it had been the same for Alex.

Had he been elsewhere to get what he needed?

But he didn't want to spoil the magic of this moment by asking that question now. He'd find out later when they were more settled. He thought they still had a lot more talking to do about the time they'd been apart. Instead, he reached for Alex again and pulled him over for another deep kiss.

Finally they pulled apart and Alex moved away to sit on the couch that they'd first made love on. He patted the spot at his side, and Sage sat down beside him.

"Melanie's been doing a lot of therapy with me, using hypnosis too. It's the first time she's been able to do that with me. She said I have you to thank for that as well, for opening me up to other possibilities in my life aside from punishing and debasing myself." He swallowed, a slight smile on his face. "She says you're a saint, that you have more compassion and patience than anyone she's ever heard of to do what you did for me."

Sage laughed. "I'm nobody's saint, Alex. You should know better than that after what we did together. Especially that bit in the stables." He grinned, feeling as if a huge weight had lifted from his soul.

Alex smiled, and Sage quailed at the look of apprehension on his face at his next question. "Do you still love me, despite all that's happened?"

Sage nodded. "Yes, I still love you, Alexander Montgomery," he whispered. "I never stopped, God help me."

Alex gave a deep shuddering sigh, reaching up to kiss Sage desperately. If Sage could have absorbed Alex, kept him close, worn him and protected him, he would have. Finally Alex let his mouth go. "I never stopped loving you either." Alex's warm fingers traced the contours of Sage's face.

"I think I can live with that. The fact you're here in my arms, that's all I need." Sage looked at Alex sympathetically. "I imagine you didn't go the police with this? Too many questions would be asked."

Alex nodded. "Not only that. Can you imagine me telling the police I was raped after what I've been doing with the man for the past two years? They would never have taken me seriously. And if it had got out, the publicity would have been too much to bear. I couldn't take that chance." He hesitated. "And I didn't want Eric to come after you because I'd reported him. He would hurt you, and that I couldn't bear. It was best just to forget what he did to me and not go back to Study in Scarlet."

"So where is Eric now?" Sage's voice was deceptively quiet but he knew even as he said the words that he wasn't averse to dishing out his own brand of justice to a man who violated the man he loved. He could think of a few choice things to do to the man himself involving floggers and whips.

"I suppose he's still there, at Study in Scarlet. Please don't go doing anything stupid. Stay away from him. It's over now and I'm here with you again. That's all that matters."

Sage nodded slightly but he wasn't entirely convinced he would do nothing about it.

"I don't like the thought of you going away to the US now I've just got you back. Exactly how long will you be away?"

"Just for about ten days. It was going to be longer but the plans changed."

Sage was relieved. "Is that it? From the way you were talking I thought it might be longer. I don't like the idea of not being able to see you for even an hour, let alone ten days." He frowned. "Alex, how are you coping now and how will you cope over there without your special sessions? Are you seeing anyone else now?" Sage dreaded the answer.

Alex shook his head as he smiled. "The therapy and hypnosis will help me through these next few weeks. I have to say it seems to be working."

Sage was quiet. What he was about to say was something he really didn't believe he would ever say to a man.

"Alex, I know you say you don't want to drag me into your world. But I've been doing a lot of research into the whole S–and–M thing since I met you and I have to say it's opened my eyes a lot. There are various levels, aren't there, and you seem to have been able to reduce yours to this flogging. If you had someone who loved you—"

Alex pulled away from him, shaking his head violently. Sage held onto him tightly.

"Alex, let me finish. Please." He swallowed. "This isn't easy for me either, believe me."

Alex raised his head, watching Sage's face.

"If you had someone who loved you doing what you needed, rather than that someone who didn't, would that help? Or is it the fact you have no emotional bond to the outside person that you need? It seems to me that some couples make this type of flogging part of their sex lives anyway so couldn't we just do the same? I know there's a big BDSM scene in the gay clubs, maybe, you know…"

His face flushed as he trailed off. He'd never offered this type of thing to anyone before and it didn't seem that bad from what he'd seen on the internet. He'd try it if it helped Alex and kept him out of another man's arms.

Who knows? I might like it.

Alex reached up, taking Sage's face in his hands, kissing his chin, his lips, his cheeks and then finally his eyes. Then Alex spoke huskily. "Thank you for that. I know it must have taken a lot for you to make that offer so I'm not going to refuse it right now. We both need to process this and talk about it more when I get back from Boston. You are the best thing ever to happen to me and I love you madly. I'm so sorry I missed your birthday last week too. I didn't think you'd appreciate a birthday card from me so I guess I'll have to think of something else to give you."

Sage kissed Alex again, weeks of pent-up frustration delivering itself in a kiss that seemed to go on forever. "What time do you leave tomorrow?" His voice was deep with desire.

"My flight's at three o'clock," Alex whispered against his mouth.

"Does that mean I can come back to your place after this bloody dinner tonight and we can talk more and I can make love to you before you leave me? I'm not sure I'll cope otherwise."

Alex chuckled. "I'd be very hurt if we didn't go back to my place and make sweet, passionate love. It will be a late birthday present. I'm all packed anyway so there's no need to get up too early." He punched Sage's arm hard and Sage winced.

"Just make sure you keep your hands off bloody sexy prissy Lance tonight," Alex growled.

Sage laughed, loving the fact Alex was jealous. "I'm not into Lance. I only said that to make you jealous. He's just my plus one tonight. And I'm going to make sure I get home to you as soon as humanly possible." He shifted uncomfortably. "Actually though, on second thought, I seem to have this little problem at the moment and I can't go out like this. Perhaps you should come back to my place first and help me get dressed?" He smiled lazily.

Alex looked at his watch. "Yes, I'll come back to your place and help you get 'dressed.' I can't have you going out in this state." He brushed Sage's groin with his hand, causing him to gasp. "And I seem to have the same problem."

Sage opened the office door and together they walked out into the studio. It was fairly empty with only a few people still milling around. In the corner, Sage could see the rigid figure of Sarah Brose as she watched them emerge from Alex's old office.

The old battleaxe probably thinks I've been diddling her 'precious.' Sage thought. *Well let's see how she likes the fact that*

I'm definitely going to be doing that in a short while and then again later.

He turned to Alex. "Shall we?" Alex took his arm and together they walked out into the cool of the evening.

Chapter 27

It was now over a week since Alex had left on his US tour and Sage was fed up. Although they texted and called each other every day and the phone sex was pretty hot, he was still missing him. Luckily he was coming home late tomorrow evening.

He sighed as he leaned back in the quiet of his bedroom at his apartment, regarding his laptop screen thoughtfully. He'd been doing a little bit of research on Eric "Man about Town" Rossi, as he liked to call himself. The man was arrogant enough to have his own website, for God's sake, but he didn't mention anything on there about his extracurricular activities raping defenceless men. Alex had told him about the lack of condom use and his re-taken test. Sage had wanted to punch something, preferably Eric's nose. From the looks of it, he was a fairly successful businessman in the beauty products industry. That explained all the men and women currently draped over him on his latest photo shoot to promote some form of male vitamin supplement. Eric was currently at some charity event in central London. Sage wondered whether he should mosey on down there and have a word with the bastard.

He thought guiltily that Alex's parting words on kissing him goodbye at Heathrow had been, "Sage, promise me you won't try and talk to Eric or go and see him." He had dutifully promised his boyfriend that without any intention of keeping his promise. Alex had also sent him a text a couple of nights ago reiterating his desire that he leave Eric alone. As much as Sage wanted to smash his fist into the man's gleaming white teeth, he didn't want to jeopardise anything he and Alex were trying to build back up or attract any publicity that may damage him. It was too risky and he was frustrated at having his hands tied like this. Sage was just too happy Alex was back with him and he wanted to make sure it lasted.

They'd also talked about Alex's excursions to the new place where he'd found some release. Sage hadn't liked it but at least he knew now that Alex had been careful while he was there and assured Sage he had nothing to worry about. The last thing either of them wanted was to go back to using condoms.

Sage sighed.

I suppose I'll just have to bloody do as I've been told even though it goes against every impulse I have to beat the bastard to a pulp.

He looked up as Dan knocked on his bedroom door. "Sage, are you decent?"

"Well, I don't know about decent, Dan, but I'm dressed at least." Sage grinned at his friend as he came in, dressed in his tux. "You look very flash. This investment dinner must be something special to get you in a monkey suit."

Dan grimaced. "Don't rub it in. I know you're used to wearing these things with your la-di-da film star lifestyle but for we plebs who aren't in show business it's a little uncomfortable." Dan smiled at Sage and continued. "I can't tell you how glad I am that you and Alex are back together. It means I don't have this Neanderthal grunting around the apartment looking as if he's going to club me any minute."

"I only do that to my men," Sage promised. "You were always safe on that score." The two smiled at each other in affection.

"I'm off now, the limo's here. Cherry's already waiting downstairs. I've left some cold pizza in the kitchen in case you wanted it. I'll see you when I get back. Stay out of mischief."

He disappeared out the bedroom. Sage turned back to his investigating. Out of curiosity he googled the latest news on the recent incidents involving Dianna and Miles. The story of the newspaper clippings sent to Alex had remained out of the public eye, something for which Sage was very grateful. DS Doyle had kept his word on that one. The press coverage had died down but there were still reporters out there who were convinced something much more nefarious was afoot and beat the drum any chance they got. The infamous "*Double Exposure* Affair" was getting more readers than it would usually deserve. He for one was glad that there had been no more events. Whilst he wasn't a great believer in coincidences, it looked like the *Double Exposure* Affair had been just that.

* * *

Sage picked Alex up at the airport the following evening. After making out on the airport concourse, amidst various camera flashes and grinning journalists, two hours later the couple were both seated side by side on the couch in Sage's cottage. Alex had poured them each a glass of wine. He watched Sage as he sipped his drink. He'd relished every minute of the ride home, knowing that soon he'd be home with Sage.

"You are the sexiest thing I've ever seen, you know that?" He reached out, caressing Sage's cheek. Sage held his breath as Alex traced his face. Alex ran his finger down the right side of Sage's chin, kissing it gently. He moved over onto Sage's lap, kneeling over him, facing him, seeing the rise and fall of Sage's chest as he breathed deeply, his eyes dark with desire. He took the wine glass out of Sage's hand and set it on the small table beside the couch. Alex was already rock hard. Sage was too, from the ridge beneath Alex's backside.

"You cut yourself shaving. You have a small scar here." Alex teased, kissing the corner of his mouth. Sage's breathing got deeper. Alex's heart was pounding so fast he thought it might leap from his chest. He licked his lips, becoming more aroused every time he touched Sage. Sage leaned back, closing his eyes as Alex started to unbutton his shirt. Alex leaned forward to push Sage's shirt off behind him and kiss his shoulder, trailing his tongue across the skin, up his neck to his throat.

"God, Alex, you're driving me crazy," Sage groaned, his left hand coming up to slip under Alex's shirt, touching the warm skin below. Alex shivered at the touch. Alex ran his hands gently over Sage's stomach. His hands slid over Sage's nipples before he reached down, sucking them into his mouth, one by one. Sage gasped in pleasure. Alex grew impatient, reaching up to lift his shirt over his head, dropping it on the floor.

Sage was heady with his need to possess Alex. The past week had brought home just how much he missed this man in his life. He watched in anticipation as his lover removed his shirt, baring his battle-worn body, scars and all, to Sage, with what seemed like no fear. To Sage, Alex's body was a tapestry of his life, showing the dark place he'd come from to where he was now. Which was here, with Sage, and he was damned if he'd let anyone take it away from him again. When Alex had finished devouring his nipples, he sat up, his lips wet with spit. Sage wanted to kiss them, taste his boyfriend in his mouth. He reached up, fingers touching Alex's sculptured chest, the ridges of his stomach and the fine hair beneath his fingers. His senses swum with Alex's heady scent of maleness and sex. Sage leaned forward, taking Alex's lips in a kiss that made Alex moan as he pressed himself closer to Sage. Alex's eager hands reached down, unzipping him then he reached in, grasping Sage gently.

Sage shifted as Alex softly caressed the tip of him with his thumb. "Jesus, I can't stand any more of this. It's been too long."

Alex moved off him, slipping out of his trousers, standing naked before him. He tugged at Sage's jeans and he lifted his backside as Alex pulled them down to the floor. Alex climbed back onto him, his mouth finding Sage's as he straddled him. His hands reached down beside him, picking up the lube, opening it and sliding the vanilla-scented stickiness up and down Sage's shaft. Sage moaned at the feel of Alex's hands on his cock. Alex reached behind him, going up slightly on his knees, and Sage saw his fingers disappear into his crease, Alex's eyes closing in pleasure at feeling his own fingers inside himself. By this time Sage was ready to blow. Anymore of this erotic foreplay and he'd be shooting his load and seeing stars.

"I need to be inside you," he growled, gripping Alex's hips and pulling him down. "That's enough bloody foreplay. I want you, Alex."

Alex took hold of the back of the couch, lowering himself onto Sage and both of them gasped as he took Sage inside him, murmuring words against his mouth as he rocked above him. "God, you feel so good. I missed your body so much, I missed *you*. I don't ever want to go away again."

Sage felt Alex's heat and smoothness as his hips met his own movements and he thought he'd rather be nowhere else other than inside this man, with his mouth on his and his hands causing havoc to his body. They kissed, rocking for what seemed like hours, and he felt the bristle on Alex's cheeks against his, heard his short, sharp breaths and the tiny mewls of pleasure he made. Sage knew he couldn't last much longer. Alex's cock was bobbing in front of him, looking ready to blow too, and Sage reached out a hand, using his guitar-strumming technique to touch his lover, playing his fingers up and down Alex's dick with mastery. Alex gasped as

Sage's hands then cupped his balls, groaning and looking down at him with unfocused eyes, his lips wet from kissing. Sage felt his own orgasm building.

"Alex, babe, I am so ready," Sage muttered. "Come with me, baby." His fingers continued their strumming of Alex's sticky, wet and heated erection and Alex cried out as he came, his muscles contracting around Sage's very aroused cock, causing Sage to press back against the couch as he climaxed inside Alex. Alex's come spattered their stomachs and Sage's chest and hand. The two men collapsed together, Alex pushing Sage against the back of the couch as he pressed against him. Sage's breathing was harsh.

They sat sandwiched together, catching their breath. Sage was having difficulties breathing with the man lying comfortably on his chest. He grinned. "Alex, I can't bloody breathe, honey. You might like to move that gorgeous body off my chest."

Alex sat up with alacrity, moving off him, releasing Sage's spent cock with a sucking sound as he moved to sit beside him. Sage saw his lover's grimace at the mess he was in; Sage's come inside him and his own semen all over his body.

Alex quirked an eyebrow at Sage. "This is the only part I don't like about sex without condoms. The mess." He laughed softly. "I think I can safely say that your strumming of my dick still feels great. That's a real party trick you have going there." He mocked a frown. "As long as you don't try it with anyone else."

Sage chuckled at the words. "No chance of that. That's reserved for you only."

There was silence and Sage thought Alex had gone to sleep. Then Alex spoke softly.

"Sage?"

"Hmm?" Sage murmured, his hand reaching out to caress Alex's hip.

"Seeing as how you're shuffling between here and my place, wouldn't it make sense to move in with me instead of staying at Dan's? It'll only be until you complete filming, so it's not permanent. There's somewhere to park your bike and you won't have to have two sets of toothbrushes and spare clothes everywhere and you'll be closer to the studio from there as well, so we'll have more time—" His speech was interrupted by Sage's mouth covering his.

Finally Sage released him and Alex looked dazed. "I thought you'd never ask," Sage murmured. "I thought it was a great idea too but I didn't want to presume. There's nowhere else I'd rather be than there with you, waking up to you every day, instead of feeling obliged to at least spend some time with Dan. And he always has a damn flat full of people."

"Oh, so you like the idea then?" The relief in Alex's voice was palpable and Sage grinned.

"I love the idea. We can make this work, lover boy." He kissed Alex tenderly. "Come on, let's get cleaned up and I'll take you out for something to eat and we can plan my moving in." He stood up and stretched, noticing Alex greedily eying his sticky stomach and groin.

"I love it when you look all wanton," Alex murmured. "Makes a man want to start all over again."

Sage reached down, cuffing his lover's head. "You're an insatiable git, you know that? Now get that sexy arse into the shower with me and let me take you out for a meal. I'm damned hungry after that all activity."

Alex seemed to need no coaxing into the shower with him and Sage laughed as he followed Alex's taut backside and long legs into the bathroom.

Time for round two…

Chapter 28

The next morning Sage went into the studio and the first person he saw was Sarah Brose, regarding him with sheer malevolence. Her small eyes glittered dangerously. Sage imagined she'd heard he was back with Alex. This time he was having none of her rude and confrontational attitude.

Time to make this right.

He pulled Luke aside. "Luke, can I have a word?"

Luke grinned. "Anything for my leading man, Sage. What's up?"

"I'm glad you said that, Luke. I'd like a late birthday present, seeing as how you still owe me one, or an early Christmas present—you can decide which. I want you to fire Sarah Brose."

Luke blinked, his face falling. "Fire her? Whatever for?"

"She's been extremely rude and insulting to me since she's been here. She looks at me like I'm some sort of bug that's stuck to her shoe and I really don't like her. She treats most people like shit and she's just a nasty piece of work."

Luke was aghast. "Christ, Sage, I can't just fire someone because you don't like them. There'd be hell to pay with the agencies and the employment people. She's been here a while now, even though she works part time."

"Then find a way to get rid of her." Sage was implacable. "Get those high-priced lawyers and HR people to find a loophole. I really want her out sooner than later."

Sage was well aware he was acting like a prima donna but he thought there had to be one time when he could play the "I'm the star" card and get people to do what he wanted.

Luke was looking at him open mouthed. "Well, I'll speak to them and see what I can do but I can't promise."

"Find a way. I don't want that woman around any longer than necessary. I'm sure you can do it." Sage moved away, leaving Luke staring after him in absolute consternation. Sage grinned at the havoc he'd wrought. It had felt quite good to be a demanding bitch.

I might make a habit of this. Next thing you know I'll be demanding Evian water, M&M's with the green ones picked out and a bottle of Cristal every night.

Alex grinned at him as he wandered over. "Are you happy now? You've been threatening to do that since forever."

Sage nodded. "That woman hates me. I have no idea why, but she gives me a really bad feeling."

Alex looked a little disturbed. "I know. I keep having this feeling that I've seen her before. It just flits into my head and I think I've got it then, wham. It disappears." He looked at the glowering visage of Sarah thoughtfully. "I can't say I'll be unhappy when she's gone. She makes me feel a little on edge too, even though she's always been very good to me." He frowned. "Too good, really, for a stranger."

Sage was about to speak when he was stopped by a sudden call from the far side of the studio.

"Sage! We're ready to go. Get your arse over here."

Sage sighed. Alex waved him off. "Go on. Strut your stuff, lover. You're in demand."

Back to the grindstone. There was no peace for the wicked.

* * *

Melanie van Pelt looked at the man sitting before her, marvelling at the transformation. She couldn't believe the figure she saw was the same Alexander Montgomery she'd met more than three years ago. This man looked healthy, relaxed and happy.

Alex saw her watching and smiled wryly. "I know. I still look in the mirror and don't believe it either. I never thought I could feel this way."

Melanie inclined her head. "The improvement is incredible, Alex. This man has definitely been your saving grace. He deserves a medal."

Alex grinned. "Sage would probably say the same thing. Poor bastard, he's had had lot to put up with but he still sticks with me."

"How are things at the film studio?" Melanie asked. "No more incidents, nothing else happened?"

Alex shook his head. "No, it's been quiet. But then it was a long time between the last ones too, so that doesn't mean much. There are no more big violent events in the book yet, and if the book is using the same timeline, we're safe for a while. Although I think this person gets off on seeing everyone relax and then they act again and cause chaos. The press attention has died off, but there's still a lot of buzz out there about *Double Exposure*. My books sales are still going through the roof."

"And the urges, Alex? How have they been?"

"I've been fine, actually. Having Sage back, having to focus on rebuilding our relationship—it's been good." He hesitated. "Before I went away on the last book tour, he told me he was prepared to help me if I had any 'special needs.' He actually offered to be the one who did things to me as long as they weren't too extreme. Sage said couples seem to do some of it in the bedroom as part of their sex life anyway and he could manage that. But it took a lot for him to offer it, I think."

"He thinks that by doing it himself he doesn't have to share you with another man." Melanie nodded. "What did you tell him?"

"I said we'd talk about it when I got back and we haven't really mentioned it again. I haven't really felt the old needs and urges."

Melanie looked pleased. "Good. So at least you know you have an out if you suddenly go all, 'Flog me please.'" She grinned. "Even though it's not quite the same as paying someone to do it and debauch you, which is mostly the attraction for people in your situation, it might be an alternative."

"I would only do that as a last resort." Alex was unwavering. "And at the moment, this man just being in my life is more than enough." He looked down at his hands. "He's moving in with me while he's still living in London. Dan is okay with it and Sage seems quite excited about it."

Melanie closed her book and tapped her pen against her knee. "That's wonderful news, Alex. I'm pleased you sorted that out."

Alex stood up. "I guess my time is up. I'll be back in two weeks for the next appointment. Thanks again for everything, Melanie."

He kissed her cheek softly and left the office.

* * *

Sage watched as Annie cantered around the field on the back of Tallulah Briar. It was a rare weekend off and he was going to make the most of it at his own home. He loved staying with Alex but he missed his horses and Miles. Mixed Jack stood in the opposite field, head over the fencing, watching his owner. Sage thought uncomfortably that it was as if he were being scrutinised by the huge beast and found distinctly lacking. He walked over to the black animal, reaching out a hand to stroke his nose. The horse whickered softly, lowering his head. Sage gave him a piece of apple from his pocket.

"There you go, you bad-tempered sod. You'll be next, don't worry. Just give Lulah her chance then I'm sure Annie will be over to fetch you. I'd love to ride you but my arse is a little tender at the moment."

He smiled, thinking of the reason his backside was sore. Alex had definitely enjoyed his bout of topping him. He didn't do it often but by God, when he did, he made the most of it.

Warm hands encircled his waist under his leather jacket and he smiled at the familiar scent behind him. Alex kissed the tip of his ear, his tongue warm. "God, your ears are cold, babe. We need to get you some earmuffs."

Sage snorted. "As if that's going to happen." He smiled as he leaned back into his boyfriend's protective arms. "Have you finished your conference call? How did the meeting go?"

"It went fine. The publisher is on board with the ideas for my new book so I suppose I'd better knuckle down and start writing soon. I'm giving you warning, though. When I write, I'm a monster. I hate being interrupted and I become all obsessive. So be prepared for the bastard from hell."

Sage chuckled. "I'm sure I'll manage. I'll just make sure to give you a good rogering now and then to keep you in your place." He cocked an eyebrow at Alex. "You will still need rogering, won't you? You won't go all solitary and withdraw all privileges because you're busy? Because I wouldn't like that at all."

Alex kissed the back of his head. "You need have no worries on that score. Are you coming in for lunch?"

Sage turned around, pulling Alex in for a kiss. They heard Annie's shout of disgust across the field and laughed. The couple walked back to the house, sitting down at the kitchen top to enjoy the lunch Alex had prepared. As Sage munched on his sandwich he switched on the TV to watch the news. Alex sighed.

Sage looked injured. "What? You know I like the news programmes."

"It's all just so much bad news, though. And they're still going on about *Double Exposure* and all the drama. I'm sick of seeing myself on the TV."

"You're just jealous because they have more pictures of me up there than they have of you." Sage ducked as Alex threw the dishcloth at him in mock exasperation.

They both heard the name "Eric Rossi" mentioned and froze. Sage quickly turned up the volume.

"Self-styled 'Man about Town' Eric Rossi was found dead in his Belgravia home this morning. Sources are saying it appears to be a suicide but at this stage, no specific details have been released. Police are investigating and we'll bring you updated news as we get it."

Sage was aware of Alex standing stricken beside him, grasping his arm with a clinch so tight it was cutting off his circulation.

"Alex, it's all right. Ow, could you just let go a little bit? That's better. Come here."

He stood up, pulling Alex into his arms, feeling his body trembling. He wasn't quite sure why his lover seemed so upset. This was the man who'd raped him the last time they'd met and Sage certainly wouldn't lose any sleep over the bastard, harsh though that might sound.

Alex finally spoke. "God, I can't believe Eric would kill himself. He just wasn't the type. He was too full of himself. I don't believe it."

Sage stared at him curiously. "Perhaps he had money worries or something else. Perhaps someone found out about his work at Scarlet and threatened to expose him. Who knows?"

Alex shook his head vigorously. "You didn't know Eric like I did." Sage winced at his poor choice of words. "If anyone had threatened to expose his S–and-M activities, he'd have told them to do it. He was proud of it. It might not have been something he broadcast publicly out of choice, but if it got out, it's not something he would have killed himself over. He would have milked it."

Sage shrugged. "Well, I for one can't say I really care. Not after what he did to you."

Alex was silent. Sage sighed. "It's happened and there's nothing anyone can do about it. If it does look suspicious the police will find out."

His boyfriend nodded but still didn't look convinced. "Can you keep the TV on please? Don't turn it off. I'd like to see what they have to say about it later."

They finished their lunch in silence, each preoccupied with his own thoughts. Sage knew Alex had known the man a long time, intimately, so it was only natural to have some level of feeling for the man. Perhaps he'd been a bit harsh. He took Alex's hands in his. They were cold.

"I'm sorry about my comment earlier. It was a bit crass. As much as I dislike the man, he was still someone you knew." He swallowed. "Someone you knew fairly well. I should have respected that."

Alex reached up, cupping his face tenderly. "You muppet, I'm upset he's dead because yes, I knew him and believe it or not, there was a better side to him in the beginning." His voice hardened. "But after what he did to me last time, I can't care about him too much. I'm more worried he left something behind the police might find, some details about what he did in his spare time and that could lead back to me. That means you could be exposed. And that scares me to death."

This was something Sage hadn't considered. He sighed. "We'll deal with it like we always do. Let's not anticipate the worst before there is one."

The next day the newspapers were full of Eric's suicide. He'd been found in his marble bathtub, his wrists cut, the razor he'd used to do it lying by the side of the bath. There'd been no suicide note from what the newspapers were reporting. The investigation with the police was "ongoing."

Alex seemed to breathe easier every day that went by without anything leading back to Eric's obsession, but Sage could see he was still tense. He tried to cheer him up by making plans for Christmas Day just over a week away. They planned on having a quiet Christmas celebration at Sage's house with Miles and Lanie, Annie and her family, Dan and Cully if he could make it. Alex had never had a family Christmas before and Sage was determined to make it special.

Chapter 29

It was seven p.m. and DS Doyle sat in his office at Chelmsford Police Station with a cup of tea and a muffin, sighing contentedly. He'd finally closed the case of the teenage burglar terrorising the neighbourhood and he thought he deserved a treat after finishing signing off the reports his constables had prepared. He took a great bite out of his muffin and a slurp of tea. His eyes lit on a folder on his desk. *Midsomer Mayhem*. He frowned. This was the one case that was eluding him, the one he hadn't managed to close yet. Idly, he opened the folder and flipped through the contents.

This had been a real rum case. Actors and authors, best-selling books, villains abounding, cults, some psycho making life imitate art…it sounded like a novel all on its bloody own!

He grinned as he took another bite of his muffin.

Perhaps he should suggest that to Alex. It'd be another best seller, he was sure.

He browsed through the newspaper clippings, casting his eyes over them again, and a freshly cut clipping caught his eye. He stopped chewing, swallowed and picked it up to examine it more closely. It was an article on the Prophet of Bohemia, Rudy Kohler. The article covered his childhood and his subsequent rise to power in one of the most nihilistic cults Reginald Doyle had ever been exposed to. There was a picture of a smiling Rudy with his arm around a short, dark-haired woman. The caption read "Rudy Kohler and his mother Sarah at the recent BNP Gathering in London."

The name Sarah tickled his curiosity. Reg peered at the picture as a chill of recognition dribbled down his spine. The woman in the picture might be years younger and a lot less weighty with a different hair colour, but he'd been trained to see the people beneath the mask, the characteristics that made people look the way they did. The jawline was the same, the same wide-spaced eyes and the slightly flattened nose. This was Sarah Brose.

He opened his drawer, taking out his magnifying glass to look at the picture more closely. He nodded in satisfaction. It was definitely her. A small piece of the puzzle fell into place. There *was* a connection between Alexander Montgomery and this woman, one that definitely led back to the past. He needed to warn the couple about this development and go out to interview the woman again. He picked up his phone.

* * *

Sage was currently sitting at a charity function next to a blonde woman with eye-catching cleavage and a predatory look that said she wanted to devour him, very slowly, using her teeth. More than once her knee had touched his under the table. It was just a matter of time before her hands starting going places he really didn't want them to go. He wondered just how polite he needed to be in staying before he could leave. He also wondered in exasperation whether he should tell the woman next to him that he didn't swing her way. He was about to take the plunge when his mobile rang. He felt relieved and excused himself politely. The blonde woman looked very disappointed.

"Christopher Sage."

"It's Reg Doyle, Sage."

"Hello, Reg. I really need to thank you. You've just saved my bacon from a fate worse than death."

"Good to hear it, but we have another problem. I was looking over the case file for all these bizarre happenings and I realised who Sarah Brose is. She's Rudy Kohler's mother. There's a picture of her clear as day in a fresh newspaper clipping my team found."

Sage grew cold. "Are you sure? Christ, I don't believe it. I knew I didn't like that woman. Do you think she's the one who's been doing all these things? God, Alex is by himself at the studio. I think Sarah is there too; it was to be her last night on the job tonight. I'm going to swing by there now and check Alex is all right."

"You should wait until I can get a unit there. I'll call the Met and get them to dispatch one. I'm coming down too. I want to be on this one."

"I'd bloody well hope you'll pick the bitch up and lock her away. If she's this psycho's mother, the apple didn't fall very far from the tree. Alex could be in danger so I need to get over there. I'll call you from the studio when I get there."

He ignored Reg Doyle's protests to wait for backup and disconnected the call. He made his way out of the Dorchester Hotel toward the taxi rank.

Chapter 30

Alex sat in his office in the studio working on his new novel. He'd found he got a lot of writing done late at night in the office when everyone had gone home. He liked the discipline of sitting at his desk with his laptop and no distractions—which meant Sage.

He grinned. When Alex tried to write anywhere else other than the office, Sage was extremely distracting as he wandered around in low-slung sweats with his chest bare. It was definitely not conducive to Alex's creative mental health. Sage was at a promotional charity dinner somewhere in the city. The studio was quiet but he'd promised Sage that he'd lock all the doors and make sure he was safe inside. He thought vaguely that Sarah was still in the building too somewhere, doing her last bit of cleaning until she left for the night. Alex was engrossed in the contents of his laptop when he heard a noise at the inner door.

Startled, he looked up into the smiling face of Sarah Brose. "Sarah." Alex smiled, closing the laptop. "Isn't it a bit late to be still here, cleaning?"

The woman moved into the office. "I forgot to clean something in the restroom. I came back to do it and saw the light on. I wanted to see you were all right." She stared at Alex intensely.

Alex felt a little uncomfortable. "You should be getting home. You're going above and beyond the call of duty being here at this time."

The woman's stare was making him feel very uneasy. He felt the slow trickle of cold sliding down his spine. Alex reached for his mobile sitting on top of the desk, drawing it toward him slowly.

He had no idea why he felt so threatened—*and by an older woman for God's sake.* "I'm quite busy and I need to get back to work. Is there anything else I can help you with?"

Sarah moved over to the window and stood looking out. "I've tried to look after you, Alexander. He would have wanted me to. I recognised you in that TV talk show you did when you published your books. I knew I had to take care of you for him. He always wanted you to be the best you could be."

Alex felt himself falling into a dark hole at these words. His head spun and he gripped the tabletop tightly. He'd heard words like those before—from Rudy. Rudy had said them when he was beating Alex, when he was ramming into him, when he'd taken his sabre and cut four deep lines into his back. He'd repeated it over and over again, his own personal mantra.

Sarah carried on, her voice sounding far away. "I tried to help you. I wanted you to be famous, to have your books made into best sellers so you'd be wealthy. We're going to need money, you and I. So I orchestrated a few incidents to get you some publicity." She turned to Alex, with a joyful expression. "And it worked, didn't it! Look at you now. Your book sales are going crazy. You're going to be a very wealthy man. Now you can share it with me. Rudy would have wanted that too."

She came over, standing next to Alex, putting a large, meaty hand on his shoulder. "I forgave you when you yielded to temptation with that man. He shouldn't have taken advantage of you that way and soiled you. You belong to Rudy."

She turned to Alex, her face thunderous. "I heard the two of you rutting away in here like a couple of animals. I heard everything." She waved at the corner of the room where the air-conditioning unit was fastened to the wall. "I had a video camera installed in there. I saw you both, fucking each other. He should have known better. You— you're used to men telling you what to do so I couldn't blame you. It's in your nature. I sent you those newspaper clippings so you'd remember your place—remember who you really are."

Horrified at the thought he and Sage had been filmed making love, Alex finally found his voice. When he spoke his voice was husky. "Who *are* you? What's your connection with Rudy?" He stood up, his hands flattened on the desk to support himself.

Sarah frowned, looking at him as if he were simple. "I'm his mother. Isn't it obvious?" Alex's world swum around him as if was falling into a plughole, spiralling deeper down into craziness.

It took a while for Alex to connect the woman in front of him—sixty-ish, grey haired and overweight—with the one he'd seen on a few occasions at the compound. The few times he'd seen Rudy's mother there, she'd been black haired and thinner. She'd also worn large black glasses, looking like a school mistress. He'd been close to her twice, both times introduced as Rudy's "pet." She'd had an inch-long scar on her jaw from what Rudy had called a "misunderstanding." Up close now he could see the scar was still there. But now he knew who she was, he could see the resemblance to the woman he'd fleetingly met.

She looked at Alex in pity. "You only saw me a couple of times when I came to visit. He liked to keep you to himself, he loved you so much. He didn't want me there too often; he was worried that I might be followed and the police would make trouble for him." She smiled. "I can see you're confused. But this is the start of something, Alexander. You and me. We're going to go away together and honour Rudy's memory and rekindle Bohemia again. Think of it! We can do so much with your money. We can start a new faith, a new beginning."

She scowled. "That bastard you were screwing got rid of me. So I won't be able to keep an eye on you anymore. So we need to leave together tonight. I came to fetch you."

"I'm not going anyway with you. You're insane." Alex stared at the woman.

Sarah stepped closer to Alex. "That actor corrupted you, made you think you're something you're not." She laughed and her face twisted in glee. "But he'll get what's coming to him."

"What do you mean?" Bile welled up in Alex's throat at the thought something might happen to Sage.

"I've got a couple of people who'll take care of him once we're gone. Show him a good time." Her face was sadistic, filled with sheer glee.

At her words, Alex caught his breath, his fear for Sage overwhelming.

"You should thank me, Alex. I heard about your trouble with that man, that Eric Rossi, so I took care of him for you. I couldn't have him think he could defile you like that and get away with it. I had to make an example of him for the members. So they could see I had the power to give them instructions. They rather enjoyed that little assignment." She smiled flatly.

"You killed Eric?" Alex's voice was disbelieving. Here was yet another person who'd suffered because of him. Despite his final hatred of the man, he hadn't deserved that ending. Acid rose in his mouth and he swallowed it back down, feeling it scorch his throat.

Sarah regarded him with a little contempt and sighed heavily. "The man was a pig and deserved everything he got. There are still plenty of Bohemia believers out there ready to do as I ask, you know. I *am* Rudy's mother after all. I needed to start growing my influence, making them aware of who I am. They loved my plan to generate money out of your books. They said it was sheer genius."

Alex wiped a cold hand over his mouth. "*That* man was a pig? What about your son, your precious Rudy? Didn't what he did to me make him a pig too?"

For a large woman, Sarah moved swiftly. She crossed the room, slapping Alex hard across the face. Alex's head whipped to one side and Sarah hit him again. Alex tasted blood. He wanted to smack her back but he didn't want to hit a woman, no matter how bitter and twisted she was.

"Don't you dare say that about my son!" Sarah hissed venomously. "Rudy was a true warrior, a man among men. He could do what he wanted and not be accountable. Men should have been glad to have been chosen by him. He really had feelings for you. You were his favourite."

Alex's temper flared and he curled his hands as he faced the mad woman. "I used to think that too. But now I know Rudy was a mad animal, sadistic, cruel and manipulative. He deserved to be put down like a dog after what he did to me and the others."

"Alex."

Alex heard his name said from the door and turned to see Sage standing there, his face white. Sage looked at Sarah standing in the room and his jaw clenched. Alex could see the pulse in his throat throbbing. "Alex, come over here. Come to me."

Sage moved forward into the room, reaching a hand out to him. Alex moved toward him in relief. Sarah snarled, her hand reaching into her jacket pocket, pulling out a pistol. She held it up, brandishing it at Sage.

"Alex. Move one step more toward that scum and I'll shoot him in the head. I'm a very good shot, I promise you."

Alex stopped moving, staring in fear at the gun pointed at Sage's head.

Sage's face was unwavering. "Don't listen to her. She won't shoot me. Just move out of the office. The police are on their way and they won't be too long; then they can take this psychopathic bitch to the loony bin where she belongs."

"I can't take that chance." Alex's voice was a whisper. "I'm not losing you."

"Alex, please. Just get out of here. I'll be fine." Sage's voice was soft and Alex saw his eyes trying to steady him, give him confidence.

Alex shook his head. "I'm not going anywhere without you."

Sarah laughed, a grating sound that echoed through the stillness of the room. "How touching. Alex doesn't want to give up his little man toy. I'm disappointed. But you're still coming with me. If you don't come with me now, I will shoot him."

Alex looked at Sage who was shaking his head violently. "Stay away from him, you crazy bitch," Sage spat at the older woman, watching helplessly as Alex moved slowly toward her. Alex needed to create a distraction to get the gun away from Sage's head and he knew exactly how to do that. By telling Sarah something no one other than Cully knew.

"Did they ever tell you how Rudy died, Sarah?" Alex said quietly.

Sarah glared at Alex. "He was killed by a bullet fired from one of the guns used by that extraction team. He died a hero, a martyr."

Alex shook his head, a faint smile on his face. "He didn't die from a gunshot wound. That was just what was reported in the newspapers."

Sarah looked at him in suspicion. "That's a lie. Why would you say that?"

"He was dead when the extraction team arrived, Sarah. I know that because I was the one who killed him."

"Alex," Sage whispered, his voice agonised. "What are you doing? Just come here, please, honey." Alex ignored him. He had to keep Sage safe.

Sarah lowered the gun slightly, unaware she was doing so as she gazed at Alex in horror. "What do you mean, you killed him? How could you, someone as pathetic as you, do that?"

"We were in the basement. He'd just raped me for the second time and he was feeling very mellow. But we weren't alone. There was a little boy with us. Rudy planned on doing the same to him when he finished with me. He was six years old, just a child, and he was scared. He saw things in that basement no adult should ever see, let alone a child. I tried to tell him everything would be all right but my mouth was so swollen from where Rudy had beaten me I could hardly talk."

Sarah was staring at Alex, mesmerised. Sage was doing the same, but Alex could see the pain in his eyes at hearing of Alex's ordeal.

"I managed to convince him it would be nice if we had a threesome. He was quite intrigued with that idea. So he cut me loose. He wanted me to start on the boy while he watched." His voice tightened in disgust. "He actually wanted me to fuck a six-year-old child." Alex heard Sage's gasp of breath and didn't dare look at him. The shame, guilt and despair Alex felt back in that room came flooding back to assault his body. "Rudy had his trousers off and he was touching himself, he was so turned on by the whole thing. His trousers were on the floor and his hunting knife was tied onto his belt. I moved the boy in between him and his trousers, so he couldn't see me. Then I bent down as if I was going to undress him but I picked up Rudy's knife instead."

Alex voice was hypnotic as he told his terrible story. He felt outside himself, as if it were someone else recounting it. Sarah's eyes grew wider and Alex felt a sense of satisfaction that she was starting to realise where the story was going. She was slowly lowering the gun. Out of the corner of his eyes, Alex saw Sage move into the room, trying to get closer to Sarah. Sarah was so focused on Alex that she didn't notice.

"He was so busy concentrating on getting his rocks off that when I stabbed him in the chest the first time, he didn't believe it. He looked at me, surprised and I pushed the kid out of the way, told him to go to the corner of the room and close his eyes. I wasn't going to let him make him into a new version of me. I just couldn't let that happen no matter what I had to do. I had to protect him. For the first time, I had to fight back at Rudy to save the child."

Alex laughed, a grating laugh with no amusement, full of bitterness. "He stopped holding onto that pathetic thing he called a penis and reached out a hand to me. He didn't believe I was doing it and truthfully, neither could I. I stabbed him again and again and again until I couldn't see for the blood and Cully pulled me away and told me it was all right, Rudy was dead and he wasn't going to hurt me again."

Alex's voice was flat with no emotion in his eyes. "He died begging me to stop, Sarah. Your warrior of a son was nothing more than a perverted, cowardly fucking demon and I'm glad I killed him."

Sarah cried out in sheer fury, raising the gun toward Alex just as Sage launched himself at her from the side, knocking the gun out of her hands. It went flying over the desk, landing on the other side.

He saw Sarah lash out at Sage, her meaty fist connecting with his chin, causing him to reel back. Sage moved forward again toward her. Alex could see his hesitancy at hitting a woman. Instead Sage glanced at the gun on the floor then his eyes flicked back to Alex.

Alex understood. Sage would keep her busy while he went for the gun. That was fine with him. He wanted the gun to stop this bitch once and for all. Put a bullet in her brain, destroy her like he had her son. He moved swiftly, heading round the desk to find the gun.

"I should have you killed a long time ago," Sarah spat at Sage. "I was waiting to take him away from you first so you'd see who owned him. Make you suffer, not having him. But now at least I can do it myself."

Sage launched himself at her again, punching her in the jaw. She cried out in pain and fell back against the table. Her hands clawed Sage's face, leaving bloody scratches as he held his hands up to defend himself.

"Let it go," he growled as he backed away. "For God's sake, woman, can't you see this is over?"

Sarah snarled, ready to make a fresh assault against him.

Alex had found the weapon. He picked it up in and stood to face Sarah.

"Stop it." His voice was quiet. "Stop now or I'll bloody shoot you, you bitch. And nobody fucking *owns* me. Not anymore." He stood, steady hands pointing the gun he'd retrieved squarely at Sarah. "Stay back, Sage."

Sarah smiled. "You have no idea how to fire a gun, you pathetic man."

Her voice faltered as Alex pointed the loaded weapon at the older woman, and clicked back the safety catch confidently. "You had the safety on, Sarah. And your son taught me how to shoot one of these. In case we ever got attacked by the police, he wanted everyone to know how to use a gun. Now move farther away from Sage."

"Make me, you little bastard." Sarah's eyes gleamed wildly.

Alex pointed the gun at Sarah, his finger poised on the trigger. "I am going to put a fucking bullet in your head, see it explode like a melon. Kill you just like I did your son. Sage, you might like to close your eyes so you don't get the bitch's blood in them."

"Alex, don't go crazy, baby." Sage watched him and Alex's hands trembled with emotion.

"She needs to die, Sage. For both of us to be safe." Alex said tremulously. The only other time he felt an overwhelming urge to wipe a human being off the face of the earth was when he'd killed Rudy. He'd forgotten how sick the feeling had made him.

Sage shook his head. "No, Alex. This isn't you, you're no murderer. Just hold the gun on her—" His eyes widened at something behind Alex, who felt the presence of someone else in the room.

"Mr. Montgomery? Put the gun down, son, and we'll take it from here."

The quiet tone of Reg Doyle bought Alex to his senses. He blinked, looking over at the door where the bulky and comforting frame of the detective stood, weapon pointed at Sarah. Alex's chest heaved, his eyes fierce as he gripped the gun tighter, shaking his head. DS Doyle moved calmly forward, holding eye contact with Sarah, reaching out a hand and slowly easing the pistol from Alex's grasp with his free hand.

Alex let him take the gun, his body relaxing. At that moment a police constable hurried into the room and Reg motioned to him as he pocketed the pistol he'd taken from Alex. The detective kept his weapon trained on the woman who was staring at them with hate-filled eyes.

"Cuff that bloody woman and get her out of my sight," he growled. The constable cuffed Sarah with difficulty as she struggled and screamed invective, fighting back. Sage moved swiftly over to Alex, pulling his body into his arms, holding him as if he'd never let go.

"It's all right, baby. It's over."

Alex buried his face in Sage's neck. "She could have shot you, Sage. I don't know what I'd bloody do if I lost you." His body was still filled with dread.

"It didn't happen." Sage stroked Alex's hair, soft, gentle strokes that soothed him. "We're both safe." He looked at Reg Doyle. "Thanks for turning up when you did. I was scared Alex was going to do something stupid."

Reg looked at them both. "I want you to go with this constable." Another uniformed officer had appeared in the doorway. "We'll mop up here, but I'll need statements from you both later."

Alex nodded, taking Sage's hand as they followed the policeman and then he stopped. He looked at Reg. "Sarah said there was a video camera in that air-conditioning unit. It may have been filming. Could you take care of it for me, you personally? I'm ready to answer for whatever I've done but I'd rather you'd see it first. I don't know how much you heard in here but I basically admitted to killing a man."

Sage hissed a breath and started to say something but Alex laid a hand across his lips.

"Hush," he murmured. "Whatever happens, happens. I'm prepared for it, Sage." He pulled Sage out of the room with him.

* * *

Reg watched as Alex left then made his way quietly to the wall. He put on his crime-scene gloves, removing the front panel of the unit. He saw the video camera, its red eye winking at him. It had definitely been filming. He switched it off, using his gloves and removed the video tape, sliding it into his coat pocket.

Alex sat in the police waiting room, exhausted as he waited for Sage to complete his statement. He'd given his already, and all he wanted to do was get home, snuggle up to Sage and never let him go. He heard his name being called and looked up to see Miles rushing toward him. The man's face was panicked, his breathing laboured and Alex worried he was going to have a heart attack.

"Alex? What the hell happened?" Miles panted out the words as his hands grabbed Alex's.

"He's in with the policemen. Come on, Miles. Sit down before you do yourself an injury."

Miles sat on the chair trying to catch his breath. He looked up at Alex. "Jesus, what happened? I got your call and dashed over here, what the hell's happened to you both now?"

Alex ran through the evening's events as best he could, leaving out the bit about the conversation with Sarah about killing Rudy. "They've got her in custody."

Alex heard his name again and looked around to see the figure of Cully standing behind him. Cully said nothing, just pulled Alex into his broad chest, wrapping huge arms around him. The hug seemed to go on for minutes and finally Cully released Alex.

"You all right?" he asked quietly.

Alex nodded. "I'm fine. It's been a bit of a nightmare though." His voice caught and he clenched his hands in frustration. Cully nodded, making Alex sit down on the chair next to him between him and Miles. "You got her, Alex," Cully said gently. "It's over."

Alex shook his head. "No, it's not." He stared down at his hands as he twisted them around. "I told Sarah I killed Rudy, Cully. I had to distract her. So I told her."

Cully's face went still. "Do the police know?"

Alex nodded. "They will. She had a video recorder installed in my office. I think it was still taping when we were in there. The police have the tape."

Cully closed his eyes in dread.

Miles leaned forward, confused. "You killed someone, Alex?"

"A long time ago, a really bad man." Cully frowned at him. "It doesn't matter now. Maybe later one of these two will tell you all about it."

They all looked up as Sage came out of the far office. He was pale but composed. Alex stood up and they embraced, then Sage gave Miles a big hug.

"They said we could go home," Sage said tiredly. "If they have any more questions they'll give us a call in the morning. Reg said he'd keep the wolves at bay that long." He smiled wanly. "He's a good man and he seems fond of me for some reason."

Alex smiled. "Who wouldn't be?" He kissed Sage fiercely. "Now let's get out of here. Tomorrow can wait. Tonight I just want to hold you and think of nothing else."

The three of them left together.

Chapter 31

The news that the *Double Exposure* Affair still wasn't quite over was front-page news the following morning and for the next few days. How it got out no one knew. It was all there: Sarah's arrest, the fact that she was the mother of a cult leader and had tried to kill a well-known actor and writer and most of all, the fact that Alexander Montgomery was actually Evan Harding, rescued from a cult when he was just eighteen years old. Jenny Miles once again did her best to contain any damage. The studio had hired a security service to keep the journalists from the building, but the streets outside were awash with cameramen and reporters.

Alex and Sage sat white faced at Alex's apartment watching the news, seeing the old clippings of Alex's past flash up on screen. Cully had appeared at the house that morning the minute the news stories broke, and he sat with them now, his face grim as Alex's old life was sensationally recycled.

Tense with anxiety, they watched for any news of Rudy's death at Alex's hands but there was nothing. DS Doyle appeared in a pre-recorded interview on the TV screen to give his comments on the recent affair. His ruddy face was calm, his voice matter of fact.

"The police investigation is ongoing. However, I can confirm that we have arrested a woman in connection with the assault on Mr. Christopher Sage and Mr. Alexander Montgomery late last night. The woman, Sarah Brose, is in police custody. Mrs. Brose has admitted to creating the incidents known in the press as the *Double Exposure* Affair. We have found other evidence linking Mrs. Brose to the attack on the actress Dianne Cunningham as well as with the death of Mr. Eric Rossi. We urge anyone with any information to come forward. We believe all these incidents are connected and were indeed events controlled by Mrs. Brose."

He hesitated and looked around.

"We realise that this is a sensational case and one that the public will be very interested in. However, with the connection to the rescue of Evan Harding, now identified as being the well-known author, Mr. Alexander Montgomery, we would ask both the press and the public to please respect both Mr. Sage and Mr. Montgomery's privacy and let them get through this ordeal. Thank you."

Alex looked at Sage then at Cully. "He didn't mention the videotape or the bit about me killing Rudy. If they have the tape they must know that."

"He's a good man, that DS," said Cully, frowning. "He at least tried to ask people to leave you and Sage alone. It's going to get very messy out there, Alex. Everyone will want a piece of you."

Alex nodded. "I know. They can ask me their questions but I won't answer them. In time this will all die down if we keep playing the 'No comment' card. They surely have to get tired and move onto something else. I'm just worried about the Eric Rossi thing. I don't want people to know about my past with Study in Scarlet. I don't really care on my part, but I don't want Sage tainted with it. Imagine if they find out he was seeing a man who liked to be debased and abused. They'll paint Sage as some kind of pervert. I don't see how this one can possibly turn out well if that happens."

Sage reached over, placing a hand on his, wanting to reassure his lover. "Alex, whatever happens, we manage it. We can't run scared on this one."

Alex's voice shook. "God, Sage, how could you say that? It could wreck your career, your life. All because you tried to help me. Look what happened to Eric. He was murdered because of me. How do I live with that?"

Sage reached up and ran a hand down Alex's cheek. "You were *not* responsible for Eric's death. Sarah did that. Alex, you can't put that on yourself too; you need to let it go. Let's not look at the dark side. Keep positive." He smiled softly. "God, you were incredible back there. I thought you were going to shoot her."

"I wanted to shoot the bitch. Thank you for trying to save me from myself. And you were my hero. You got the gun out of her hand." Alex's voice faltered. "I was so scared I thought I was going to lose you."

Sage's hand gripped Alex's tightly. Alex lifted Sage's hand, kissing it as he held it to his mouth. "I'm just glad you're here, talking to me. I can get through anything as long as you're here." There was a loud knock on the door and Cully stood up to answer it. There was some soft muttering and finally he appeared.

"DS Doyle is here." As he said the words, the detective appeared in the doorway. Alex stood up and moved over to shake his hand.

"Detective. Good to see you again."

DS Doyle nodded. "Good to see you too, gentlemen. May I ask you some more questions?"

"Of course, take a seat." Alex gestured to the chair at the other side of the couch.

The policeman sat down. "Please call me Reg," he said quietly. "I think we all know each other well enough by now."

Alex smiled. "I'd like that, but then you have to call me Alex. He's Sage. No 'Mister.'"

Reg looked at them both as Cully watched him carefully. "Did you watch the news?"

Alex nodded. "Yes. I wondered why there was no mention of the videotape. I would have thought I'd have been arrested by now for Rudy's murder." His voice was wry. "I've been expecting the boys in blue to turn up and cart me away."

"There was no mention of it because it didn't exist." Reg's voice was quiet. "I destroyed it."

Alex's mouth dropped open. "You destroyed it? Why?" Sage saw hope flare in his eyes. It flared in his heart too.

"I was the only one to see that particular tape in the office. I removed it and burnt it. There was no need for any of that stuff to get out. You've been through enough, Alex. I think you've paid your dues and this Rudy character was a real bastard. I didn't see any need for you to have to go through all that again. I'll take the consequences if there are any, though I frankly doubt there will be. No one even knew that tape was there. The only part I can't get a handle on is your connection to Mr. Rossi. I wasn't sure why he was killed."

"He was killed because he hurt Alex." Sage knew he had to make this believable.

He was an actor. He could do this.

Alex, Reg and Cully turned to look at Sage. Alex took his hand and Sage saw the question in his eyes.

"Eric Rossi attacked Alex at a function. He was drunk. Alex said something he didn't like and Eric got physical with Alex in the bathroom, punched him. Alex told me about that little incident here in the office. He said it was done in the heat of the moment and he thought nothing of it. But Sarah didn't like people messing with Alex, present company included. She told us Eric needed to be punished." He squeezed Alex's hand tightly in warning.

Alex took his cue and followed Sage's lead. "I didn't want to tell the police about the incident and risk it getting it all over the papers. I'd had enough of that. And it was really wasn't all that big a deal to me. The man was an arsehole and he'd just had too much to drink." He shrugged in apparent unconcern, and Sage thought he'd done very well.

Reg looked at them both strangely then nodded. "I see. We do have other tapes in our possession that I couldn't do much with, I'm afraid, as the team who went into to Mrs. Brose's apartment took custody of them. They'll be watching them and reporting back to me."

Sage's heart sank. That meant the police would see all the sexual activity in Alex's office. His face flamed at that thought. He cleared his throat, clutching tight to Alex's hand.

"Um, there might some compromising stuff on those tapes." Reg Doyle regarded him thoughtfully and Sage's face grew warmer. "I'd appreciate it if you could make sure it doesn't get leaked. Alex and I wouldn't want our private home movies appearing on the porn channels on YouTube."

The light dawned in Reg's eyes and he nodded, his face slightly amused although going pink. "I'll try and make sure that the viewing team keep it under wraps and as little as possible gets out to the papers," he said primly. "And no one is going to believe this psycho woman if she tries to tell her side of the story, whatever that is." He smiled nastily. "There are plenty of ways to discredit anything she says. I have my own arse to cover as well."

"Reg." Sage held up a hand and Reg took it. "Thanks for what you did for Alex, for getting rid of that tape. I appreciate it."

The policeman clasped Sage's hand warmly. "You two have been through a lot together. I think you both deserve a break." He smiled. "Think of it as an early Christmas present. You haven't forgotten it's in a week's time, have you?"

Sage laughed. "Actually, with everything going on, Christmas hasn't really featured much on my list of things to do. I guess we need to some emergency shopping."

Reg turned to Alex. "Alex, I'm sorry to hear about your ordeal at the hands of Mr. Rossi. I'm not sure I believe that whole story, you two, but it's the one I'll be telling. You two look after yourselves and Sage, please try stay out of trouble. My case load is bad enough as it is." He grinned and walked into the corridor.

Sage watched him go. Alex cuffed his chin affectionately. "That was a stroke of genius. I just hope it gets left there."

Sage shook his head. "We had to make some excuse for now. Reg isn't stupid. When Sarah starts spilling the beans about you and Eric and Study in Scarlet, and why she actually killed him, he'll know the truth then. The whole damn police force will know, no doubt. I just wanted to buy us some time. From what Reg said, he won't want details being made public either, as it might put him in the spotlight. But if the worst happens and everything comes out, Alex, we'll have to manage it. Together like we always do."

Later that night when everyone had gone, Alex lay beside Sage in bed, stroking the hair back from his forehead, his strong hands gently caressing his jawline.

"I'm glad everyone's gone home," he murmured in Sage's ear as his tongue delved into its depths. "I really want to make love to you."

Sage shivered, his cock hardening. He had been tired but Sage's sleepiness disappeared the minute Alex whispered his sexy message in his ear. He watched as Alex nibbled his nipples and Sage's cock grew harder with every deliberately sensuous movement his lover made. Alex grinned at his greedy expression. "You have a bit of a tenting thing going on under there," Alex observed with a sly smile. "Happy to see me, are we?"

Sage scowled. "Shut the hell up and get busy, you teasing bastard." God, Alex naked turned him on like nothing else. His sexy torso, his beautiful cock, his shaven groin—Alex was just perfect. He held his breath waiting for the next step. Alex sniggered, his hands gently stroking Sage's erection, making his body ache with need.

Alex whispered. "Strum my strings, Maestro. I promise it won't take long. I'm really horny today. Then I will suck you dry."

"As opposed to other times?" Sage said lazily, his heart skipping a beat at the words coming out of Alex's mouth. His strong fingers grasped Alex and he slowly stroked him, playing his now-familiar tune on his lover's dick. "I seem to remember you attacking me more than once in your desire to have my body."

Alex's body tensed against his, his warm skin sending thrills of sensation through Sage's, his deep, panting breaths in Sage's ear an indication of just how needy he was. Sage kept up his movements, finding Alex's mouth and sliding past his lips, his tongue meeting Alex's ravenous one. Sage loved the way his man tasted, all minty toothpaste and blackcurrant from the sweets he sucked throughout the day. He moved his mouth to nuzzle Alex's neck, licking the sweat from his skin. Alex gasped and huffed beneath him, his hands slowly stroking Sage's shaft, cupping his balls and driving him to distraction. The two men played a slow ballet of touch and release, a symphony of emotion and physical contact that left them both gasping as each one tried to please the other. Sage smiled against Alex's mouth as he finally felt him pulse beneath his hands, hot fluid soaking his hand and arm, wetting the bedcovers and the sheet. He revelled in Alex's moans as he came, his mouth hot against Sage's ear, the breath deep and warm.

"God, Sage, your fingers are bloody magic," Alex gasped. "I still say it must be the guitar playing. Every gay man should learn to play the guitar. Maybe we should open a master class." Sage chuckled as Alex made his way under the bedclothes and Sage's thighs tensed in anticipation as Alex's mouth encircled his hardness, flicking his tongue over Sage's shaft, nibbling the tip of him then rolled his tongue around Sage's cock like a man devouring a lollipop. Sage closed his eyes, giving into the sensation as Alex's fingers stroked his taint, cupped his balls, and slid a finger slyly inside his arse, causing Sage's hips to rear up, pushing his cock into Alex's mouth. Alex took Sage deeper, his throat muscles working around Sage, his expert movements causing Sage to grip the bedcovers and try to stave off the orgasm he knew was soon coming. Sage wanted this to last a little while longer. This slow sexual tango continued for what seemed like hours until Sage could hold out no longer, feeling his groin heat up beyond boiling point, the prickling in his backside intensifying. His cock swelled, and with a deep grunt he climaxed. Alex sucked him dry, his mouth hungry for more and finally Sage was spent and Alex raised his head off Sage's now-spent cock. He smiled in triumph. "You tried to hold out, lover, but you had to blow sometime. That was pretty awesome."

Sage reached down, pulling Alex up toward him, kissing his mouth which still tasted of Sage's come. "You really know how to suck a man dry, babe. I love your bloody mouth, you know that?"

Alex kissed Sage tenderly as he moved to lie beside him. "I hope that relieved some of the tension, at least."

Alex's face grew serious as he moved onto his elbow, lifting himself up, looking down at Sage with eyes that told him everything about the depth of Alex's feelings for him. "You saved me, Sage. I can never tell you how much I love you for that."

Sage kissed him. "I love you too." His tone was tender. "Now settle down to sleep and stop molesting me. We can start again in the morning."

Chapter 32

Alex smiled as he watched Sage lead Annie and Tallulah Briar around the courtyard. It was good to see Sage back in his element with his horses. The snow fell gently, covering the ground in white, frosty flakes. Sage turned and waved to him as Alex watched out of the kitchen window. Miles came up behind him.

"It's good to see him out there, looking so well," he said quietly. "After all that the two of you have been through, this Christmas Day is turning out to be a real family affair. I can't believe you got everyone together for it, Alex. It must have taken some doing."

Alex had organised this one in record time. He'd sat Sage's godfather down and told him everything about his past and what he and Sage had been through. Miles had wept, telling Alex he'd done the right thing in protecting a child and that there was no way he would ever judge him. It had been an emotional time for both of them and Alex was glad he had Miles in his life too. This was starting to feel like family to him.

"Oh, it wasn't so bad." Alex waved through to the lounge where Reg Doyle sat with his wife Lily, arguing with Dan and Cully about the merits of the latest football heroes. "Sage has some good people in his life. It wasn't that difficult to convince them all to come and enjoy the turkey, even if I've never cooked one before. Thank God Lanie's here. She's a real treasure, Miles."

Alex watched fondly as the small, stocky figure of Lanie Grainger bustled about preparing the table and the food for their guests.

Miles grinned. "She is at that. I don't know what I would have done without her." He looked at his partner in affection and she smiled at him from across the room. The door swung open. Sage came in, his breath frosty, his black hair speckled with snowflakes.

"God, it's bloody freezing out there! I don't know how Annie does it. She's just taking Lulah for a ride then she'll be back in." He lifted a lid to one of the pots on the stove and sniffed. "Smells good. When will it be ready to eat? I'm starving."

Lanie tapped him across the knuckles with her wooden spoon. "As soon as it's ready, young man. About another half an hour and then we can sit down to it."

Sage grinned, pulling Alex close for a hug. Alex kissed his bristly cheek. "I'm glad to see you're hungry. There's plenty to eat, that's for sure." Sage released Alex and wandered into the lounge. Alex grinned as Dan waved his glass of wine at his friend. "Sage, my man. I was just telling Cully here about the time we chained ourselves to those railings. He seems to be quite taken with that story."

Sage grinned, sitting down and soon the group were immersed in a lively conversation. Alex watched from the kitchen doorway, his heart full. He still couldn't believe the point he'd got to, when he actually had people to call family. After everything that had happened, he'd found a sense of peace he'd never known before. Alex watched Sage as his blue eyes sparkled and his hands waved animatedly as he talked. An enormous surge of love for this man coursed through Alex's body. Sage would never know just how much Alex owed him. He'd changed Alex's life irrevocably for the better.

Alex went back into the kitchen to fetch a beer from the fridge. Filming for *Double Exposure* was now complete and now came the hard work of editing and reviewing the footage to make sure the series aired on time in June next year. Sage had already been offered the lead role in another TV drama series, which he was considering, as well as a fairly large supporting role in a new thriller movie being made. He was definitely going places, Alex thought. Everyone seemed to want a piece of him.

Reg Doyle came up beside him and smiled gently. "Penny for your thoughts, Alex."

Alex smiled. "I was just thinking how lucky I was to have all these wonderful people here today for such a special time. I've never celebrated Christmas like this before."

Reg laid a warm hand on Alex's shoulder, squeezing it. "After what you and Sage have been through, you both deserve every happiness you can get. I'm just glad the media frenzy has died down for you both, although there may still be some hurdles to face as the case with Sarah Brose goes to trial. Personally I think the two of you will be fine. We managed to wrap things up quite tightly and I have a feeling no one will believe any ramblings that come out of that crazy woman's mouth to question either of you."

Alex knew that when Reg said "we" it was actually all due to the man standing in front of him that things had been managed so well and that the sordid details of his past had been kept under wraps.

"The videotapes we found at her place were watched and the necessary evidence on them were what we used to put her away. But they're safe in lockup and I've made damn sure no one goes near them without me knowing. They won't see the light of day if I have anything to do with it."

Reg glanced at him. "I'm glad you and Sage finally told me the truth about Eric and your—situation—and the whole Study in Scarlet thing. While I'll never understand why someone as tough as you felt the need for that, I certainly don't judge it. And knowing about it made it easier for me to manage the situation for you." He grinned. "I think I headed that one off at the pass. I painted Sarah Brose as a completely crazy lady, who had no idea what she was talking about." He shrugged his shoulders guilelessly. "They found a whole load of really weird S-and-M literature and shit in her apartment. Some fairly dodgy stuff that lent credence to my story about her being a rather kinky bitch who liked to make up stories and had a few strange S-and-M habits of her own." His tone was implacable. "I know it was wrong. If anyone found out I staged that I'll be behind bars a long, long time. But it was worth it. And I know that I managed to keep things under wraps as far as the Rudy thing goes."

Alex nodded. "You put a lot on the line for us, Reg. I'm still not sure why you did it all, but I'm not going to question your motives. Sage feels the same way. I can't believe you put yourself at risk like that for us. You know we'll never say anything to get you into trouble don't you?"

He nodded fondly. "I know, Alex. As for my reasons"—Alex saw his fond glance at Sage—"let's just say I like seeing two young people get a second chance to have a future they deserve."

Alex nodded gratefully. "Sage and I owe you a debt of gratitude, Reg. Thank you."

Reg shrugged. "It was a pleasure. Everything is as it should be. You and Sage are safe together. Sarah's in prison—for the long haul, I hope—and justice has been served. It's like one of your happily ever after romance novels." He grinned wryly. "Talking of which, how's the new book coming along?"

"Second in the series, fifty thousand words and counting. I've still got a long way to go but it'll be in the stores next year at some time."

Sage sauntered into the kitchen with an empty wine glass and smiled when he saw Reg and Alex together. "Anything I should know about going on between you two?" he teased as he opened the fridge to refill the glass with white wine.

Reg grinned. "Sorry, Sage, your young arse had just been usurped by a more mature man of experience and charm. You've lost out. I'm switching teams for Alex."

Sage raised his eyebrows. "Really? Well then, I'd better try and convince him otherwise, hadn't I?" He reached out, pulling Alex closer, kissing him hungrily.

Reg shook his head and left the kitchen to give them some time alone.

Finally Sage released Alex and grinned wickedly. "Could you really give that up?" he said softly in his ear as he nuzzled his neck.

Alex shook his head as he leaned into him, enjoying his scent and the warmth of his body. "I could never give you up. I love you far too much to do that."

Sage pulled away, his eyes regarding his lover anxiously. "It's been so hectic, what with Christmas preparations and everything, we've not had a real chance to talk about the really private stuff much. I've just assumed you're okay, and as you're still seeing Melanie, I thought you were doing fine. Am I right? Are you okay?"

Alex chuckled. "I'm more than okay. Melanie is over the moon." He looked guilty. "She *was* very mad at me though for not being honest, because I never told her about killing Rudy. She says if she'd known it would have made a difference to my therapy, that I was punishing myself with Eric for killing Rudy. I suppose she was right. I never thought I could do without it. All I need now is you. The needs I had seem to have disappeared."

Sage hugged him close. "I'm glad, babe," he whispered with emotion. "But my offer still stands if you ever feel the need. Don't forget that."

Alex reached up to caress his face gently. "I'll remember. Thank you, Sage."

Sage let him go and Alex saw him take two small pieces of paper from his pocket. He watched as Sage laid them in an ashtray on the kitchen tab and bought out a box of matches from the kitchen drawer.

"What the hell are you doing?" Alex asked, puzzled. Sage kept quiet, picking up the two pieces of paper to show him what was written on them.

Chrysippus. Tallulah.

Alex looked at him with wonderment in his eyes as Sage lit the match and slowly set fire to the two pieces of paper.

"No more safe words." Sage muttered. "It's not going to be that easy to get rid of me a second time. We work together on whatever happens from now on, regardless of what it is."

Alex pulled Sage into his chest, holding him tightly, feeling the beat of his heart against his own. They stood together in the kitchen for a while, until Lanie came in and frowned.

"The stuffing is burning! Sage, for goodness sake, get your lanky body out of the way so I can get it out of the oven."

He grinned, moving aside, taking Alex's hand and drawing him into the lounge. They sat down to join in the conversation and Alex cuddled up to him on the sofa. This was the best Christmas present he could ever have had. A family, a wonderful man in his life and finally some peace from the demons that had plagued him since he was eighteen years old. Alex looked around the room, marvelling at his good fortune. Maybe there was some truth in the happily ever after idea after all.

AUTHOR NOTE

S&M can be a healthy, happy choice between consenting adults. *Saving Alexander* is about one man's punishment and self-torture, and should not in any way be construed as a condemnation of the lifestyle.

ABOUT THE AUTHOR

Sue Mac Nicol was born in Leeds, Yorkshire, in the United Kingdom. At the age of eight, her family moved to Johannesburg, South Africa, where she stayed for nearly thirty years before arriving back in the UK in December 2000. She now lives in the rural village of Bocking, in Essex, with her family. Her plan is to keep writing as long as her muse sits upon her shoulder, and her dream is to one day be able to give up the day job and get that big old house in the English countryside overlooking a river where she can write all day and continue to indulge her passion for telling stories.

Sue is a PAN member of Romance Writers of America and also a member of the Romantic Novelists Association in the UK. She is also a member of a rather unique writing group called the Talliston Writers Circle.

BOOKS BY SUSAN MAC NICOL

<u>The Starlight series</u>
Cassandra by Starlight
Together in Starlight

<u>M/M Romance</u>
Stripped Bare

<u>Short Romance fiction</u>
The Magic of Christmas
Confounding Cupid

Boroughs
Publishing Group

Did you enjoy this book? Drop us a line and say so! We love to hear from readers, and so do our authors. To connect, visit www.boroughspublishinggroup.com online, send comments directly to info@boroughspublishinggroup.com, or friend us on Facebook and Twitter. And be sure to check back regularly for contests and new releases in your favorite subgenres of romance!

Are you an aspiring writer? Check out www.boroughspublishinggroup.com/submit and see if we can help you make your dreams come true.